GIRESUN ISLAND

GIRESUN ISLAND

BY: JOHN M. MCKEEL

NEW DEGREE PRESS

COPYRIGHT © 2021 BY: JOHN M. MCKEEL

GIRESUN ISLAND

ISBN   978-1-63676-754-3   *Paperback*
          978-1-63676-755-0   *Kindle Ebook*
          978-1-63676-756-7   *Ebook*

For Jennifer, Cameron, and Kaitlyn

You are always with me.

Contents

GIRESUN ISLAND AUTHOR'S NOTE   9

GIRESUN ISLAND   13

CHAPTER 1.   FROM THE ASHES   29

CHAPTER 2.   A SNAKE IN THE GRASS   41

CHAPTER 3.   THE END IS THE BEGINNING   51

CHAPTER 4.   THE CRUCIBLE   61

CHAPTER 5.   TERRA INCOGNITA   71

CHAPTER 6.   NOTHING BUT A GOOD TIME   85

CHAPTER 7.   BLOOD IN THE WATER   97

CHAPTER 8.   BIRTH OF A NATION   105

CHAPTER 9.   THE WOODSHED   117

CHAPTER 10. REST AND RECOVERY   125

CHAPTER 11. A PATTERN OF SHADOWS   133

CHAPTER 12. ROLLING THUNDER   141

CHAPTER 13. CHECKMATE   151

CHAPTER 14. SALVATION   157

CHAPTER 15. AN INCONVENIENT TRUTH   171

CHAPTER 16. THE PRICE OF ADMISSION   179

CHAPTER 17. THREAT OF VIOLENCE   189

CHAPTER 18. CONFRONTATION   195

CHAPTER 19. STAND YOUR GROUND   213

EPILOGUE WHAT LIES BENEATH   233

ACKNOWLEDGEMENTS   237

APPENDIX   239

Giresun Island Author's Note

An asteroid is hurtling through space to obliterate the Earth. The best chance we have is not to blow it to smithereens with a nuclear arsenal, but to use small nudges that produce enormous effects later. Liet Kynes in *Dune* changed the face of Arrakis by slowly planting tiny stubborn grasses, eventually converting the desert planet into an oasis. Small, intentional movements—what British diplomacy called "soft power"—can create revolutionary change over time. Tiny differences in starting conditions can result in a consequence chain as chaotic as Edward Lorenz's butterfly effect. Imagine a world just out of reach, one we might get to if certain changes are made. "What if?" is the best part of science fiction, and it is more than technology or far-flung futures. Its strength as a genre is in the interactions between people and what happens when they meet a challenge. People, the true power in any human endeavor, experience, or change. The small interactions we all have over a day can have a profound effect on those with whom we come into contact.

Millions of people today are already displaced by regional conflict, with unchecked atrocities sanctioned by recognized governments and terrorists alike. Climate changes are destroying impoverished cultures around the world as people struggle to find food and water. Diseases have exploited our unsteady upper hand in prevention. Financial systems of consumer-driven economics are finding it hard to cope with these insecurities, and other political-economic systems have fared no better. In our return to isolationist, protectionist policies, we have vilified our national neighbors to the south. In our America-centric world, the countries of South America are frequently denigrated as hopelessly rife with poverty and corruption, dominated by drug cartels. These situations do not exist in a vacuum, as anyone affected can tell you. Relationships drive these evil things. When their fallout is left to crystalize rather than resolve, otherwise normal developmental milestones in people are perverted, in societies as in people. Toxic traits fester without a narrative of reinvention, without context to put experiences in perspective.

Ironically, this stunted growth is often used to chastise people who follow their own instincts. Women who take on traditionally male roles face even more malice and reproach than men who fail to live up to some imagined standard of machismo. I admire many women who compete athletically at a level few men could only dream of. The physicality does not detract from their chosen expression of femininity, it enhances it. The CEO, scientist, lawyer, or statesperson role does the same, just as it does for men. Women just have a better average at maintaining their humanity above all of it. The point is, these roles are all choices. They are open to us all. The segregation we may expect is simply a construct, and it should be regarded as such. My hope is that the readers of *Giresun Island* will see that reflected through the characters, and maybe experience some of how a ubiquitous truth is obfuscated by a millennia-old system of tradition and sometimes subtle pressure. Hopefully, we can all come away from the story with Wheaton's Law, "Don't be a dick," engrained in our behavior moving forward.

I have seen what happens to the people living in a war zone. Women are powerful examples of opportunity trumping stigmas in the way that they strive to protect their own—as a fighter, as a mother, as a provider. The prejudice of men does not stop them from doing what they feel is right. In *Giresun Island*, a Kurdish female Peshmerga fighter named Carsem is lost after her last stand results in the destruction of her village and the deaths of her children. How do these shared, genderless experiences fit into the biases of the people around them? What about those whose wars are fought in their own countries? What do we do as humans when we return from war without a home to go to? With nothing to connect her—no family, no country, no unit—she wanders until haplessly stumbling into an assassination plot. The only thing left of Carsem that she recognizes is her iron core, the drive to protect and defend. She foils the attack, then is rewarded with a new life on a mysterious island rife with technological innovation and ruled by women. Across a wide strait from her new home, a cultural revolution and resurrection are taking place in South America. What would happen if a toxically masculine government, full of bravado and machismo but structurally poor, collided with a matriarchal society that held a severe technological, competitive advantage? Rather than dealing with the island as an equal, the nation next door plans to invade. When her new home is threatened with destruction by men, will she risk returning to the abyss? What would happen if old ways of looking at the world disappeared? What is possible if the reality of the world was no longer able to be ignored? Not everyone will take kindly to their preconceptions being shattered, either. Some will try to stop it by brute force.

Beyond the lies that we all see the world through, *Giresun Island* is a story of what is possible. Veterans, especially women, have experiences where the façade of social order failed. I hope they will enjoy this book. So will anyone who feels that opportunity is more important than biology in determining the course of a person's life. It is a science fiction story, if only to shine a light on what is possible beyond convention.

CHAPTER 1

Giresun Island

The engines of the submarine groaned as the boat pitched toward the surface. The jump jet's systems were spinning up from the back of the sub in preparation for a catapult takeoff. In the cabin, the triumvirate leadership of Giresun Island tried to ignore the interference in their preparations for a diplomatic meeting on the mainland.

Gro-printed burl wood lined most of the interior, with soft ambient light bathing the cabin. A deep blue carpet dotted with gold emblems of Giresun Island's standard was bordered by a waist-high wall of textured off-white hemp fiber plastic. The whine and vibration of the aircraft's electric engines was barely noticeable. The chairs matched the miasmic weft and warp of the burl paneling in a deep brown of simulated leather. The pressure compensating system underneath was concealed in luxury. Like most Giresun products, art masked function. Three women sat in scattered seats, as separate as they could be in the small aircraft. Keiko's face was bathed in light seeping from her glasses. Her fingers tapped almost rhythmically on her thighs as she haptically navigated the augmented reality browser. Chris fidgeted between smoothing her pants and twisting the modest jewelry around her right wrist. Columbia read the brief again on the delegates they were to meet from Gran America.

"Prepare for launch," the aircraft's pilot said over a loudspeaker. The biomimetic sub rose to the surface while the railgun catapult emerged from what otherwise looked like a whale's dorsum. The pilot counted down. "Three… two… one…"

The small aircraft launched and achieved its cruising speed in seconds. The acceleration was absorbed by the specially designed seats. Chris, caught off-guard, was thrown against her bench. Once her body achieved the same velocity as the aircraft, she redoubled her attempts to smooth herself and preen.

Columbia smiled. Every time she made a jump flight it took her back to her wild days in the Security Forces. She could feel her body react like it was going back to the fight. Columbia took several deep breaths to bring down the rush. As the First Consul she had a burgeoning nation to represent, not an incursion to lead.

Keiko was barely disturbed from whatever she was doing, pausing only to anchor herself during the launch. Once her equilibrium was reestablished, she remained in the same blue-lit trance as before. Under the cover of sea spray, the submarine dove into the deep waters off the coast of Guiana.

The cabin was all business as each woman rehearsed her role to play in the trade negotiations ahead. Columbia rehearsed over flashcards that hovered over her outstretched palm, streaming from a device wrapped around her wrist. Everyone called them "screens," but the data was projected into the air while a sophisticated array of sensors interpreted the wearer's movements to interact with the image. Keiko streamed hers into a headset that allowed for a more immersive interaction, as well as maintaining privacy. Chris used it as a mirror.

"Prepare for descent," the pilot interrupted half an hour later.

"Everyone ready?" Columbia asked.

Keiko emerged from her separate reality and nodded. She neatly folded the glasses and put them into her case before taking a bottle of soju from her fridge. "Minibars on transports?" she asked Chris.

"They're convenient and cost-effective," Chris said.

Keiko wore a poker face for a second too long before breaking into a quiet laugh and raising her bottle.

"Good idea," Columbia said. She removed a pre-mixed Caipiri1 from the fridge under her bench. She twisted the top off and rais _ a toast. "To progress. May all roads lead to Rome."

CARTAGENA, COLUMBIA, CAPITOL OF GRAN AMERICA

1025 28 FEB 2075

As the door to the plane folded down, the Giresun representatives squinted behind their sunglasses. The heat rolled in over the women. It had a flinty edge to it that made for an unpleasant background to the chemical exhaust smell of the tarmac. Unlike the fuel-fed turbines spinning elsewhere on the runway, the *Remora* silently waited. Its engines were already shut down but ready to spin back up at a moment's notice.

"Presidente de Gran América y delegados. Buenos días desde la isla Giresun. Encantada de conocerte," Columbia announced without aid across the tarmac to the mostly seated delegates. She offered her hand to the president. He attempted to turn it palm down but could not overcome her grip. Without hesitation, she gestured with her open arm while holding his hand.

"These are my fellow consuls from Giresun. Keiko Tangawa and Chris van Buren," Columbia said. She released the president from her grip and joined him walking side by side to usher the party off the airfield. President Calderone kept trying to take the lead from Columbia, but her long muscular legs were more used to triathlons than sitting behind a desk like her competitor's. Rather than make a scene of his weakness, Calderone relented before he started panting for breath. Columbia slowed her pace to help him save face. The other states' representatives filed in behind the president and consuls without any recognition of the duel that had been fought and lost in front of them.

In moments, cleaning staff arrived in red polo shirts, bandanas, and khaki shorts to clear the space. The Giresun pilot returned the safety lock on her holstered sidearm. She motioned for the security sensors to disengage weapons and monitor the area around the plane. To a casual observer, the pilot just climbed aboard without doing a thing.

~

The airport terminal stood a hundred meters away, a hulking mass of stained concrete and glass. Like most things here, function was all that had mattered when it was constructed. Financial profiteers brought civilization to the continent, so they said, but the reality was every dime spent was designed solely to turn a profit. Few architectural beauties existed here. It wasn't Brutalism. It was merely brutal.

Walking through the main airport terminal, Columbia remarked, "I hope you didn't suspend flights for our visit, sir."

"No, we just finished making some renovations that were well-timed with your visit. Otherwise, we would have used the private airport for diplomatic reasons."

"Thank you. It's quite nice. Do the people in the countryside or the barrios outside of this side of town have so much to choose from?"

"I'm afraid with our best efforts, the harvest suffered from the unfortunate weather again. We try, but there is always a shortage at the bottom, you know."

"It's the way, isn't it?" Columbia said. "What we propose could change that, though."

"Something that would surely make my constituents more at ease, *Señora Honalee*," he said.

While a short walk, the oppressive disparity was in stark contrast to the equality and comparative opulence of Giresun. Columbia held her mask of composure easily. She had personally been running interdiction missions against the deSilva cartel for years in the Security Forces. She knew the score. Gran America was like every other state—resources at the top were abundant, while those below fought tooth and nail for their scraps. Chris caught a face she recognized and dropped back in the entourage.

"Excuse me, you're Ignacio Guzman, aren't you?" Chris said.

"Yes, hello, Ms. van Buren," he said, turning to offer his hand. She folded hers into his grip.

"Pleasure to meet you, sir," she said.

"Likewise," he said, catching her eye.

Keiko's hand buzzed. She turned her wrist over and back. She caught up to Columbia and knocked her hand against the First Consul's, then dropped back into the following crowd. Columbia flicked two fingers in rapid succession where Keiko could see.

"Ah," President Calderone said. "Here we are. The motorcade will take us to the proposed sites, and the relays you sent over have all been installed. We are at your convenience."

The delegates followed the presidential party into their cars. Keiko put on her glasses and began tapping on her lap.

"Good morning again, esteemed delegates of Gran America," Columbia's voice announced across all of the delegates' car interiors. "As you know, Giresun Island is an independent state with a high investment in innovative technology. We are here today with a goodwill proposal. A historic problem in this part of the world is growing food crops for an increasing population. It is fate, because of geography. Vertical farming can overcome that."

A transparent animated schematic appeared in front of the passengers of each car in the motorcade. The audible shock made Keiko smile as she continued to tap her fingers in syncopated rhythms. Columbia kept time with Keiko's tapping. They had worked together in the Security Forces operations division long before turning to politics. The tempo kept their physical actions in synch during the presentation just as they'd synchronized their movements in the field years before.

"Gran America also has a long history of innovation and technology, including the hybridization and dissemination of corn—staple grain only second to rice in the world. This semi-automated structure can be constructed in the middle of a neighborhood or town and provide dozens of hectares of food and meat production, with a minimal energy investment. Through aquaculture and solar capture, it is a ten-fold improvement in energy consumption compared to current monoculture agribusiness. Placing the food in the communities that rely on it brings the food and the production jobs to the same people. Our offer is simple. We will provide the technical experts and designs; your communities provide the raw materials and workers. The only money we request is in recognition and payment of our patents, for these and however many more farms you build. We will donate the expertise in exchange for establishing diplomatic ties between Giresun and Gran America.

"As you all have no doubt received already, we have drafted the proposal and given each state a copy to review. This is as we agreed during our last meeting with your contracts administration. Your governing bodies have also received the document, in the interest of transparency. Thank you."

Columbia's address was paused across the network.

"*Señor Caldarone*, the floor is yours. I believe this is the first site. Can you tell us more about the neighborhood in relation to where you live in the capital?" Columbia said privately.

Hubert Caldarone sat speechless for a moment in his air-conditioned, leather-appointed town car. The technology of the presentation alone was overwhelming. The fact that these women could display it so seamlessly in cars without so much as a telecom connection was alien. He admitted to no doubts that they could make good on their proposal for infrastructure projects, but his face betrayed his racing thoughts. What else were these Amazons holding back?

He suddenly realized he was losing the initiative. He cleared his throat. "This is one of the Bolivarian neighborhoods. You might remember..."

1730 05 MAR 2075

"They ought to be in our airspace in five minutes," the flight control officer said.

"Ought to be, Sam? Since when do you make guesses?" Columbia asked.

"Since they keep varying airspeed, boss."

Columbia borrowed the control officer's binoculars and stepped out onto the catwalk. She sighted along with the plane's projected flight plan thanks to an augmented reality overlay. The interior of the flight control tower was littered with holographic overlays tracking multiple flights, conditions, and even satellites. Sometimes there was no technological substitute for the detail of direct experience. The day on Giresun Island was much more palatable than the week previous in Gran America's state of Ecuador. Here the horseshoe bay reached out like a bull's horns, driving the wind up through the jungle and across the open fields that perfumed it with the scent of a million different living things. The air pressure change kept the air cool and humid from the ocean as it rose. The sharp rise of the mountain crest took the brunt of the sun's tropical heat, shielding the small city below. From the main control tower on top of the mountain, everything looked small and tranquil, wrapped in a blanket of green on a cerulean sheet.

Keiko slipped through the doorway and joined her. Columbia took the hint. She handed off her field glasses to the officer of the watch, then followed Keiko down to the shuttle. This sun-soaked side of the island was occupied mostly by industrial traffic and the airport. A mag-lev shuttle ferried air traffic crews up to the tower, and in seconds it arrived in the airport. The passenger terminal where the official reception was to be held looked like the inside of the *Remora*, but the ceiling was faceted cut quartz. Columbia knew it was strong enough to withstand a hurricane, or a direct hit from a mortar shell.

It looked like a glittering jewel throwing light and rainbows across the blue carpet and wood paneled hall.

"Popular opinion is overwhelming on the net," Keiko said.

"That's all you, Keiko." Columbia smiled, still scanning the flight path for the small private jet. "It's quite an opportunity. I mean, liquid fuel turbines… c'mon."

"They may give us the in, but they may hate us for it, you know."

"I know. When is the second party due?" Columbia asked.

"Any time now. I went and sent out a pilot to keep them off the reefs," Keiko said.

"Probably find their way with a fish finder," Columbia said.

"Now, now, don't be a hag," Keiko said. The door closed after her.

"Gotcha," Columbia said. As she walked out of the passenger terminal, she could hear the engine's roar. Representatives of Giresun's industries mingled in the reception area. The major presenters—agriculture, manufacturing, and construction—formed a tight clique at the center. "Okay, folks. Let's make a good impression," she announced.

The ground crew directed the late model jet across the tarmac to the end of the red carpet. The door opened. A gangway moved into position. A quintet played the Gran America national anthem as the dignitaries walked down the stairs. Presidente Caldaron led the procession, waiving conservatively.

"Welcome to Giresun Island, President Caldaron and representatives of Gran America. May I present representatives from our industries, including our mining, power generation, mineral refineries, and agriculture? We also have representatives from our undersea ventures along the coast."

"You mean under the coast, right? We saw the lights on the way in," Mez Calla said. The representative of Ecuador looked like someone else had dressed him. As if these permanently pressed slacks and blazer were a costume he'd been forced to wear. From the look of his weathered skin, old fashioned denim and a well-worn western shirt were more his fit. He offered his hand to Columbia and shook it firmly. His eyes were assessing her as a fighter might, not in the way some of the other men looked on.

"That's right, we have operations underwater and are experimenting with permanent settlements there," Columbia said. "All within our borders, I assure you. Not sneaking up on the coast."

"Heh, no doubt. Of course, you'd have to be a nation to have borders, yes?" Maxim Torres said.

"Wrong side of things to encroach on Brasil, *meu amigo.*"

Maxim and Columbia slapped their hands together to shake. Maxim drew her in with a pat on the back. "I'm working on it. They hate you so much, *garota.*"

Columbia smiled at being called a girl as they parted. She slowly removed a thin wire from a concealed pocket in the side of her dress. Staring straight at Maxim, Columbia drew it taut through her other hand and snapped it between them at neck-height like a garrote. Maxim's face froze, concern hanging on his face behind the handlebar mustache. Columbia winked and artfully twisted the wire around her hair to pull it into a ponytail. Maxim's shocked expression melted into a toothy grin, and they laughed.

"What's funny?" Chris asked.

"Maxim was telling me he's already looking forward to sampling the food from our farms."

"Nothing beats a free state dinner!" Maxim said.

As Mez Calla was led away by Maxim, Columbia picked up on the extra stitching his tailor had used to cover a waist-holstered sidearm, and from the bend in his belt, she knew he was usually armed.

"Columbia?" Chris said. "Dinner?" Chris offered Columbia a hand.

"Right, coming," Columbia said.

Keiko was already inside, preparing to dazzle the guests. Columbia could see the delegates from the ship walking into the promenade across from the airfield entrance and into the opulent conference center.

～

"I hope everyone brought their appetites. While we indulge in the best food and drink that Giresun has to offer, I should add it is all from within our island—even the fish!" Chris announced to the guests. Cloches rang like bells as the wait staff removed the hoods from the platters.

"We know you all have vibrant food traditions of your own. All we are offering is the means to produce the ingredients your people require," Chris continued. "While you enjoy the food and drinks, let's make the most of our time together." A three-dimensional hologram floated in the middle of the square, surrounded by tables.

"These images are coming from aerial vehicles that took off as you landed. As you can see, we have converted the constructed materials of the island into a tropical landscape as verdant as our other island neighbors," Keiko said as she nodded to the representatives of Trinidad and Tobago. As the newest members of Gran America, they were largely excluded from the decision-making bodies within the confederation. Keiko subtly played every advantage. "The soil is repurposed from the domestic mining operations here." Keiko's image highlighted the mining facilities at the center and in the waters of the island. "Our proprietary method replaces the traditional mining operation with volcanism and pressure wave technology. It allows us to essentially call forth the elements. We can refine ores without the slag and toxic waste pools like Mongolia and elsewhere," she said.

The picture flew over vast jungle foliage at tree-top level, circled the mining operations with capped fumaroles and active but controlled lava flows. The drones powered on after a few passes to a ring around the middle of the island.

"Here you can see the farms themselves, in full production as we discussed in our last meeting. We will take a tour of the nearest one, once everyone has finished their meal." Along the coast, we capture energy from the geothermal runoff from our mines, as well as wind and wave generators. Our latest development is a bioengineered surface for solar power. Not only does it currently produce thirty percent energy capture, but it also acts as a pressurized second skin, adding an additional protective layer to anything… under the waves."

The scene blew past the surf-laden beach and dove into the Caribbean-clear waters around Giresun. Habitats gleamed beneath the waves like shiny pockets of coral. Inside, the delegates could see people working and going about their daily lives fathoms beneath the surface.

"Astounding," the Guyana representative said. The silence had been deafening, now a crescendo of applause built its way around the table until it reached President Caldarone.

"Thank you, to my friend from Unified Guyana," Keiko said.

"Yes, yes. Absolutely amazing, thank you ladies," President Caldarone said. "I very much appreciate the food and wine. I am looking forward to seeing these wonders where I can touch them for myself." He smiled. "Father, forgive me, but I'm in the boat with doubting Thomas, I must admit… but I am most impressed." Calderone turned. "If you will indulge us, Representative Herrera has something to thank you for your hospitality."

Pepe Herrera rose and lifted a briefcase onto his seat. The Triumvirate stood. Columbia held back while Chris and Keiko moved forward toward the Peruvian delegate. Señor Herrera removed a jade statue from a foam-lined case. The ambient light flickered and reflected off the polished green surface like it was dancing. The smooth surfaces pooled the light in languid flows as the triumvirate stepped closer, as if the sculpture was fluid held in shape by some unseen force.

"Surrounded by so much new, exciting things, we would present to you this jade jaguar, recreated by an artist we hold as a national treasure from a historical artifact in our *Museo Nacional de Arqueología Antropología e Historia del Perú*, our museum of antiquities in Lima," Señor Herrera said.

Chris reached out to accept the gift while Keiko bowed.

"With the greatest pleasure, we will place this marvelous sculpture in our public archives for all the people of Giresun Island to see and appreciate. Thank you," Columbia said. The other Consuls returned to their seats, and the Triumvirate sat as one.

~

"Could you feel the envy?" Keiko asked. The Triumvirate sat around the salon overlooking two-thirds of Giresun's horizon. The penthouse sat on top of the tallest building in Giresun Island, at the end of the wide boulevard from the harbor. From the air, the crescent-shaped lagoon was connected by an eight-lane parade strip ending at the Forum and Archives complexes, with the Triumvirate's residence on top of the Forum. Behind the seat of government rose a volcanic ridge like a shield wall. The arable land and industrial areas spread out from the city below in tracts of light, like tentacles in the night. In the common room of the penthouse, music played in the background while electric torchlight danced in shadows over a collection of eclectic furniture and accent walls.

"It was thicker than the kudzu vines invading the north estuary," Chris said. "Should make next month's meeting in Cartagena fun."

"Well, a girl always likes to be wanted," Columbia said. Her somber expression cracked into a laugh.

Keiko refilled her wine glass.

"Anybody catch the aides nearly vomit when the recruits were running through the brambles course?" Chris asked.

"I got a vid," Keiko said. "Check it..."

"*Why are all the women scarred? Why don't they hide it?*" a man asked. His face was twisted with the effort of trying to understand why the island of women was so full of physical challenge rather than cosmetic shops and boutiques.

"Yeah, real macho. Pretty sure Guzman had a hard-on," Columbia said, refilling her glass.

"We didn't exactly behave our best all the time, either," Chris said. "And you can't expect them to understand our customs, like running through the acacia thorns..."

"Yeah, someone make sure the staff knows not to tell foreign dignitaries that they'd 'be more handsome if they smiled more,'" Columbia laughed. "And oh, how cute was it about the statue?"

"Hey, that was a nice gesture," Chris interrupted.

"Yeah, but the bug hidden in it wasn't," Keiko said.

"Can't blame a *gaucho* for trying," Columbia said.

"Then there's this—" Keiko flicked her fingers over the back of her hand. A surreptitious recording of President Calderone appeared against the night sky silhouetted by the twenty-foot-high cantilevered ceiling.

"*What would you do if someone, not us of course, came and took all this from you?*" he asked.

"*I wouldn't want to be the fool who tried. I'm so glad we have you as a friend,*" a recorded Columbia replied.

"Think it's a threat?" Chris asked.

"If he could back it up, sure," Columbia said. "Just can't stand that a bunch of countryless barbarians have the tech edge, or that an island of women isn't what he'd hoped for."

"Get a load of who's using a tanner," Keiko stretched out the video image of Calderone. The color was a shadowless flat brown. She changed the spectrum. "See? That's artificial UV."

"Heh," Columbia guffed. "Gotta get the natives on your side."

Chris stared in the general direction of the image but said nothing.

"Keiko, what does it look like—the deal?" Chris asked, after a moment. The displayed image changed to a still frame taken from surveillance. Mez Calla was reaching for a second dessert off a tray in the hallway outside the lav.

"Ecuador's a hard ass, but he is a true believer. Wants a united continent and then some," she said.

"He's got the time in the fight to prove it. Just look at those hands," Columbia said. The picture zoomed in to show chapped, calloused skin.

Keiko shifted the image to the Peruvian delegate.

"Pepe's going to go with whatever the president says, unless it erodes prestige and scientific credit, particularly for Lima," Keiko said. "Colombia is still trying to separate themselves from the image of drugs and corruption, so he'll make an effort to show support for the margins and end up going with this guy—"

Maxim Torres filled the space, his loud suit almost making the consuls squint.

"So, since Maxim is such a friend," Keiko nodded to Columbia, "We've got their money and resources in the pocket.

"Unified Guyana, Trinidad, and Tobago will all vote as a bloc, not that it matters much so far."

The pictures were replaced by a series of charts.

"Did you notice, Guiana, Trinidad, Tobago were all barely given time to speak? When they were, Brazil, Colombia, Peru constantly cut them off or interrupted?" Keiko said.

"Almost indistinguishable from Unified Guyana representatives too. Were they dressed that way out of solidarity, or just their version of khaki?" Columbia asked. "Chris, you're on the fence?"

"No, just looking at faces and thinking about lines of power," she said. "UG is the money pit of the GA—they add continuity to the country but constantly rely on it for financial and material support. Trinidad and Tobago recently joined the GA, so they're about broke. They emptied their reserves to buy into the confederation, so they have no choice but to follow with their bloc. They're going to be desperate if the confederacy falls. Keep Colombia and Brazil happy, appeal to Peru's vanity, and follow through right off the bat with your promises, and Ecuador is in."

"Agreed." Columbia slapped her hands down on her lap and rose from the divan. "Been a busy day. See you tomorrow." She sauntered out of the common area to the First Consul's penthouse door.

"'Night," Keiko said.

1845 06 JUL 2073

Carlos stood behind the truck, out of sight of the other men. He pulled up the latest message from their employer. "Object and location confirmed: 2-0-0-0-0-6-0-7-7-3." He turned off the display and picked up the ammo crate at his feet. Carlos waddled around the tailgate of the truck with the heavy box before heaving it onto the bed. The over-sized storage unit was dank. The night sky was taking over the last sunbeams. It was still hot and humid, sun or no. Now the insect chorus was building up, even here in the city. "Okay, *muchachos*. We're good to go," Carlos said. He wore a stained and wrinkled green field shirt and matching pants, every inch the would-be revolutionary. Standing next to the other two men in their red shirts and tan shorts, he felt ridiculous.

Juan sneered. He never took his eyes off the soldering iron. The rental storage unit smelled of open-air toilets—the bucket in the corner—and a diet of preserved food. The translucent plastic skylights dripped condensation on the stained concrete floor. Their rusty wire bunk beds were in four rows by the main door. A side door, by the toilet bucket, was open for cross-ventilation. It wasn't helping.

"Ours is not to question why," Carlos said. He stood apart from the men, commanding.

José zipped up three duffle bags of munitions. "That's it," he said. "'We've got plenty of explosives, a rifle, and *pistola* for every man."

"Political theater," Juan said. A puff of smoke rose from the circuit board. "*Soai...* I'm going to need to switch that gate out."

"Keep your attention on what's at hand," Carlos said.

"I'm going to go check on the truck. God help us, I don't know if it'll make it so far," José said.

CHAPTER 2

From the Ashes

DE SILVA OPERATIONS HACIENDA, AMAZON BASIN, BRAZIL

1939 17 MAR 2075
"The Cartel infrastructure is more or less unchanged. They look to you as the new leader," the lawyer explained. "Señor de Silva, I am sorry for your loss. Your father was a great man."

The papers sat on the table in the middle of the suite's sitting room. The lawyer stood up and took his valise out the door with the punctuality of movement that belied his desire to avoid a secondary attack. A vacuum sucked the air out of the hotel's posh conference room behind him. Baroque moldings glinted in the electric candlelight. A fanciful green carpet ran from wall to wall with a barely noticeable jungle motif woven into the fibers. Armand's shock-ridden gaze absently drifted to find monkeys and jaguars, snakes and fruit hiding in the pattern. A fluted tumbler sat before him, untouched on the table while condensation pooled at its base.

"Now the real work begins," Elana, Armand's teacher and sometimes confidant, said. Her typical pantsuit was replaced by a navy pencil skirt and blazer, while a striped shirt with a riot of color spilled out between the dark fabric and her dark skin. Oversized eye glasses softened her features in concert with bangs that threatened to drape across them. "The hypotheticals I used to give you, you excelled at in the classroom. But this isn't practice anymore. If you want me to stay, I will."

Armand slumped back in the Queen Anne chair and sighed. Every time he closed his eyes his body went into survival mode like a cornered rat. He sat back up.

Samuel Brönner, head of security, checked the windows again. His lean but large body blocked the light as he passed by each one. The crewcut he wore made his shadow look bald. Brönner stopped at the sitting area on his way to the door.

"You must now become a man. Force yourself and decide what to do next," Brönner said quietly.

"I know who did this," Armand said. "Yankee cowards." He picked up the glass of dark liquid but stopped short of his lips. "There's nothing I can do. Nothing that would mean anything."

"Are you alive?" Brönner said.

Armand turned and stared at him. His boyish looks belied a charisma he'd inherited along with the reins to the de Silva empire. He wore designer clothes that made him look like a fashion model, and his shoulder-length hair flowed like black tendrils in the breeze of the air conditioner. Loose and flowing today, his hairstyle changed like the clothes he wore. The effect drew people into his orbit, as inescapable as gravity.

"Are you alive," Brönner repeated slowly.

"Of course," Armand said.

"Then you can act," Brönner said. "You can always act while you still draw breath. It is a matter of will. Of creation."

Armand returned to face forward, brooding over his still hovering drink. Something broke in his countenance. Armand's eyes came into focus, and determination drew across his features until he vibrated with purpose. He drank deeply from his glass.

"I know what to do. It is time to come to our senses. We must all become men. Not just me." Armand stood. "Call a meeting of the remaining district heads. I need a prospectus based on our greasing wheels, projections, and effectiveness as well as the costs. Can you do that?"

"I'll have it for the meeting. Day after tomorrow," Elana said.

Brönner turned away to hide his smile. He checked the exits again.

DE SILVA OPERATIONS HACIENDA, AMAZON BASIN, BRAZIL

2114 18 MAR 2075

"They work for you now. Don't forget." Elana Chavez straightened Armand's tie. "Let Brönner be Brönner. He can keep the dogs in line until you're settled."

"Señor de Silva," Samuel Brönner said. He stopped at the rough-hewn double doors in a summer retreat on the Amazon upstream from Iquitos. The occasional stink of the turgid river made the aides and lackeys pinch their noses while their linen suits wrinkled and collars fell. It barely registered to Brönner. Just another detail in the tapestry of his home. The droning hum of the insects competed with the croaks of the frogs along the jungle's edge.

Armand nodded. Brönner opened the doors and stepped aside. The men inside the conference room were in tailored suits. Hulking bodyguards stood behind them. The chairs shifted back as the men rose to their feet and sized up the young de Silva cartel head.

Before Armand could sit, one of the drug lords laid into him.

"*¿Qué soy? ¿Un perro, que debería seguir la llamada de este chico? Po-gai eso—*"

[What am I? A dog who should follow this boy's call? Po-gai that—]

Suddenly a knife hilt appeared in the red-faced drug lord's right eye. Brönner's right arm dropped as he readied to draw his Makarov with his left in one counter-balanced sweep.

The deposed drug lord's body guard stood by as the body hit the table and slid into a lump, halfway landing in his seat. For a moment no one moved. Then Brönner nodded to the unfazed bodyguard, who picked up the corpse bodily and lugged it around the table to the opposite door. The bodyguard glanced at the knife, then looked back at Brönner.

"Keep it," Brönner said.

Armand cleared his throat quietly. "Take your seats," he said. The men glanced at each other, then settled back into their chairs. "I know this is a trying time for us all. My family is dead. I was buried alive, left for dead. The imperialists didn't like where we were heading, so they did what they always do: regime change."

Men who were accustomed to power shifted nervously in their seats. Brönner smelled the change in their sweat as fear spread like a wave around the table. He stayed behind their point of view so that the fear was focused on his young prince, the new power in the room.

"The Americans are really gonna hate this," Armand said through a mischievous grin.

A paper chart was brought in behind Armand.

"I know, I know, it's not flashy and high tech. But you know what I love about paper? Can't be hacked. If it gets out, I know who saw it, *simón*?"

The crowd shifted in their seats almost imperceptibly.

"My father, God rest his soul," Armand made the sign of the cross, "made you all very rich men. Made the men who work for you very rich too."

Nods and murmured agreement bounced around the room.

"I plan to do the same. It's time for a change, though. Let's take it to the *imperialistas*, those damn Yankees, and show them how much they need us!" Armand said.

A sporadic applause built its way around the room, crescendoing until the assembled dons were on their feet, pounding on the table in their enthusiasm.

The death of one of their own was a powerful motivator. The questions would eventually come, but his authority was established. Armand let them burn off their nerves for a minute, then motioned for the crowd to sit back down. The sweat was pooling, bleeding through their jackets, as the subject turned to familiar business. Their collective breath was still effectively held, but the tension was easing. Armand gestured to the chart. "This map is our network, our cartel. It is vast. But it is a trade route, a supply chain. I know more than a few of you have advanced degrees in business and finance. Is this not so? But this is, after all, only business."

He smiled, encouraging the others to let out a nervous laugh.

"We sell products, like any business. But as any good Bolivarian will tell you, people make it work, and when you control the means of production, it's personal. I say it's time to make it personal," Armand said.

Staying seated, the dons cheered. A file of young people in business casual clothes—odd for the Amazon—strode in through the doorway. They placed portfolios in front of each of the cartel leaders. The cordon of aides exited the room from the opposite side of the table. The effect was hypnotic.

"We're going into the business of *la Revolución!*" Armand announced. "We're going to march out and create a new world. Don't worry, I see your worry. I went too far, eh—it's like this. The business hasn't changed. What we do is what we have always done, but why are we always pissing where we eat?" He shook his head. "We can make the system our own instead of fighting it, but it's just a different way of getting to the same ends. We're a business. Business is about profits, no? If the people support us, if we become the government, we cut costs. How much did we spend on greasing the wheels last quarter?"

"More than ten billion US," the head accountant said.

Armand shook his head. "More than ten billion. Who of you doesn't want a piece of that?" he shouted. "If we're the government, then they're our wheels! Someone doesn't do what we want? Gone. Not like that poor bastard just now, but fired, out of the way, replaced in the day with someone we can use."

Nervous laughter skittered around the room.

"We've been going the right way for years, obviously." Armand waved his hands around the room. "But we can grow, and this," he said, holding up the portfolio, "this is how we start. Get smart, I want financials and projections turned in tomorrow. I'll see to incorporating your new figures into the budget and set a date for trials. Worst-case, we burn it to the ground, we go back to the way Papa had it, and forget this."

~

Samuel Brönner was waiting at the doorway and closed the two massive panels behind Armand's exit. They walked down the terracotta-tiled hallway. The Amazon languidly drifted across the embankment. Their footsteps echoed slightly under the Moorish arches of the veranda. The air was stifling, thick with the afternoon heat and intense humidity of the rainforest.

"*Soai*," Armand said, sighing.

"Found your voice," Brönner said.

"You don't want your knife back?" Armand asked.

"Don't care. It's just a thing."

"Okay," Armand said. He sat down on a rattan couch. A servant brought a pitcher and glasses. She poured for the men, then backed away and slipped into the house.

Armand took a drink and coughed.

Brönner was on his feet, gun drawn. "That's not agua fresca," he said.

"*Soai!* No no no no! It's fine! I'm fine!"

Brönner looked down at him, the gun disappearing.

"Just not used to this homemade *cachaça*," Armand said, trying to stifle another cough. "Do you think they'll go for it?"

"Too early to tell. We scared the *soai* out of them, and they aren't easily scared. Fear won't last. They're greedy little men. As long as they're getting what they lust after, they'll play along, unless someone convinces them they can do better," Brönner said. He stared across the river and silently catalogued the signs from the environment. He heard the dons' vehicles peel off from the other side of the hacienda.

"Can't just keep killing them off," Armand said. "That was an observation, not a command."

"Good. There will be more of that. I wasn't sure," Brönner said with a chuff.

"I'm not naive," Armand said.

"Give them just enough of what they want, even if it means a leading loss."

"And you…" Armand said. "What do you want?"

"That's not your concern, Prince."

They sat on the veranda, sipped the rough homemade rum, and watched the jungle thrive.

PERU, AMAZON SIDE

2114 24 MAR 2075

The jungle night was impenetrable from the window. The glow of the headlights from the truck behind failed to illuminate anything more than flapping grasses and leaves as the convoy passed. Armand stared into the darkness, brooding.

Elana touched his arm. "Individuals are intelligent; they can be smart. People, on the other hand… People are dumb, stupid even, like animals. They react to emotion, and that can be aroused and guided through the simplest of things." She smiled softly. "Ideas rule. Like a ragged dog, you feed them, play with them, make them feel accepted, and they will be loyal—until a better offer comes along."

Armand pushed his well-worn western shirt's rolled sleeve cuffs above his elbows. The front was mostly open, showing the clean T-shirt underneath. His moleskin pants broke in uncouth folds over the dusty hiking boots. He looked all the part of the country worker, like some golden age American President in ranch wear trying to convince the plebes that he was one of them.

Elana reached across the cabin of the car to fuss with his shirt sleeves. "When you're up there, in front of the crowd, watch how it moves. It's made of people, but it's like its own living thing. When you're talking, you can see it. You can see an idea infect a crowd. It spills from person to person. You can literally see it from up on the dais. It reaches a critical mass, then explodes. Then the pitchforks and torches come. Maybe it takes on a pseudo order, like guttersnipes in powdered wigs and guillotines. Here, it's more like rocks and Molotov cocktails."

Armand kept staring out the window.

"You remember how it works?" Elana chided. The car at the head of a procession of trucks bumping along as the jungle gave way to another collapsing hovel of a *barrio*.

He turned from the window to her. "*Sí*, of course. You practically made it part of my nightly routine, *señora*."

"Humor me," she said.

"We show up out of nowhere, no fanfare or big to-do. We give gifts, entertainment, food, and shower the people with riches. We turn no one away. We are just visitors passing through, looking to make the acquaintance of the people," Armand recited.

"What comes after that?" Elana asked. "Let's just run over the details."

"Then we come back and do the same again, except we run out. We say, gee, it'd be nice if we had somewhere to store stuff. Maybe we could stay for a while and get to know you better. Next time one of our people passes through, just let us know. You know the deal, give them a silver coin and they'll work like a dog. These locals will be shamed and, what's more, greedy. They'll build us a foothold because we asked. We show up, and this time we talk about their lives and bemoan their fate with them, and gee, wish we could help. Here's some stuff to help in the meantime. Too bad your leaders aren't able to provide better for you."

"And if they take the bait?" Elana asked.

"Then we've got them. We can exploit the failings of their elected officials. We fix things without their doing anything… at first. Then we ask for a little help, then wash, rinse, repeat. We take control from the ground up, and the government officials will have no actual control before they know what's happened. Then we just walk up to the residence and ask for the keys."

"About sums it up," she said. "And if they don't bite?"

The destitution and poverty outside in the barrio was magnified by the sudden eruption of detail. Buildings crumbled into their neighbors, surrounded by a warren of makeshift steps and alleyways. Tall, rusty rebar jutted from the sky from half-built cinderblock walls. The promise of homes that would never be. Ragged tarps flopped in the breeze, trying and failing to stand in for walls and doors that remained unfinished. The structures seemed slapped together, like the architect had an idea of what made a building or house without understanding the order in which they came together.

"Are you certain this is the way forward?" Brönner interrupted.

"As a cartel, we have no standing on the world stage. But as a government, as a nation, or a continent? They will listen, and we can do as we want!" Armand said. "As for the plebes, we appeal to their neighbors and call out their selfishness, their greed and their dishonesty in the face of charity, then their neighbors run them down for us," Armand said before opening the door.

Sunlight beamed in as the sun rose over the surrounding canopy. It formed a preternatural outline around the young man like a vision. "Just the sort of special effects the Inca were so proud of," Elana said under her breath as she scooted across the padded bench and reached for his hand, bangles chiming. "Watch that ridiculous pompadour hair of yours."

The truck doors opened. Men jumped down and started tossing out boxes of fresh vegetables and dry goods. A crowd quickly grew, hemming in Armand and his trucks. Armand shook hand after hand. Men passed out bottles of water purification tablets, filtration straws, medical kits. Women distributed cards with link codes to the crowd for their devices. Soon people were leaving with more food than they could honestly carry. They returned with their neighbors.

Standing in the open maw of one of the empty transports, Armand held an amplifier and commenced another address.

"*Buenos dias!* My name is Armand. I couldn't find a market, so I came back with one. I hope you like it. I'm no Guevara. Do I end my sentences with 'che?' I'm no Bolivar, either. I make no promises, I have no shining sword. I'm from Cusco, not Argentina. I grew up all over this land." He shook his head as he looked over the crowd. "I've seen how we're treated, by the privileged, by the world. We're better without them. Let's do it ourselves, for ourselves. They can come to us and wait for us." He pulled one of the cards from his pocket and waived it. "Check out the links we gave you. I hope to see you all again real soon!"

Enthusiastic cheers and raised hands waved as Armand climbed back down. His men made a cordon between the truck and the car. People still managed to poke their hands through, between the bodies forming the gauntlet.

~

The motorcade drove up to a simple concrete dock off the Amazon. A powered barge waited, slight smoke drifting over the water downstream. Armand and Elana walked across the gangplank, followed by a few staff. Armand was nearly into the cabin when a scuffle spun him around. Brönner had a man pinned on his knees.

"*¡Por favor señor, no me dieron opción!*" he cried.

[Please sir, they gave me no choice!]

Armand slowly turned and slipped into the deck below. A heavy splash against the hull sounded as the motor revved. The man disappeared. Brönner sauntered down into the cabin wiping his hands on a towel before pouring a glass of ice water and sitting in the corner next to the ladder.

"I wonder how much of that food is going to spoil before it's eaten," Armand muttered as the boat started back to Iquitos.

"Your name is all over it, so it doesn't matter. Mission accomplished," Elana said. She smoothed her pantsuit against its fight with the steaming Amazon. "I'd have met you upstairs, but at least there are fewer insects down here."

Armand stared out at the river. "The same thing again at the n‹ town over?" He sighed. "This is tedious."

Brönner shook his head. "No, the network is handling it. We start small. Enough to test the waters, not enough to arouse suspicion or bankrupt anybody."

"So while my name and face are the ad campaign, we're hitting enough targets to make progress around the GA." Armand nodded to himself. "If it's successful we'll snowball into a massive takedown. Like a *lucha libre* flying off the ropes." He flexed, mimicking a wrestler's pose.

"Mm-hmm," Elana said, opening her screen. "You do ten percent of the glad-handing, the cartel's network will preach the message to the other ninety. Of course, we only broadcast your appearances."

Brönner raised an eyebrow and looked the other way.

Armand snorted. "We get so stuck on the cost of our lifestyle. It's easy to forget how cheap some chicken and a can of tomatoes are. It's true, people are loyal to their stomachs, *viva pan y circos*."

Elana looked up and narrowed her eyes. "Don't get lost in the process, Armand. Every prince who has been overthrown by his own people was seen as betraying their trust first. The obligation you're courting and bending to your will is based on reciprocation."

"Of course, professor," Armand said, staring out a window.

CHAPTER 3

A Snake in the Grass

PERU

1646 03 APR 2075
The old man refused to meet Brönner's gaze. He stared at his feet, hat in hand, and spoke softly. "The last Bolivarian revolution brought us proper housing and sanitation, but eventually graft and greed got the better of them too," the old man said. "The food and supplies have always been welcome, but we cannot join you. This is our home, this is where we make the best good. We do not care about who prints the money. What are we on, the nineteenth republic or something? The worker is who we support. No *señor*, we will not move."

The leader of the Chávez XXI village's neighborhood council stood in the nighttime light, with its golden color from the strings of bulbs between buildings in the barrio. The once tall three- and four-story buildings crumbled around them. Their rough moss-covered brick edges and destroyed walls left black blank spots against the stars. Bullet pock-marked plaster played in shadow under the electric lights. Weeds slowly worked to split the road under their feet. Decay crept through the village, and Brönner could reconstruct the once beautiful town in his mind as the old man droned on.

"I am sorry to hear that," Brönner said. They stood in the street as the rest of the neighborhood watched. "Be well."

Brönner whipped his hand over his head in a tight circle. The men started their trucks behind him, and he slipped into the cab of the lead vehicle. A screen lit up, its blue glare highlighting the hatchet man's face from below. Armand's face appeared.

"They did not agree," Brönner said.

"They will be missed at the table." Armand gave a curt nod and turned off his screen.

Brönner typed in a command code and turned his screen off as well.

A pellet the size of a papaya dropped from the lead vehicle and skittered across the broken road into the gutter.

～

"They've gone. We've made ourselves clear, comrades. They won't be back, and the world watches." The old man gestured around the sky above. "The days of *Caracazo*… they're still held to public opinion, they're too exposed to do anything like that. So go back to your homes, sleep well. I'll see you tomorrow."

The old man lowered his hands and walked back into the house. Strands of lights turned off along with their gasoline generators. Under the moon and stars above there was still light enough to see the scattered members of the town council. He turned up his head at two men, like a reverse nod. A cat call shrieked from someone's two-fingered whistle. Delegates from different neighborhood families filed out. They picked up rifles from the shadows and took up watch posts on top of the end buildings. At sunrise, four men huddled in the center of the barrio where the meeting had taken place.

"Nothing has come or gone all night," said one.

"Me neither," said another.

"That's both ends," said the third.

"No one is sneaking around either. I heard a cat and a dog get into it, but that's it," said the one.

"Then we're in agreement? The guys on watch before us saw nothing. We saw *nada*," said another.

"We have to wait and see, but not up there on the wall," said the fourth.

∼

The sun beat down on Chávez XXI, an intense heat away from the shade. Two different kinds of heat—the sweltering humidity of the jungle, combined with the sizzling sear of direct sunlight—kept the adults away, and for a little while at least the children played. Two girls played with rocks at the side of a stone-filled gap in the road. The light was so intense that they bowed their heads to play in the shadow created by their own bodies. The rocks alternated as people and cars in their game of make-believe. Something twinkled in the storm gutter. Patrice slipped under the hand rails down into the concrete spillway.

"Patrice! Not suppose to do that," Izzy scolded.

"Shut it," Patrice said. "It's fine."

Patrice reached down into the leaves that accumulated at the grate to the sewer.

"It's some pieces um metal." She shrugged. "Look like one uh dose runners lef some of a fancy car passing trew," Patrice said. "Bad quality. Te car's prolly dropping more parts erwhere."

She brought the scrap metal up with her. The pieces fit like a clam shell.

"Prolly like a muffler. You know, BRRRRRRPPPT psse-ewwwww BRRRPPPT!" Patrice said.

Patrice chased Izzy around the road making the obnoxious impression.

"Eww, te inside's all slimy," Izzy wiped her hand on the ground.

"Be'er go wash it off before *tia* catch you wid a stain on your *vestido*. C'mon," Patrice said.

ECUADOR

"Welcome to Ecuador," the driver said. "Call me Manny."

Brönner said nothing as the highway became rougher before falling away completely as the mountains of jungle overwhelmed the infrastructure of man. Rolling hills of vegetation backed by mountains and spotted with high plains, Ecuador was beautiful in its rugged terrain. Peru was more extreme in its geography, but the two countries were similar in Brönner's eyes. Savage wilds dotted with concrete jungles.

"We should be in Santo Domingo in a couple more hours," Manny said. "Protest should be really fired up by then, *señor!*" Manuel said.

Brönner tried to ignore his insinuations of conversation.

"Want me to turn on the radio? Want to take a *siesta*? I'm good. I can wake you later."

"People never know what they want. Not really," Brönner finally said.

He pulled his hat down over his eyes and leaned back in the truck's seat.

The driver was nervous. "I'll just wake you up before Santo—"

"Wake me up before San Gabriel," Brönner said.

"San Gabriel del Baba? Sure, sure. I didn't take you for a *tourista*."

Brönner raised his hat slightly.

"Never mind. I'll wake you," Manuel said. His knuckles were white as well as his face.

The landscape rolled on, alternating golden-brown brush and thick jungle foliage. Manny tried to stay focused on the drive. He was used to cartel gigs; not a gang member, just hired transport with a steady set of driving skills under pressure. This passenger—if he'd known who the ticket was, he would've broken his own arm to get out of it. Samuel Brönner's reputation was that of a ruthless killer, coming from the merciless predators of the de Silva cartel. Two hours passed before he dared turn on the radio. Brönner's hat inched up.

"We're coming up on San Gabriel," Manny said quietly.

"Turn here and stop before the next corner," Brönner gestured at a folded map in his hand. The area he'd marked was a de Silva compound. It was surrounded by dense jungle, a hidden depot off a nondescript dirt road, odd in the fact that the road was perfectly maintained.

"Straight to business," Manny said. "I take it we're not making an official visit. Should I keep the engine on, or power down?"

"Power down," Brönner said. "You're coming with."

Manny retrieved his revolver and checked the cylinder. Moments later the truck was parked, facing the way they had come. As he opened his door, Brönner cleared his throat.

"Bring an automatic magnerifle," Brönner said.

The imposing figure of Samuel Brönner melted into the brush as he entered the jungle. The animals didn't miss a beat, as if he were just another jaguar on the prowl. Manuel tried to be quiet in his footsteps but was haplessly cracking twigs or rustling leaves. He stumbled on the uncleared brush, clearly unused to the weight of the magnerifle's electromagnets and block of refined iron. The denizens of the forest noticed him. Birds squawked, some flew. A couple monkeys dared to swing above and howl. Past the initial tree line, Manny lost sight of Brönner.

Manny began to panic, then the hairs on his neck stood on end.

"Don't move," an unfamiliar voice said callously behind him.

Brönner cleared his throat behind the stranger.

The man spun around, puffed out his chest and shook a beat-up magnerifle menacingly toward him.

"Now you're both gonna—"

The other man suddenly fell at Brönner's feet, blood pouring fast from a wound at his left neck, his right ribcage, and right inner thigh. He gasped as Brönner dug through his pockets and took his rifle. Manny stood in shock, his brain trying to piece together the scene he had just witnessed. Brönner started walking back into the woods. He snapped his fingers. Like a hypnotist's subject, Manny turned away from the corpse with a vacant expression and followed.

Manny picked up the other man's magnerifle and saw it only had enough charge for a few burst shots. The iron block was nearly depleted.

"At least it's not as heavy," Manny said.

Two kilometers later Manuel caught up with Brönner as he scaled a tree.

"Manuel, what did you do today?" Manny asked himself in a gruffer voice. "No *soai*, there I was. This guy, big, bald *gaucho* I'm walking around with gets jumped. But the *bandito* was cut to ribbons in the blink of an eye. I walked with him into the woods, because he said to. Then, he disappeared!"

Soon Brönner dropped quietly down onto the jungle floor trailing a wire behind him.

"Of course, only to drop out of the damn trees like a jaguar a minute later. Probably to eat me," Manny said to himself.

"In ten minutes, exactly, pull this until you hear the magnetic accelerators going off. Then lay down behind those bushes. I'll be back. If I run, you run."

"Ten minutes," Manny said through the shock.

Nine minutes and fifty-nine seconds later, Manny pulled on the wire. Automatic gunfire erupted from the canopy. The slices of iron were accelerated at thousands of meters per second, shaved from the weapon's block in a nanosecond. The friction in the air caused each round to look like a bolt of lightning. Their incredible velocity shredded the jungle in their path. Explosions in the distance concussed through the underbrush. People shouted, then stopped.

Three minutes later, Samuel Brönner walked through the forest whistling. Manuel got up from his hasty position and stared at the other man. Brönner had embers glowing on the back and sleeves of his shirt. Manny could see blood drip over splotches of mud.

"You're on fire," Manuel said.

"I don't have time for that," he said. Brönner slapped at the back of his sleeve. "Just smoking. It's a pity, that could have been so simple. People naturally assume they're the top predator. Makes them inherently biased."

Manny kept looking up at the canopy like a haunted house 'til they made it back to the truck.

"That gun in the trees didn't hit *soai*, did it?" Manuel asked. His eyes were on the smoke rising above the trees as he started the truck's fuel cell. He thought of the de Silva depot and what carnage would make a fire like that.

"What?" Brönner said.

"Santo Domingo?" Manuel asked.

"Quietly," Brönner said.

∼

Manny turned down the radio, drove into the center of the small town of Santo Domingo, and parked near a gathering crowd. The town was better preserved than most, with stretches of ancient cobblestone and neo-gothic arches. Large blocks of townhomes dominated the downtown area, bathed in light by decorative streetlights against the falling sun. The smells of the countryside faded away under the perfume of progress. Someone with a blow horn announced the procession amidst chants against everything from corruption to police brutality.

"Stay here. Be ready to drive away—"

"Quietly?" Manuel interrupted.

Brönner walked off into the crowd with a duffle bag from behind his seat. The march departed, leaving the large square littered and abused. Manny stood by the truck watching. An hour passed, and warnings blared from loudspeakers in the direction of city hall.

"All civilians are ordered to return to their homes or businesses," they announced. "Disperse or you will be fired upon."

Manuel got into the truck and cracked the windows. Shouting drowned out the loudspeakers. Police gunfire echoed through the streets, but not what sounded like crowd suppression.

"*¡Viva el Pueblo de Ecuador!*" screamed the speakers.

[Long live the people of Ecuador!]

Manuel saw billowing black smoke rising from the direction of the government seat. Flames gathered and spread. There was no need for high-tech bombs when it was easy to get alcohol, fuel oil, soap, and glass bottles. Just hand them out with a match to a crowd and let nature take its course.

"*¡Po-gai los conspiradores!*" they shouted again.

[Po-gai the conspirators!]

The predator slunk back down the road after an hour and a half. The sirens and smoke had started thirty minutes ago. Manuel noted that the duffle bag was gone.

Brönner slipped into the passenger seat, and they drove south in silence, back into the darkness.

PERU

1646 17 APR 2075

"Oddly enough, we were just there," Armand said. He looked beyond the camera's view. "...a few weeks ago now, yes."

"Yes, odd," Pepe Herrera said. "I was hoping you'd maybe heard something when you were there."

Armand shrugged.

The decayed village of Chávez XXI now had a smell to match its broken walls and crumbling buildings. No children played in the streets, and no congregation of tenants to appease.

"Ah, here's the update. The aid we've sent should arrive in the morning," Armand said, scrolling through his screen's feed. The tailored news, commentary, advertising, and social networks flowed through the air, projected against his outstretched palm.

"Well then, *buenos noches*, Señor de Silva," Pepe said. "This plague is wiping out whole villages, and it's catching in cities now. The body count is unimaginable."

"No clue where it came from?" Armand said. His eyes flicked to his truck. He smirked and thought, *Bronner and his cruel weapons have scored again...*

"Just showed up in a couple pockets around here, along the jungle," Pepe said.

"*Via con dios, Señor Herrera. Adios.* Please let me know if we can be of further assistance in this time of tragedy."

Governor Herrera stared at his screen after Armand de Silva's image disappeared. It was replaced by scrolling information from his feed. He read none of it.

The ambulances came and went, though streets choked with detritus and mobile morgue wagons. The dusky twilight obscured the body bags being loaded into the refrigerated vans. The actinic blue lights from the command center glared in the dimness. Pepe wiped away a stream of tears before anyone noticed. The barrio of Chávez XXI was decimated. Nine out of ten residents had collapsed over the last three days. The first to go were the family of an old man, the village elder. Pepe nearly collapsed with the viewing. A pair of little girls, sisters, laid side by side. The sight had nearly killed him by itself.

There had been no fever, no respiratory distress, just a sudden catatonic attack followed by systemic collapse and death within three hours. The local hospital was little more than an aid station with an old chapel converted into a ward. Even if they had the capacity, there was no way to stabilize the cascade of organ failure quickly enough here, and patients were dead before they could reach Lima or Cuzco.

Herrera walked into the command center when he was certain his eyes were clear. He squinted as his eyes caught up with the harsh white light. It gave everything a faint blue hue and obliterated the outside world.

"Any change?" he asked.

thing new, señor," the attending physician said. "Our virolo-
Lima and the infectious disease team have come back with
ng. It's like the old stories of the jungle spitting something out
at the villagers. It's already gone, and we have no idea what hit us."

"No further transmissions?" Herrera said.

"Not for at least twenty-four hours," the physician said. "Deaths
are slowing down, but no one is recovering. We don't even know how
it's transmitted, when it was, or why it stopped."

"Thank God it did," Herrera said. He made the sign of the cross.

"What god?" the physician asked. He passed the governor a clip-
board with the names of the dead.

CHAPTER 4

The End Is the Beginning

CUZCO, PERU

1127 15 MAR 2075
The cobblestone cul-de-sac was more or less full. People gathered around the raised platform and politely paid attention to the woman speaking. The political speech was more like a lecture than a sales pitch, and the pedestrians responded in kind. The night air was cool, and the stars fought to overcome the brilliance of the nearer street-lights. The people milled about play-acting at paying attention. The production was a de Silva matter. People who showed poor manners toward such things paid a price, but there was no requirement to actually pay her any mind. Like similar lectures in the *escuela*, just keep your eyes more or less upfront, nod, and smile. Maybe clap when it was over.

"...in conclusion, we must unite the people, as our ancestors did, and reclaim our Incan heritage that the conquistadors and Europeans and Americans have taken from us along with our relics. I know this is an old song, and that everyone has heard it before. Greed has always kept us from achieving this. We are not at the mercy of the imperialists anymore. They have seen their decline. Now it is time for us to rise up and take back what should have been ours all along!"

Elana Chávez held her hands up from the makeshift podium in the cul de sac.

People all applauded politely if not enthusiastically, then as if by cue moved on, trying to escape any further notice. This barrio was just another blur of rich drug dealers surrounded by destitution and squalor. The de Silva cartel allowed her to have these political speeches and rallies because she was Armand de Silva's private tutor. The education of his only legitimate son had been of personal interest to the drug czar, and Elana Chávez was the finest political science doctorate that Peru had ever produced. The boy loved history and politics, so she was invited to the hacienda to pursue her work and make sure Armand was properly educated. Evidently, she was not just given a platform for her pet political science project, but an audience too.

Elana shook hands with the people still in the street. The crew packed up the platform and sound equipment.

"We even had a news van tonight," a crew member said. He coiled up the electrical cords from the podium.

The cameras were closing up after shooting a closing segment with their reporter. Suddenly, the high-pitch scream of metal parts ripped across the sky. The cameramen furiously tried to bring their equipment back online. Fireballs erupted from the hills above—the de Silva hacienda. They were immense, orange, and red, like the afterimage of the sun when closing your eyes from it. Then the heat and concussion swept through the courtyard. Glass windows blew out, littering the ground in shards. Useless car alarms wailed. Elana stood dumbfounded in shock. The air around her felt like she had opened a furnace door and left her to struggle for breath.

～

Two blocks away toward the de Silva hacienda, a woman got up from the bed and dressed. The air was humid and still hot, drifting in through the open window. The orange of unglazed terra cotta tiles gridded the floor of Brönner's small studio apartment. They off-set the Navajo white of its textured plaster walls. A rough-hewn wood beam ceiling and scant rustic pine furniture gave the long, narrow room a cloistered feel.

"*Diosa de la Muerta*, why ain't you got *ayecee* in here, man?" she asked.

Samuel Brönner said nothing, lying under the crumpled linen sheet. The woman clutched her platform heels and slipped a roll of bills into her vanishing waistband. She closed the heavy wooden door behind her. A draught of chilled air flooded the room and fluttered the window coverings as it left as quickly.

Brönner lay still until he could no longer feel her presence. He paid the going rate but did nothing. The potential energy was thick as she had lain next to him in the simple room. She had touched him a few times, but he willed himself not to respond. He was master over himself and refused to be moved.

The blast shook the tile roof. Dust rained down on Samuel's spartan room while his ears popped under the sudden pressure. He could see the light of the fires through the curtains. A switch flipped in his mind, and in that instant he was ready for war. With whom he did not know, but whoever it was would pay for disturbing his lair. Brönner sat up and slid his clothes on as his feet met the insoles of his boots. In seconds he was fully dressed and on his way to the de Silva hacienda, or whatever was left of it.

∾

Elana pulled up to the hacienda's grounds amid the police, fire, and paramedic crews.

Brönner stood, silhouetted by spouts of flame between the rubble. The ground was already wet from the firehoses' drainage. The previously manicured gardens were in unrecognizable tatters.

She heard a man in a hard hat yell, "Did you cut all the breakers?"

"Yes, all the panels are off for this side of the house," replied another.

Blue lightning flared as a grounding rod was attached to the main electrical cable. The man in the hard hat was blown back five meters, landing in a cloud of dust on the pile of rubble.

"*Señora*, it's not safe! Please, we will call for volunteers. I can't fix the electrical if I have to keep ushering people back, please!" the engineer pleaded.

Elana gingerly picked her way back down through the rubble along a path-in-progress, strewn with masonry and broken things, toward Samuel Brönner. He looked paler than usual, practically cachexic. The rescue effort's coordinator was with him.

"When did you sleep or eat last?" Elana said as she joined him.

The other man took his cue to leave.

"Doesn't matter."

"You're no good to us dead," she said.

"Neither are they."

〜

Armand's four-poster bed suddenly dropped eight meters down. For an instant, he was floating, wrapped in a silken sail, riding through the air. The next he hit the mattress hard, like a *luchador* body slam. The sides clam-shelled over him and locked into place. The cocoon was a composite of metal reinforced ceramic, designed for the protection of sleeping occupants during a natural disaster. In the palace of the world's largest drug cartel, it was a panic room capable of withstanding a military assault. In an instant, the bed converted into a life pod, and any sense of control Armand had entertained before was left behind.

Outside, everything was on fire. The elegant Spanish-colonial compound was reduced to charred ruins. Pockets of fire billowed from ruptured gas lines once the gas and heat met with the oxygen above the rubble. The garden was a smoldering wreck. Buried under it all, Armand heard the rapid clacking and rapport of weapons fire as it resounded throughout the hacienda. Armand's bed had swallowed him whole. He fought and struggled against the steel coffin. Hours seemed to pass. The lighting turned on, and off, on and off, as he played with the light switch controls in the security hideaway. Food, medical supplies, and even entertainment other than the electronic toys he was used to were anchored under the mattress.

"Everything except a way out," he mused.

Instinct said everyone above was dead. His dad, Alejandro de Silva, had powerful enemies.

"Who would make such a bold move, though?" he asked the audience in his head.

None of the previous cartels were lacking for profit or peace. Señor de Silva had seen to it, uniting all of the factions under one roof, like Alexander the Great with the Greeks. It was his life's work to legitimize their agribusiness and throw off the two-faced bias of the Anglo-Europeans.

"It was not enough for someone."

Stuck inside a two and a half meter by one and a half meter steel box, sealed away from the destruction, Armand de Silva vowed to take whoever it was to test over this insurrection or attack.

"There will be hell to pay," he swore.

Armand struggled with the latch. The lid was pinned down by something.

"Probably the whole godforsaken house up there," he said.

He began to hyperventilate, slowly enough he did not notice it until it was unstoppable like a hiccup. His mind searched for something to hold onto, anything to calm the rising panic. A song his mother sang to him when he was a child came like a ghost into his thoughts and worked its way through his lips.

"*De Colores,*" he wheezed. "*—de colores se visten—*" wheeze, wheeze, "*—los campos en la primavera,*" he went on.

[The colors. The colors dress the fields in the spring.]

"*De Colores, de colores son los,*" he sang, pausing for breath. "*Los pajarillos que vienen de afuera.*"

[The colors, the colors of the birds that come from outside.]

Armand closed his eyes and took two long breaths. He sang louder, forcing the air from his lungs in controlled blasts.

"*De Colores, de colores es el arco iris que vemos lucir.*"

[The colors, the colors are the rainbow that we see shine.]

The wheezing passed.

"*Y por eso los grandes amores, de muchos colores me gustan a mi. Y por eso los grandes amores, de muchos colores me gustan a mi.*"

[And that is why I have a great love for many colors. And that is why I have a great love for many colors.]

While the clock shone an hour and a quarter had passed, it felt like days. Armand could hear machinery thundering outside as the rubble was cleared from somewhere out there. He choked back panic. He began the next line in an infinite round of song.

"*Canta el gallo, canta el gallo con el quiri, quiri, quiri, quiri, quiri. La gallina, la gallina con el cara, cara, cara, cara, cara. Los polluellos, los polluellos con el pio, pio, pio, pio, pi. Y por eso los grandes amores, de muchos colores me gustan a mi.*"

[The rooster sings with a quiri, quiri, quiri, quiri, quiri. The hen, the hen with a cara, cara, cara, cara, cara. The chicks, the chicks with a tweet, tweet, tweet, tweet, tweet. And that is why I have a great love for many colors.]

Something sounded like it scraped the side of his coffin. Armand struggled bodily to keep his frantic mind under control.

"*Y por eso los grandes amores, de muchos colores me gustan a mi. De Colores, de colores brillantes y finos se viste la aurora, De Colores, de colores son los mil reflejos que el sol atesora!*" he yelled. The scraping intensified and was now coming from all around him.

[And that is why I have a great love for many colors. The colors, the colors so bright and fine the aurora is dressed. The colors, the colors are the thousand reflections that the sun treasures.]

"*De Colores, de colores es el diamante que vemos lucir. Y por eso los grandes amores, de muchos colores me gustan a mi. Y por eso los grandes amores, de muchos colores me gustan a mi.*"

[The colors, the colors is the diamond that we see shine. And that is why I have a great love for many colors. And that is why I have a great love for many colors.]

"We've got you! We're going to work to free you from the rubble," someone outside was calling.

Tears dripped from Armand's cheeks and his breath came in choking sobs as he listened to the people digging to unearth his tomb.

GIRESUN ISLAND

1130 15 MAR 2075

"There's been an incident," data analyst Sim(on) said. Giresun Island's Security Force's World Operations rarely had anything good to report. His voice broke the hum of cooling fans in the analysis room. The cold room was surrounded by walls of server racks. The floor provided ambient lighting through lit tiles separated by a black grid. Overhead was a vaulted ceiling with a concourse and glass office fronts in a tiered border.

"What'd you say, Simian?" Nancy said. She was a hulking monster rising from her command chair.

"Someone just leveled the de Silva organization," Sim(on) said, ducking the insult.

"What do we care about drug cartels themselves?" Nancy said.

"Power vacuum that big next door could be of interest?" Sim(on) shot back.

"Fine. You type up the products. I don't care," Nancy said.

Sim(on) returned to his display and rolled his eyes. He knew that the performance monitoring software would annotate his HR file, but everything in the Black Box was collected, collated, and recorded by the AI. Anyone who pulled up his eye roll was going to see it was the direct result of working for a troll.

∼

Three hours later, at the end of his shift, Sim(on) walked out of the Black Box building. Inside of the onyx Brutalist cube, all of the intelligence services of Giresun Island parsed, indexed, and reported on the world's deeds and failures. An artificial intelligence coordinated efforts by way of probability projections, identifying the potential threats, weaknesses, and opportunities for Giresun to leverage. It was housed deep under the complex, and while its existence was well known, details of its construction and maintenance were practically nonexistent. The AI simply was. No one gave it another thought, because it had always been there. Sim(on) turned from his mental reveries where he'd been more heroic in facing Nancy's abuse, to why she was even necessary with the AI controlling everything.

"Just gonna keep walkin', eh ?" Abby said. Her SF ID badge had a yellow smiley face decal covering her photo, right above the title "Maintenance."

"Hey," Sim(on) said. "Sorry, I didn't see you standing there. Lost in my thoughts."

"As usual." Abby lightly punched his arm.

"Sorry, long day." Sim(on) said.

"Nancy?" Abby asked.

Sim(on) grunted.

"Buy you a drink?" Abby asked.

"What, at that dive?" Sim(on) asked.

"What's wrong with the Admiral's Daughter?" Abby said.

Sim(on) turned around so fast his backpack kept swinging.

"What?" Abby said with a smile.

"I could see if René can meet us there…"

"Ugh, she's probably off at some rally to save a 'vital part of our marine ecosystem from undue harm caused by island expansion' or some *soai*," Abby said. She stuck her hands in her pockets and canted her hips from side to side.

"Like you really think that's a bad thing."

"Just more toilets to unclog and chillers to fix for the prissy mavens," Abby said.

"Society would collapse under its own weight if it weren't for you," Sim(on) said. "Fine. You're buying."

"It's cool, I'll pass the free drinks to you. Win-win. What are you talking about, there're dudes there too, not like you'll be all alone with the girls."

"I'll take the free drinks from your admirers. They can't expect anything with your rep though," Sim(on) said.

Abby walked with a shuffling step so Sim(on) could keep up.

"Invite sent," he said. "Did she have work tonight? I'm sure some socialite has a party that needed organizing."

A shrug barely registered as Abby picked up the pace.

CHAPTER 5

The Crucible

NORTH WEST IRAQ

1539 04 JUL 2071

Even the dust in the air was burnt. Carsem could not smell anything over the chemical soot falling around her from the explosions. Her hearing was shot through with a single tone and a constant pressure like her ears were packed with the clods of dirt raining down on her and her two children. They dug into the newly formed crater, burrowing into the side as deep as their broken fingernails would allow. Sand rained down and pelted them with embers of flaming earth. More gigantic helicopters passed over, pushing out pallets of explosives packed with ball bearings. Carsem had seen the men fall right out with their makeshift bombs, only to dangle from harnesses below the aircraft when she fought the Turks and their genocidal allies. Her resistance was covered in a mire of terror as she knew her family was in the enemy's crosshairs along with the remnants of her village. Carsem pulled her arms from the cascading dirt and saw Ani and Anan. Her heart exploded.

"Ani! Anan!" She screamed their names, pulling them onto the top layer of the crater's scorched earth.

Neither child breathed. She placed her two fingers against their necks, one at a time. Neither... wait... Anan's pulse was thin and erratic.

"Help me! Medic!" she yelled.

Forced into an impossible choice, Carsem began pumping Anan's heart and filling his lungs with her breath. His pulse faded despite her best efforts. She looked into his eyes and saw the thin red lines of raised blood vessels against the white. Dirt fell across his face, and she wiped it away, remembering all the times she had soothed him back to sleep in the night.

"Stay with me, Anan!" she screamed. "Anan!"

Men and women from the village, battered and torn, dropped down next to her.

"We're here," an older man, Farouk, said. Carsem saw his lips moving but barely heard him.

The women carried her away from her children. Carsem was helpless in their arms, with no strength to fight back to her ruined life lying there in the pit. As they left the crater, there was a yawning emptiness trying to swallow her.

NORTH WEST IRAQ

1830 09 JUL 2071

Carsem sat alone in the dark. A hot, flinty breeze fluttered the bedsheet drapes in the room. She had lost track of the days and did not have the courage or strength to move beyond the bucket that served as the toilet. Women from the village brought food, left it, and took away the dishes. Everyone was lost in the doldrums of gray mourning. No one had disturbed her beyond the dishes for days.

"We're going to bury the dead in the morning," a Yazidi woman said. The bodies were already buried. As customary, within a day of the attack. This was the ceremony to mourn their collective loss. She changed out the trays in the doorway.

Carsem spent the day trying to build up the courage, the strength, to leave through the same door.

⁓

Women sang *kilamê ser* for the village as the men laid the shrouded bodies to rest under a final layer of dirt. Prayers to *Tawûsî Melek* were also given to Allah, and God in Kurmanji so that no one was left behind. The desert wind was picking up speed as it traced its way through the decimated community. The day's heat was rapidly fading, except the boulders and rocks against the box canyon that surrounded the village ruins. The sunset drew shadows across the orange rock and khaki dirt, turning small shrubs and gaunt trees into rivulets of darkness creeping up the walls.

The oldest survivor addressed the ragged community in their mourning.

Carsem quietly slipped in between rows of survivors.

"My dears," he began. "We have suffered a great loss, after loss and more loss. Our people are used to such things, but this does not make it easier."

The old man had to catch his breath.

"We are all in pain, and it is the pain of loss that hurts us the most. Love is what we must strive to find as the pain softens," he said.

The old man shook under a fit of coughing. Another man came to steady him, and the old man patted his hand as he recovered.

"I guess we don't have much in the way of books now. You all know I loved to read. There is an open place to explore ideas that do not fit in our regular lives. Questions we might not dare to ask. Such as how people do not understand love, how it eventually distills into hate, and so love is eventually corrupted in the mind.

"It is easier to die than to befriend life at times. The biggest problem is not a lack of love but the inability to love. I was a boy when we stopped the honor killings after the rape wars of the Islamic State, and people thought we were giving up our culture to foreigners. But here we are. There is no shortage of people trying to kill the last of us—because of our enduring culture. We became more open to love, and that makes some hate us more.

"But here we are. We still stand," he said.

Women started their heart-wrenching song for the dead again as the men buried the last bodies.

The Yazidi woman from the doorway found Carsem in the crowd and took her hand.

"We are all *mirî* now," Carsem said.

[We are all the Dead now.]

~

Carsem gathered the small things from her home that survived the bombing campaign. Toiletries, a few clothes, a digital frame of family photos. All in all, it barely filled the bottom of a courier bag. She stood stock-still in the common room for an eternity. Suddenly, she took a deep, ragged breath. Her steps to the door were inordinately heavy and mechanical. At the doorframe, she met an invisible force field. It was as if she couldn't cross the threshold, despite leaning into the doorway. A tear slipped over her lashes, and the spell was broken. She stepped through into the night.

SYRIAN DESERT

2339 09 JUL 2071

The night air was full of the scent of herbs and flowers as Carsem struck out. The moonlight was impossibly bright, reflected off of the sands after the hard-packed earth gave way to open desert. A billion stars shone down on the panoply of life around her as creatures fought for survival against the harsh, arid landscape and one another. Like the prophets and sages of countless centuries before her or those who wished to unburden their families from their sins or infirmities, Carsem walked out deeper and further into the *choł*.

A United Nations soldier had once given her a fat book in English about a boy who becomes a man after he traveled to a far-flung desert planet. She understood his death wish, after the fall of his family and the loss of his drive to remove himself from society and disappear into the dunes like she was. He became a god. When she had gone to school in America, the New York Public Library was her favorite place to be. Surrounded by everything imaginable, what she wanted to do most was escape into more such tales of adventure and odyssey. All Carsem wanted to do now was die where no one would miss her and she would not have to feel alone surrounded by people. No godhood, no fabled return. Just peace, and in it, release from her pain.

When the sun came, it beat down with a vengeance. Carsem dug a trench in the high side of a dune. She slipped into a shelter sack with thin ribs, lay in the trench, and piled the sand over her cocoon. Even with the insulation from the sun, it was still sweltering. She woke as the temperature shifted and dug out like any other desert creature. She examined her pack and saw that she had four days of water rations left, but there was a *waha* another two days out by foot.

Carsem arrived the following night. The reported oasis was dry and deserted, left to the elements. She found plenty of shrubs and even a couple of young palms. Unfortunately, the plants carried no tapable water but did offer plenty of room to rotate a solar still. A nearby row of dunes gave her respite from the heat of the day, as well as cover.

On the second night, an albino desert monitor lizard came out to warn her from encroaching too far into its territory.

"I'm not interested," Carsem said. She charged the lizard back into its burrow.

Days went by. Carsem's ability to sleep was soon outmatched by the length of the day. She began watching the tiny outcrop of plants, her still, and the creatures she shared it with. The albino came around, but so did a darker brown lizard. During the day, Carsem slipped out of her hovel and made a closer inspection of the burrow. Before an adult chased her away, she saw eggs inside. The following night, Carsem stalked the male.

The large lizard made a show of hissing and whipping its tail. A bite could be fatal, depending on species. Carsem cared less about her

ety, but a fast death was preferable to starvation or heatstroke. Not
anting to attract anyone's attention, she drew her long *jambiya* and
waited for the tail to whip around. When it passed her, she grabbed
it on the weaker return sweep.

Carsem hauled it in as the lizard turned to snap and claw at her.
Dust billowed up from the struggle, like a miniature sandstorm. As
its jaws snapped shut again, Carsem gave the tail another heavy pull,
then drove her long dagger into his side, behind the left foreleg, and
toward the other side of its neck. The lizard died quickly, rolling in
the sand with the hilt of Carsem's *jambiya* sticking out of his side.

"Now you know how the mouse feels," Carsem said.

She quickly skinned and gutted the lizard, leaving the entrails
for her neighbors. The solar still became a multi-tasker and allowed
her to dry out the meat and hide. It wasn't a perfect way to tan the
skin, but the end result was useable and possibly something to trade
with later. The meat added several days to her food rations, and
when her water reserves were restored, Carsem continued on into
the wilderness.

When winter came again she felt the desert winds shift, pushing
her inland. Her first task was to check on her accounts. Her husband,
Rumi, had set up their finances. With the uncertainty of life in the
desert, he had broken with society and included her in both accessing
and teaching her about the process.

Once Carsem fully reached civilization again it was deep in the
heart of her enemy's country. She kept to herself with her head covered for anonymity. Her husband's uncle, Raz, lived in the north
toward the border with Armenia and Georgia. Raz had arranged for
her to go to school in America years before, so that she could raise
strong, well-educated children for his favorite nephew, Rumi. Carsem
had been a sponge of American pop culture, absorbing everything
she could in New York. An idea slowly formed in her head. To start
over, she would see it again, and more: The great American road trip.

1027 20 JAN 2073

A bus hauling people, furniture, and animals with no sense of order to it nearly ran Carsem down. She only heard the horn honking when it was less than ten meters away. Carsem knew her hearing was damaged in the attack a year and a half ago, but until she was around the world of man again it had not been obvious.

Switching from the isolation and margins of the desert to the bustle of cities and commerce was as nerve-racking as anything she'd encountered. Cultured people in the streets gave her a wide berth, customary for visitors from the desert. Like the patterns on a snake, her clothing and mannerisms displayed a warning that she was not to be trifled with. Here she moved through the day and slept at night. As harsh as the cycles of nature were in the desert, there was a reason for violence. Nights in the world of men were chaotic in their dangers. Carsem wanted none of that blind rage anymore. Her family was gone, taken from her by the very people surrounding her now. The sand and wind had taken the hurt, the sorrow, and burnt them clean away.

Unable to sleep long in even the hard beds of anonymous hotels, Carsem spent most nights learning about the world at large on her new screen. Food and information were just as important here as they were to survive the open dunes and wilderness. Splaying the fingers of her upturned left hand with a wrist snap turned the device on. It projected from a wrist cuff in a curve toward her fingers. A menu allowed her to expand the projection beyond, though the extremes of projection depended on the manufacturer and model. Alternately, Carsem could project the display on the inside of her arm for environments where greater contrast was needed.

Within the projection, she could gesture for changing the foreground object or scrolling through menus. If she ever encountered a larger advanced display, she could send her selected information, videos, or pictures from her screen to it with a flicking motion toward the other device. Her skin chaffed under new clothes and electronic comfort.

Carsem started a program in American Sign Language, the best bet for signing wherever she went. She was surprised to find how much had been co-opted into her small unit training. Many of the signs were the same for moving silently, or without a need to shout over noise, from her training.

∼

She reached out to Uncle Raz and caught him up on her position, careful to encrypt her location and messages as the Peshmerga had taught her in battlefield communications—"only broadcast in the clear what you wanted the enemy to hear." She learned about the decades-long economic decline of the West and the utter destruction of Southeast Asia from a combination of environmental collapse and loss of the world's petroleum reserves. Entry visas for the remaining United States were now a simple matter of showing up and signing in, while each state controlled its own border. Uncle Raz would provide passage to anywhere she wanted to go, as well as access to the full investments Rumi had made with their meager soldiers' pay. It would be enough to get started. She was not sure she was ready to reconnect with civilization, but the desert no longer held her thoughts.

"Too many memories," she muttered, searching for her next adventure. All her life, America had captured her thoughts in the tales of foreign agents who trained their combat troops. While the United States was a shadow of its former self, Carsem settled on Boston. Raz's shipping ports turned back to Africa after that. He had no contacts in South America or the Caribbean, sadly.

"We have family there, in Boston," Raz wrote. "I can make the introduction?"

"Yes, please. Just looking to get my feet on the ground and then take a road trip like Jack Kerouac," Carsem wrote.

"Always dreaming of adventure, like when you were a girl," Raz wrote.

"A castaway still," she wrote back. "Thank you, Uncle."

～

Reaching the green hills of the Black Sea, she walked through the northern cities of Turkey until she reached the port of Rize. They alternated between impoverished villages not too dissimilar to her own, and full-fledged cities of modern sophistication. Carsem became used to the aerial drones and wheeled delivery robots zipping about. In fact, they paid her more attention than the average human on the street. The one constant across her trek was the earthy, acrid smell that rode on the ever-present dust. It worked its way through her clothes and everything else, like an olfactory passport stamp.

One day, with the sun high overhead in a cloudless sky, her screen buzzed. Carsem looked up and picked out her destination in the industrial park of high, cheaply made warehouses from her displayed augmented reality view. She walked into the dim cool of Raz's import-export warehouse office. No one was smoking, but the scent of tobacco still permeated everything. Like a signature of coming indoors in opposition to the outdoors smell. It was a strange juxtaposition, a unifying constant linking the transition, like her arid desert morphing into these green rolling hills and mountains. Carsem tried out signing.

"Hello?" she signed.

The secretary gave her a shrug. Frustrated, Carsem typed out "RAZ?" on her screen and showed it to her.

"Just a sec," the woman replied with an exaggerated, melodramatic pantomime. She walked over to a door with closed blinds. The secretary knocked three times, then opened it. A young man came out, and after a few seconds the secretary waved Carsem in.

"Hi Raz," Carsem wrote on her screen.

"Hi kid," Raz signed. He sat back down at his desk facing her and leaned back.

Carsem smiled and sat down opposite.

"Voice, translate and display," he commanded aloud. "You can sign. It will know,"The words appeared between them on a holographic projection. "Neat, eh? Those Germans keep coming up with new toys, only for the Chinese to make them cheaper," Raz said. "Same as it ever was."

"These are pretty good too," Carsem signed, pointing to her wrist cuff.

"Okay, brass tacks?" Raz asked.

Carsem nodded.

"Good, you're always so practical," Raz said.

"Details matter," Carsem signed.

"I've got news for you—you've got quite a nice nest egg now. The village divided the accounts among everyone. Very generous," Raz said. He sent over code authorizations to Carsem's screen. She read through the documents and signed them. The accounts were now solely in her name, and everything Rumi had set up was liquidated into an international fund.

"At such a price," Carsem signed.

"I know, and I am so very sorry for your loss, my dear," Raz said. His eyes began to water before he could wipe the tears away. They shared a moment, then he dabbed his eyes with a handkerchief and it was past.

"Okay, sorry. I thought about what you were saying about a road trip. I have an idea, but I'll have to work it out with our cousins over there. Anyhow, road trips are dangerous, but you know that. I have no doubt you're up to whatever comes. I hope it brings you what you're looking for, whatever it is," Raz said. "Let's go eat. I've got an office container on the ship for you to stay in on your journey. It's stocked with food, water, clothing, even has its own commode. It'll be an adventure," Raz said. "They're in port until the wee hours tomorrow, so if there's anything you need before leaving..."

The old man stood up, and Carsem followed suit.

CHAPTER 6

Terra Incognita

0532 07 FEB 2073
The shipping container was a small apartment on the inside, well lit and spartan but comfortable. A simple mat and what felt like a buckwheat-filled mattress made for the sleeping arrangements. There was a carton of rations, far more than Carsem needed, in the near corner. In the opposite corner behind a screen was a chemical toilet. A holographic display on the wall across from the toilet and wash stand gave the illusion of an outside world.

Carsem spent the first days sleeping, but the dreams kept waking her up. Her long-dead husband Rumi was with her and the children in the attack. In the dreams, after the bombs passed, she was the only survivor. She dug her way out of the crater only for the dead to reanimate. Like an old horror movie, they came for her to make them whole again. She woke up crying and scuttling herself across the floor of the cabin.

Despite the nightmares, Carsem made the most of the time she could not sleep by catching up on the havoc wrecked on the United States since her last stay, via the screen projected against her palm at the flick of her fingers. Climate shifts and rising seas continued to erode the old coastlines and flood plains. The American South was transformed, like a knit work of suspension bridges with dangling cities underneath. Texas had finally seceded, though it read like they left before being asked to go. Carsem wondered at it all, and slowly one dream replaced another.

The ship sailed through the straights of Gibraltar before Carsem ventured out of her apartment. Rumi's uncle had arranged the cruise, medical clearance, and manufactured the passport. It wasn't smuggling if you technically didn't have a country to start with. Raz simply updated the papers from her teenage visa, even if she was never officially from the African Union.

"*A gift from the people of Kurdistan for your sacrifice,*" *he'd written on a scrap of paper with the bundle as he handed the documents to her.*

"*Uncle Raz, thank you. Rumi—,*" *she'd said.*

"*Never mind that,*" *he had said loudly but kindly. He'd pulled his phone out of his pocket and spoke into it. The words appeared on the screen.* "*You were, are the virtuous woman we always tell stories of. Your time of fighting is over, I hope. May you find peace somewhere in the world where the Turk does not know you,*" *he said.* "*Now go. Never look back, but know we all hold you in our hearts.*"

"*Thank you, Uncle,*" *she remembered saying.* Carsem wiped a tear from her eye.

The shipping vessel was crewed by eight men and women, but mostly controlled by machine intelligence. The humans all kept to themselves. It gave them plausible deniability of whatever was actually being shipped. Occasionally, parts of the crew would run into Carsem at meals in the galley. After hustling across the Syrian desert and threading her way through city warrens, Carsem felt like the proverbial long-tailed cat in a room of rocking chairs. She focused her senses in the confines of the ship to build herself back up. She had to beat the demons in her head. She started healing the physical degradation of desert life 'til she had the strength to face her emotional trauma. Carsem got used to pushing through the pain, leaving as many tears as sweat on the floor of her room. After two and a half weeks alone with a screen and solitary confinement, she could read lips and do push-ups standing on her head.

⌦

Eighteen days at sea took her to the port of Boston. The city sprawled around the harbor, a strange mixture of working docks, high-rise towers and old brick buildings. The smell of civilization was different here than it had been transitioning from the desert. Here there was a putrid decay of the busy port and industry along the shore. It was rot and machinery instead of the dust, tobacco, and low-tech manufacturers of Turkey. She immediately thought of her early teen years in New York but knew better than to mention it when she went ashore. Carsem was to be greeted at the dock by local, distant relatives. She walked down the gangplank onto the docks, then to the passenger terminal. With only a tiny duffle bag and coat, there was not much for Customs to inspect. On the other side of the fence, a couple waved to her. She recognized them from the screen which had been her only companion on the journey. The projected interface from her hand was everything she needed it to be—entertainment, information, education, or confidant.

"Welcome to what's next," a late-middle-aged woman said. The air was cold, and a light frost sparkled in the late sun while they walked out of the terminal. The streets of Boston were like walking into a parade of angry goats, with cars loosely obeying the traffic laws and people pushing right back against the angry motorists. Fewer of the cars were combustion engines than she remembered from New York. The air was easier to breathe than she expected.

"Thank you, *pûr*," Carsem said. She pulled her threadbare coat around a little tighter.

"Of course, *biraza*. You can call me Janice if you prefer. Don't get me wrong, *pûr* is nice too," she said.

"Well, Boston has a history of throwing off oppressors and being a new foothold for immigrants," an older man said. "David," he said, offering his hand. He looked her over in assessment rather than the appraisal she was used to.

"First, you ladies need to get this in order." David waved his hand in a cloud around Carsem. "You look like a refugee."

"David!" Janice chided.

"In the nicest way, of course. But seriously, we need to change your clothes... and burn these," David said. "What? I can say that. We're family."

"But first, food. You must be starving!" Janice said.

"And cold!" David said.

Carsem realized she did not feel cold, hungry, or self-conscious. She nodded to all their offers. They were easy to hear, even in her state.

They dined in a corporate chain restaurant with decorations trying to simulate an early twentieth-century understated elegance. Electric lights were purposely dim and yellow, producing a reflected glow on the simulated wood paneling. Coarse woven napkins sat crumpled among the dishes of pasta and red sauce as the conversation drifted. David decided to stay and work at the table over coffee while the ladies went for a walk after their meal. Janice passed a wrapped Havla candy bar into Carsem's hand, and the women left David in the mall restaurant toward the multi-story block of shops around them. They barely cleared the doorway before Janice was pulling Carsem through another and into the arms of a butch saleswoman.

"What do you want to do next, dear?" Janice asked, stacking tops in over Carsem's arm.

"It's a big country, America. I think I will see it," Carsem said.

"You'll need a car then," Janice said. "May need a job to raise the money first."

She added several pairs of pants to the pile. "There, now we see what fits," she said.

Carsem leaned against the door of the changing room. She released a sigh so pent-up, her stomach hurt. There were so many things to choose from, she was overwhelmed. After a few truly ridiculous looking combinations, a scoop-necked top, dark blue jeans, and a flannel deck shirt were the closest she came to approval from Janice. "Shoes. And you're going to need a new jacket. I'm afraid the old one fell apart when I threw it in the garbage can," Janice said.

"Boots, good leather ones, and a jacket like Joan Jett," Carsem piped up.

"Like who?" Janice asked.

"Only the best rock star to come out of the original punk scene! Like, a hundred years ago?" Carsem said. "C'mon, you've got to know 'I love Rock n' Roll'? I used to get beat for singing along to it."

An hour later and with several bags in tow, Janice and Carsem rejoined David at the restaurant.

"Well, cleaner. Army roots are definitely showing," David said. He set down his small cup of coffee. "But it is you, and a definite move in the right direction." He smiled.

Janice jabbed Carsem in the ribs and smiled. She nodded toward the empty seats.

"Tomorrow we'll see about a car," Janice said. She gestured to a waiter for more coffee.

BOSTON, MASSACHUSETTS

1651 08 MAR 2073

"How do you like it?" David asked.

The night was dark, punctuated by halos around streetlights. The cold had everyone bundled up, their breath smoked in the night. The suburbs were strangely quiet. Carsem briefly wondered what had happened to all the hustle and bustle she expected from the city. Suddenly, like an epiphany, Carsem was transported out of her reality as David walked her around the corner. The streetlights reflected off the avocado green and black sport stripes of the retrofitted muscle car. For a moment, she was experiencing no death, no nightmares, simply the overwhelming fantasy of driving an endless highway toward adventure in the unknown world.

"It's perfect," Carsem said. She ran her hands over the edges of the car's body. Cold as it was outside, her hands tingled in delight. "Oldsmobile 442..." she said in a quiet, reverent tone.

"Your uncle said muscle, space, and self-reliant," David said.

Carsem couldn't tear her eyes away from the avocado green paint, black racing stripes, and chrome to read his lips.

"It was retrofitted with a diamond battery. There's enough room to sleep in it, and true to the original, the beast can do a quarter-mile in 10.4 seconds." David said. "The batteries basically recharge themselves. You won't need to plug in this baby for about a hundred years."

"Turn it on," Carsem said.

David slid behind the wheel and started the power supply.

Carsem splayed her fingers over the hood, then slowly lowered her face and pressed her ear to it. "I can feel it, but not hear it. So weird," she said

"The doctors said you might regain more hearing as time progressed," Janice said.

"Maybe." Carsem shrugged.

"It has all the old tech stuff, synchs with your screen, lane depart assist and automated braking... you know, pretty basic. Nothing new, but it's sturdy. It'll get you to all that you want to see if it's still there. You'll just have to drive it yourself," David said. "Now, about the price. I was able to get it down, but it's still pretty hefty."

Carsem stood up, beaming.

"I'm sure. Just send me the tag, and I'll take care of it. Raz already brought over my accounts. Side effect of being my kind of refugee," she said. "Thanks to communal inheritance, money isn't one of my problems."

~

"It's been four weeks," Carsem said the next morning. She stood with David and Janice on the sidewalk outside their flat. The fall was giving way to winter. "Your hospitality has been beyond anything I expected. Like, fairy tale good. But all good things must end. It's time," she said.

"We know. We don't want to see you go," Janice said.

"You know where to find us," David said. "There's something in case of emergency in the trunk, behind a false wall past the spare tire. This land of ours isn't what it once was, but it isn't like the old one either, no matter how much we're starting to look like it."

"I packed you some food. It's in the cooler. There's tea in the jug," Janice said. She held on to Carsem, maybe a little too long.

David gave her a hug in uncharacteristic silence. He straightened his tie and jacket before opening the driver's door for her.

"Be well, *gyan*," he said.

Carsem sat in the bucket seat and buckled the five-point harness, checked her mirrors, and slowly pulled away from the curb. As she watched her hosts in the rearview mirror, she adjusted her posture. The leather jacket squeaked against the seat. She caught a look in the mirror of her now blood-shot eyes, before accelerating onto the interstate.

～

Carsem wound her way through the freeways and out into the country heading south, toward New York. She thrilled at the feel of the car. David hadn't told her about the "sim" button. When selected, it gave the feeling of driving a perfectly tuned 442, from the vibration in the steering wheel to the purr of the engine Carsem felt through her bucket seat. She offered a little prayer to Tawûsê Melek for their continued good fortune.

"Suggested route," the screen blurted.

The deviation took her around greater New York City, swinging in a wide western hook starting in Westchester. The collapse of the city was as momentous as the rise of them during the eighteenth century. Pollution control and support systems failed under the weight of the population and its resurgent diseases. Generations without vaccinations led to the mutations of old viruses while the overuse of antibiotics and antiseptics created new strains of bacteria, pushing people out into the vast spaces in between. Telepresence allowed even factory and warehouse workers to "port in" from wherever they wanted. It was the reverse process of the industrial revolution, with anyone who could get out of the city leaving. What was left was a wide chasm between the excessively wealthy who stayed behind pretending not to notice, and the desperately poor who left to fend for themselves. New York, Los Angeles, Chicago were essentially prisons. As exceedingly violent and hazardous as they had ever been. It was better not to look, even if the hills between Westchester and the city didn't offer much of a view.

"No thanks," she said, following the navigator and taking the loop right, away from the Big Apple. David and Janice's parents had escaped early on in the disasters that brought down the Empire, and for a change they had enjoyed success despite the calamities all around them.

∽

Carsem motored on through the southern border before taking a break. She sat under a Banyan tree, eating from the stockpile Janice had sent with her. After a stretch and bathroom break, Carsem gave in. She opened the trunk and pushed against the panel supposedly separating the trunk from the back seat. It clicked and pushed further out. Carsem lifted the false wall and discovered an eighteen-inch pump-action shotgun, a cleaning kit, an advanced medical kit, four boxes of double-ought buckshot, another of deer slugs, and an antique US Marine Ka-Bar field knife.

"Thanks, David," she said, before closing it all up.

New Jersey, in contrast to its northern neighbor, was now an honest garden state. Tropical transplants began sprouting up along the freeway. As the tropical zone moved north, previously untreated helminth and other parasitic infections spread. So did the lush fruiting trees and canopies of once equatorial regions. Banyan and mangrove trees now encircled rest stops for added shade. The Mid-Atlantic states looked more like rainforests than ever as the estuaries reclaimed land inward from the rising seas. The long pylon bridges created a ribbon of vehicle and train traffic floating over acre after acre of estuary.

Late in the night, Carsem slipped south of the nation's capital into the Blue Ridge Mountains, as full of people keeping to their own business as ever in its history. The descendants of people who fought the law in the 1920s still knew how to leave well enough alone. Carsem found a reasonably safe place to take rest for the night. She pulled a cover over the car. It reflected the light from the linear opposite side. From just feet away and with up to five points of view, the car was invisible. Carsem slept in the backseat with the now loaded shotgun on the floorboard, next to a box of shells.

The following morning Carsem slowly peeled herself off of the vinyl bench seat, then used her screen to check the outside through the 442's exterior cameras. Everything looked clear, but she still did a sweep of five and fifteen before stretching out and taking the car cover down. Today was the long slog out of the Appalachians and into the deep south.

Carsem ate 'til she felt ready to burst. She had no intention of stopping from Georgia 'til she reached the latest incarnation of New Orleans.

∾

For every ill the major cities had fallen to from their hubris, the southern half of the United States suffered through a transforming planet. The temperatures were typically in triple digits year-round with a burning humidity that untrained lungs found hard to breathe. Rising sea levels and flooding deltas converted the deep south into a patchwork of island cities connected by high-rise multi-tiered bridge systems. People who could not afford the price of living on land, or in the floating communities below, lived in suspended clusters of units under the bridge system. They hung like grapes in the wind.

Hurricanes were kept at bay as the flooded ruins created thousands of miles of transitional wetlands where they normally lost their power.

Louisiana, through a combination of repatriation following the Reparations and Reconstruction movement, had rebuilt New Orleans before the water permanently rose. A feat of engineering to surpass ancient Venice was contrived to raise the city with the rising water. Megalithic pylons cycled rising water levels to push sections of the city above. In floods and storm surges, the city stood above the water while canals channeled water through. The result was the birth of new tourism as Cajun gondoliers pushed their boats through the floating Wards to and from the French Quarter.

As Carsem rocketed across Lake Pontchartrain, the floodwaters had receded leaving the multistory levees looming over the horizon. Enormous sea walls protected the rest of the reclaimed land with a touch of ominous foreboding of what lay beyond.

Just beyond the banks of the Sabine River, earth and steelworks massive enough to see from space separated the Republic of Texas from the rest of North America. Originally constructed to cut off immigration from Mexico, the border was then extended as a combination of unfettered capitalism, unchecked freedom, and self-sufficiency imploded with the conversion to diamond cell batteries collapsing the fossil fuel industry. Texan pride denied the ensuing anarchy until its border was militarized. The ruling state then created a fortified border to blockade the troops stationed on the other side. Texas was trying to bootstrap itself out of the morass, but the right to self-protection and unrestrained freedom had become the grim reality of the wild west romanticized for so long. Death was in the streets. Precious few were willing to serve the common good.

Rather than taking her chances in the wide-open Libertarian nightmare of wanton destruction the Lone Star Republic had become, Carsem booked passage on a ferry from New Orleans to Cancun, Mexico, on her screen. She made a slow roll into the city after the long climb to its current height after Lake Pontchartrain. She passed under a magnificent archway abutted by the tops of derricks. A carved banner under the archway read, "In Memoriam of the Ninth Ward."

~

Carsem pulled into a hotel on Magazine Street, for all the world looking like a perfectly preserved reenactment of the previous century. Her screen said there were vacancies, and she picked up a room on the second floor. The trees still lined the street, and retro trollies occasionally rambled past down the middle of the road. Her hotel had the same decadent neglect permeating New Orleans. She could barely hear the sounds of the Garden District as she walked out into the afternoon sun, but she was hit full in the nose by the magnolias. Everywhere was green, alive, and warm with the undertone of life's eventual decay. It had been a very long couple of days. She stretched her legs out of the Garden District, away from Lafayette No.1 and toward the downtown.

Carsem nodded and shrugged her way through the pedestrians. She ate from stalls and drank concoctions that seemed to change flavors with each sip before finally settling down at a back- alley bar where her screen told her she could get the best food from the most underrated chef—read cheap, good eats—in town. Despite the snacking, the street vendor drinks made her hungry.

She sat at the bar and was left alone. The more aggressive clientele was still hours away. This was effectively still day drinking. While that was New Orleans *de rigueur* for centuries, since she was out of the popular scene etiquette declared to speak only when spoken to.

Carsem nodded to the bartender.

He finished polishing a coupe glass and side-stepped to her end, away from the door.

"Hi," he said.

She smiled, picked up a menu, and said, "Special, fried oyster po'boy, Sazerac, and an Abita lager, please."

He smiled and cocked his head slightly to the side.

"Jus a minit," he said.

She shrugged minutely and smiled.

Carsem could feel music playing, but not enough to catch the melody.

The drinks arrived first. She took down the beer in five gulps, then nursed the rocks glass. The barman smiled, turning mostly away from her back to his never-ending polishing.

A young woman brought her food from her side of the bar. She left a pile of napkins weighed down by a clean but battered fork and a bottle of Crystal hot sauce. She left with a curt nod. Her lips had moved but Carsem couldn't make out the words. She didn't try, either.

With a full belly and a slight buzz, Carsem walked out of the bar labeled "Eats" into the darkening dusk. She'd pocketed the hot sauce as a memento, leaving an exaggerated tip for the inconvenience. The incandescent dayglow of Bourbon Street's tiered levels and arched overhead walkways radiated down the intersecting boulevards and across the giant traffic circle where vehicles, trollies, and pedestrians met. Milling around the circle was as close as she wanted to get without ears or a preexisting friend.

Carsem walked back to her room on Magazine Street. Magnolias perfumed the air, which was warm and dark. Humidity turned the occasional streetlamp into a shining nebula. The hair on the back of her neck bristled between the gaps in arc lamps. Movement caught her eye as someone stirred in the dimness. Her body reacted to a subconscious threat, forcing her eyes to look at shadows shifting in front of her own outline against the disheveled pavers. As if she were seeing a time-lapse replay vid, a different body contour emerged from the side of her own. Carsem stopped, dropped to a crouch as she spun, and threw the momentum into a punch aimed past her would-be assailant's anus.

The man with a stubbly beard and gravestone teeth was confused as his sap missed the back of the woman's ear. The small leather bag of lead shot skittered across the broken sidewalk pavers. His shoulder hurt from the lack of impact, overreaching his target and twisting his torso around. The erection he'd had at the thought of his prey was suddenly evaporated as his balls exploded in pain. It seared his vision and threw up his lunch of meth and Southern Comfort. Carsem popped up so fast her feet left the ground. She took advantage of the height, throwing all of her weight into a double-fisted hammer blow to the atlas bone in the man's neck. He sunk to his knees before she redoubted with an ear strike to both sides of his head simultaneously. Carsem could not detect a pulse if there was one. She picked through his pockets carefully. She had smelled the amphetamine stench of meth mouth before she had even turned around. Carsem found a .380 automatic and a steel shank with four holes drilled in it. She easily fit her fingers through the knuckleduster, while the edge of the bar fit in the palm of her loosely held fist. His stash of drugs was gingerly tucked back in his pants pocket. The sap was left where he dropped it. Obscured by shadows between the street lights, he looked like a passed out drunk on the curb. Carsem casually straightened the errant hair out of her face and walked on as if nothing happened.

~

The next day Carsem woke and ordered breakfast to be delivered to her room. She was nearly done packing her things after taking another shower when her screen alerted her to a drone outside her window. Automated window delivery allowed concierge services to be offered to multiple locations without additional infrastructure— including breakfast from Galatoire's, in this case. Eating breakfast in bed, she watched the view screen on the wall and was sure there would be a noise complaint from her neighbors as she enjoyed skipping through the channels at full volume.

~

Carsem melted into the seat as the 442's simulated feedback rumbled through her body. After 1,500 miles, the road beast was feeling like a worn pair of shoes. She drove down Magazine to Jackson and along the Mississippi to the port. The line was already deep for the ferry. Carsem parked and turned down the air conditioning until a young man in a pale blue uniform and brown pants walked up, tapping on a screen. She rolled down the window with a preset announcement on her screen for him.

"Good morning, ma'am," his screen displayed in turn. He smiled. Carsem waved politely.

"Where are you headed today?" he asked through the device.

She smiled and said, "Cancun, Mexico."

"I'll just scan your car ID, and send me the link for your docs, please."

Carsem flicked a finger across her screen toward his.

"Thank you," he signed.

"You're welcome," she said.

"Enjoy your time across the border. It never changes, like how they used to call Rome the Eternal City," he said loudly.

"Have a pleasant trip," he sent from his screen with a montage of life in the Cajun Navy. While formally adopted decades ago by the Coast Guard, other than their primary objective of search, rescue, and disaster relief, they were tasked with the safe transport of travelers around the Republic of Texas's territorial waters in the Gulf past the Sabine delta. Carsem drove the 442 onto the ferry, while thoughts of sunshine and tropical beaches radiated from her smile.

CHAPTER 7

Nothing but a Good Time

GIRESUN ISLAND

1843 15 JUN 2075
The Admiral's Daughter was hopping. Women lined the bar and every booth. The two billiards tables had a row of quarters nearly across the balkline on a side. Likewise, the karaoke booths and dartboards were occupied. The room was painted in navy blue, so dark it looked black. Real neon signs hung at regular intervals, while a large mermaid sitting on a rocky outcrop looking toward the sea illuminated the middle of the bar itself. The bar top was zinc with a brass rail, the floor was a gro printed yellow pine. Abby couldn't see much of either with the press of humanity spread across both. The floor's finish was battle scarred, permanently scuffed despite the best efforts of the circulating cleaning bots. Dance music was punctuated by flashing lights and reflections from a complex array of mirrors and laser effects. Abby closed her eyes to get away from the crowd and exhaled as her mind flooded the open sensory channel. There was a fade to white, and she was transported to a scene from years ago. Seeing her old crush, Sarah, again made her want to leave, but not as much as she wanted to stay.

~

"Snitches get stitches," the woman with the scarred arms said. She side-stepped around the octagon mat's inner circle, arms poised like talons facing Abby.

"So do slitches too big for their britches," Abby said.

Half the other woman's height but equal in weight, she swatted the outside edge of the woman's left hand, feigning a grapple. As her opponent countered the blow easily, Abby slid under her stance and wrapped their legs together from the bottom up. Planting her arms and twisting her hips, Abby felled her opponent. Abby locked the other woman's leg with an arm-bar backed up with the tangled limbs. The security specialist tapped out.

"Nice corkscrew," she said while recovering.

"Mm-hmm," Abby said.

"I'm Alice," she said.

"I'm fine, thanks," Abby said.

"Cool. Well, next time," Alice said.

"Yep," she said. "I'll make sure they keep the mat clean."

Abby walked past the weight stacks other women were using. Nearly all of them had official Security Forces insignia on their clothes. Those who didn't were probably the Security Forces' mates. She walked with purpose to the door of the women's locker room. She paused before pushing through and took a breath before ramming ahead.

The room smelled of sweat and body odor, covered by a miasma of scents. Women everywhere were in various stages of changing into or out of clothes. Here and there ladies worked to get noticed for one reason or another. Most were just moving on to the next task. Abby was in the latter category, but this was a perfumed den of vipers.

She ignored everyone, whether they were watching or not. Abby deftly switched from her gym clothes to a towel with barely a peek for anyone to see, other than her collection of tattoos. An old tradition from the Founders of Giresun Island, Abby's programmable inked artwork morphed with her body's autonomic reactions, like advertising for her unconscious mind. As she waited for a free shower stall, Abby started lathering shampoo into her hair.

"Nice ink," a middle-aged woman said in the next line over.

"Thanks," Abby said noncommittally.

The woman had rough scar tissue above her towel on her back and shoulders.

"We all wear our stories, huh?" she said, catching Abby looking.

"Truth," Abby said, stepping into the stall and closing the door.

Two minutes later, Abby was walking back to her locker's alcove. As she performed the earlier quick change in reverse, the older woman appeared already dressed. She stood casually at the open end of the U-shaped enclave of lockers. A double-wide bench formed the center of the changing station.

"Hey Abby," the woman said.

Abby was suspicious—she didn't know the woman personally, but she wanted to. Her name was Sarah Kelly. She was a legend in the Security Forces, part of the do-what-you-want special projects division.

"...you're always welcome to come down to the Black Box if you get tired of roughing up my girls. It's your call."

The woman left a calling card on the bench, keeping her distance from Abby as she continued rummaging in her locker.

"Let me know when you're available for a drink with me, Sarah," Abby said in false baritone after the woman had turned the corner. She exhaled sharply and slammed the locker door shut.

～

Sim(on) nudged Abby out of her daydream to catch a dirty table as two lovebirds were slowly making their way toward the door. He quickly sat down and stacked dishes.

"You know, even in a place like this, they have people or bots to do that," Abby said.

"Last thing I expected to hear from you, really."

"Just checking," she said nonchalantly. Abby scanned the crowd.

Sim(on)'s screen chirped.

"I'll leave you to it. Tom Collins?" she asked.

"If someone else is buying. Otherwise, just a black tea, no—"

"No sweetener, I know," Abby said. She smiled and gave him a wink.

Two Norse goddesses made moves on Abby at the same time. From Sim(on)'s viewpoint, she played into it. Ten minutes went by after they melted into the crowd. Sim(on) could make out the tops of the other women's heads bopping over the rest. They stayed at the bar.

"...and here you go, Tommy-boy," Abby said, sliding a frosty tall glass in front of Sim(on). He raised his fruit festooned drink in a toast to her.

"Sláinte," he said over the rim. "René'll be here in, meh, ten more."

"Minutes or drinks?" Abby said, returning the toast with a tip of her glass. "Snacks?" she asked. "Snacks. Snacks!" Abby chanted with a fist raised in the air and returned to the bar.

Sim(on) went back to his screen.

Abby returned this time with a sampling of the mostly fried delicacies the small kitchen offered.

"I don't even want to know what you did to get those," he said looking up from the screen. His dark skin was lit with blue light from the table height, making the whites of his eyes glow in the artificial light of the bar's booth.

Abby giggle-snorted as she dipped a chicken wing in blue cheese dressing.

About the time half of the plate was gone, their screens chimed together. They looked toward the door as René walked through.

"Oh *soai*," Abby said. "Shark attack—"

René was in a billowing cream satin blouse with peaked lapels and large buttons dancing in the dark glow of neon. Her dark tweed pencil skirt barely registered against the shuffle and bustle of the bar floor. Modest four-inch heels clacked their way, expertly dodging dance steps and drunken laziness while ensuring all eyes were on her within the transit to their table.

"We've got about ten seconds before there's a feeding frenzy, miss," Abby said.

"Nice to see you too, short stack," René said. "Hi Simon, thanks for the invite. How was work, guys?"

The two giantesses were moving across what passed for the dance floor, and several others watched to gauge their position in the queue.

Abby stuffed half of a cheesesteak egg roll into her mouth, swallowed, then announced, "She likes boys."

René glared at her playfully.

"She likes boys *today!*" Abby corrected.

René broke into a laugh.

Abby saw the two women from before wondering if they should continue on.

"Jesus, would you just scoot over a little more together, please?" Abby said to Sim(on) and René. "Thank you. Drink?"

"Radcliffe's punch. They use real Ceylon tea here," René said.

"I ordered it for you. Things are getting weird over there," Sim(on) said. He nodded toward the bar. "Left my little buddy at home?" he said to René.

"No dogs allowed. How's it as 'every man's jack' today?" René said to Abby.

A few raised voices ended up with a separation at the bar. It made enough of a wave to clear some space between there and the table.

A waiter brought by refills for Abby and Sim(on)'s drinks along with a baroque teacup filled with an amber liquid and a glittering shard of ice. René smiled at the waiter, who was distracted by the commotion.

"My day was the ush," Abby said. "You know, squeaky doors and clogged toilets. Hard work being a Jack of All Trades on an island of women—not counting you of course, kid. What about you, princess? Get up to the tower today?"

René dropped her gaze for a second before flashing her striking almond eyes up at Abby with her head still down. Abby smiled and laughed a little too loudly, as the tension at the other end of the room caused heads to spin toward them.

Abby reached across the table and erupted in laughter as she clutched René's fists. René's reaction to the insinuation about Columbia faded with her eye contact. The jab had unintentionally struck something, and Abby was clueless.

"Sorry, I know you do more than consort with the heads of state," Abby said.

Everyone else went back to trying to ignore the fight brewing at the bar.

"Hey, where did the jalapeños go?" Sim(on) asked.

"Sorry," René said. She held a napkin up to her lips.

"Fine, nachos are fine," he said.

"Help yourself. Last thing, slowpoke," Abby said.

"All yours, dear," René said.

Sim(on) scarfed down the loaded chips. Then he gulped the rest of his drink.

"What's going on?" René said.

"Scarborough," was all he said.

"*Soai.* Oh *soai,*" Abby said. She wadded up her napkin and threw down her drink too. "Stay behind me."

"One of your codewords, or a someone?" René asked.

"Person. Primeval beef with—" he said, nodding at Abby.

"*Soaiiiii,*" René said over the top of her glass. "Damn, that was good too."

René slipped off her heels, and discreetly tucked her earrings into a hidden waist pocket on the way out of the booth.

"Time to go," Abby said.

Sim(on) had just cleared the booth when the space around it cleared out like a drop of soap in oil.

"Alley Cat! Is that you?" a high-pitched growl called out.

"Nancy. Oh hi, Colleen, Susan… look, the whole gang's here," Abby said.

"N'gono here was having a little trouble getting a drink's all," Nancy said.

"Mind if we sit with you?" N'gono asked. She was a powerfully built, two meter tall sprinter with a light brown biker jacket and Kevlar paneled pants. She did not ride a bike.

"We were just heading out," René said. She politely offered Susan her seat.

"That's too bad. Heard you were talking some *soai*, but I know you don't have anything to prove. Right, Alley Cat?"

"Stop this now," Sim(on) said.

"Or what, Simian? Go curl up in a cubicle. The grownups are talking," Nancy said.

René reached for the back of Abby's forearm with the back of her fingers. Abby's fist relaxed.

"The lady said we're leaving. Have fun," Abby said with a smirk.

"Oh, but we were hoping to see some of your sick moves! You know, since you're too good for the SF's... or is it you're just a coward?" N'gono said.

"Can't throw in all the way, might have to commit to something," Nancy said.

N'gono reached with a leg to block Abby. Under the table René slid her leg from between and around as she got up from the booth and knocked N'gono into the edge of the table.

"Oh dear, I'm sorry!" René said.

Abby launched a double-fisted strike in the distraction. Nancy barely dodged the lower punch, missing her solar plexus and landing square in her breast. The impact bent Nancy's head down to meet Abby's upper fist between the eyes.

Sim(on) guarded both their backs as he pushed Abby and René toward the door.

"After them! Idiots!" Nancy screamed.

The two Vikings blocked N'gono's way.

"Geb oud!" Nancy tried to push past as blood streamed down her face. The crowd joined in to hold them back.

"Ewe thaw, dey hid furst!" she yelled.

"You brought the abuse," the first giantess said loud and clear.

"You cornered them," the other announced.

"Had it comin'," said a voice.

Others chimed in, screaming and hurling insults at N'gono and Nancy. The circle closed around them.

⁓

Sim(on) directed them into an awaiting AutoCab.

"Whose ride did we jack?" Abby asked.

The car accelerated away from the curb. The bar looked quiet from outside.

"No one's—I called it before the goon squad showed up," Sim(on) said.

"Dang, you're bright," Abby said.

"Tell my boss. Better yet, let's keep it our little secret," he reconsidered.

"Where to now?" René asked. She touched up her makeup in a hand-held compact.

"Let's go to your place," Abby said. "Mine's trashed."

"On it," Sim(on) said.

After driving to the Northside of the island, they pulled up to a luxury high-rise apartment building.

"Glam... I always forget what a crap hole I live in until I visit you," Abby said. She stepped out of the cab and craned her neck to look up at the top. "Man, Columbia really likes you, for some reason." She walked to the door.

"A slitch's gotta make a living," René said.

"I just like the connection here, no judgment," Sim(on) said.

René smoothed her skirt and followed after, quietly using the windows' reflection to make a sweep behind them. Abby waited by the automated door guard for her.

"Like the Wizard of Oz," Abby said.

"See? She gets it. We're just out of time," René said.

"Yeah, like a hundred years," Sim(on) said. "It's really kind of sad that you two are so locked in the past. Come on into the future. The world's smaller, but we have cooler toys."

An Art Deco face gently lit up in the door frame as René approached.

"Good evening, Miss Anderson. Are these two people with you?" the door asked.

"Yes, they're with me."

"Very good. Have a nice evening," the door said.

The maglev elevator pushed them into their heels as it accelerated up the rails to the twenty-first floor. The door chimed, then opened. The floor was a deep green diamond weave carpet bordered by cream, and the walls were a burnt umber wood from a gro-print facility on the island. Chrome hardware accented the hallway, shining in the recessed light. The ceiling simulated the sky outdoors, despite several more floors above them.

"That looks better than the actual sky." Abby snorted.

"Yeah, I went outside once. The graphics sucked," Sim(on) said.

"It's nice to have friends," René said.

"What *do* you do for her, and will you teach me?" Abby said.

"C'mon, do I look like a tattler?" René said. The break in confidence before was nowhere to be found now.

She reached for the door handle. There were only three others on this floor. Abby knew there were panels for cleaning supplies and a fire exit here somewhere, but the night had already used up her finer observation skills. René's dog was already making chuffing noises behind the door.

"Good boy," René said as she pet the dog.

"You know the drill, make yourselves at home. Pizza, or smorgasbord," René said after opening the fridge.

"Pizza?" Sim(on) asked. He was already down on his knees next to the dog, playing on the floor.

"Beer?" Abby said.

"Sounds like a plan. You know your way around. Don't be shy."

Sim(on) flicked his screen toward the wall. A holo display lit up, and he pulled up a scrolling feed of world news.

"Sound off," he said before the automated reporter had chimed in. "Last of the petrol reserves just about out," he said to no one in particular. The dog joined him on the sofa watching the holo.

"I'll give you ten minutes, fifteen tops. Then if there's not a *telenovela* on, I'm going to throw this empty bottle soundly at your head," Abby said.

Sim(on) was caught between chewing a mouthful and a report on the mounting freshwater crisis in North America when René sat down by Abby.

"You okay?" she asked. "That seemed personal..."

"Just came at a bad time—memories," Abby said. She closed her eyes to quiet her head, but it didn't work. Abby's brain filled in the quiet.

∽

The computers gave the room a burnt smell, worse than the dusty air usually drifting through the remodeled aircraft maintenance bay. Old aircraft parts and grease added chemical notes to the miasma, in a strange counterpoint to the open sewers outside permeating everything else. The heat was barely kept out by the painted-over windows.

"I need to talk to you," the supervising officer said.

"Yes sir," Abby said. She pushed away from the makeshift desk and terminal.

Standing up, her sweat-soaked shirt peeled from the chair. She pushed it back under the desk and took her uniform top off the back. The dried sweat gave it the feel of cardboard as the fabric cracked and bent over her body. Abby buttoned the front as she walked after the officer. Around the corner, shielded by rows of dangling cables and computer parts, the officer stopped.

"I need you to run a trace," he said.

"Sure—what target?" Abby asked.

The officer passed Abby a slip of torn paper.

"This is a local number," Abby said.

"Yeah," the officer said.

"That's outside of our targets."

"It is. But we need it done," he said.

"I get that. It's illegal," Abby said.

"I need it done," the officer grew impatient.

Abby stiffened and locked eyes dead ahead, away from the man.

"According to our mandate, what you are asking is an illegal order, sir. I respectfully cannot follow your order."

The officer stood close enough to Abby that his chest rested against hers.

"If you can't do this, I don't need you. You can go back out on patrol, soldier."

"I understand," Abby said. "I will not do this. I will get my gear and report to the motor pool."

∽

Abby pulled away from the memory and leaned in on René's shoulder.

"You know you're my best friend, right?" René said. "You can tell me anything you want."

"Yeah," Abby said.

"Need to talk?" René said.

"Not now. You know the drill," Abby said.

"Yeah," René said. "*Po-gai* goons."

René let go of the last bit of tension in her shoulders from Abby's barb about Columbia and took a deep draught of her beer.

CHAPTER 8

Blood in the Water

MEXICO—REPUBLIC OF TEXAS BORDER

0940 24 MAR 2073

Carsem put the car into manual mode on the wide offloading lot after the Cajuns returned control to her from the ferry. The air was a different humid from New Orleans, and while the passage around Republic waters was smooth, she was eager to get on the road again. The signs offered her frontage roads to the left and right, the 1800 West or the new 307. When her light changed, Carsem gunned the simulated motor onto the 307 South toward Tulum.

Vast ancient ruins appeared and disappeared by the windows with regularity. The sight reminded her of her home. Hours passed in a blacktop tunnel through a green blur over her headlights. Carsem crossed through Belize and Guatemala before stopping in San Pedro Sula, Honduras. The city was like any other she had visited along the road, another bland menagerie of Spanish colonial architecture and bland modern buildings. She reserved a room through her screen and went looking for a place to eat nearby. A crowd of children, probably herded by the couple of young teenagers she saw, swarmed around her. She tossed a couple coins away from her, and while she couldn't hear them, she felt their feet chasing away. A ratty-looking dog stayed behind, sat on its haunches, and watched her.

Carsem was touched—the kids at least looked like they knew the score and could manage. This dog seemed utterly hopeless, but it still panted after her. She moved and it moved. She stopped, and it did too. It had no obvious wounds or limp she could see. She tossed it a scrap of a protein bar. The dog smelled it, then ate it. She started to walk away, and it barked. Only once. Carsem held out her hand, and the dog carefully came to her. It sniffed at her. She started to walk again, and the dog followed just behind and to the left of her feet.

They dined on grilled meat, vegetables, and stuffed corn flatbreads. Carsem ordered four plates, though she only ate one and a half. They were spotless before she returned them. Carsem couldn't hear if he made more noise during their feast, but the animal was suddenly attentive to her movements as if it knew her limits. She got up to leave, so did the dog.

"Have a nice night," she said to her companion.

The dog locked step beside her.

"Typical man. Fed you, now you think I'll take you home."

It looked up at her.

"Ay, c'mon."

Carsem walked back the way they'd come. She stopped by a *farmacia*, its green neon cross hanging from the row of eves.

"*Perros no*," the attendant announced. He'd meant for his voice to carry from the register to the door, but fortunately, it worked for Carsem's needs all the same.

Carsem motioned for the dog to stay put. It did its best while she walked through the door. Using her screen to translate the labels through augmented reality, she picked out some multi-purpose pet shampoo, dog meds, and a collar.

"Fine," she said to herself and walked to the register.

The attendant waved a wand over her and the sundries. Her screen alerted her to the transaction.

"*Buenos noches*," he said.

"*Adios*," she said, hoping he was done.

~

By the time Carsem hit the state of Panama, Gran America, she was getting seriously road-weary. The Pan-American Highway stretched out ahead, hypnotizing her with the monotony of lines, dashes, and dots.

"Come on, come on, you can make it to Panama," she said. The city was a few kilometers off still.

She ended up pulling over after the car buzzed from her hands slipping off the wheel.

"Ugh. Fine." She parked in *El Valle de Antón,* just shy of her goal for the day. "Just a little rest. Eh, Sancho?"

Sancho rolled his eyes to her without lifting his head from the console between the front seats.

Carsem felt the thump-thump of his wiry tail wagging against the bench seat in the back as he sat on the floorboard.

She woke suddenly to a knock against the glass of her car. Eight men surrounded the outside. One held the side of his needler pistol against the window.

"*Fena.*" She hit the start button.

The retro-style slap shifter threw the car into reverse, and she floored the accelerator. Blue smoke filled the air as she flipped the 442 into a reverse J-turn, side-swiping a vehicle she couldn't identify through the cloud. Other impacts rebounded off the fenders—they felt like garbage cans. Carsem smoothly transferred into drive and peeled out again toward Highway 1. When she made it to the median lane, her adrenaline shakes kicked in. Sancho poked his head up to check on her.

"Thanks for the head's up."

The Oldsmobile drifted slightly. Her eyes flicked away from assessing the damage when garish neon paint and idiotically bright lights picked their way toward her in the sparse traffic.

"Great."

Seconds later, the collision alerts started beeping as the suped-up rally cars started to flank her. She saw the guns before she saw the men holding them as windows rolled down. She shot a glance at Sancho and pushed him down into the floorboards. With both hands on the wheel, she slammed on the brakes. Three of the cars playing at ramming her from behind folded into one, with the chrome bumper of the 442 acting as part battering ram and part cowcatcher. The rest of the traffic seemed to evaporate into the mist along the highway. The drive train of the Oldsmobile turned off.

"Come on, come on, come on!" she said, pushing the start button.

The instrument panel came to life after the third try. The vibration was offline, but the readout registered full power, and the suspension problems were only minor. With a little back and forth, she pulled free of the wreckage behind her.

"There you are!"

The two cars who had flanked her were now racing toward her in the wrong direction. Carsem saw the tiny pocks of smoke and flame flashing from their weapons. They wouldn't be out of effective range for long. She reached for the shotgun under the backside of the passenger seat. Sancho was clueless about what she was after but did the best he could to get out of the way without climbing onto the seat.

"Gotcha." She pushed the safety button to fire.

Carsem estimated time and distance, then as the *drogas* were too close to maneuver at their speed, she accelerated. She was careful to hit just at the top of her tires' grip to keep from advertising her takeoff with the blue smoke of a high-speed burnout.

"*Qirika we* çikirîne," she spat, diving between the on-rushing cars. [Go choke yourself.]

Bullets flared wildly. Carsem felt them hit the car, but they missed the glass. Her opponents turned in her rear-view mirror, circling the wreckage of their *compadres*, and emerged on reverse sides. Carsem kept her speed at 80 percent of the 442's top speed, pretending to make a run for it. At two hundred kilometer per hour, it was a convincing dodge.

The light, whiny cars soon caught up to her. This time they waited to have her in their sights. Their minds were made up to make her pay for her audacity before ending her. She took advantage of the passenger on the left's obscene pantomime to sideswipe his ride. Carsem tapped the brakes. She avoided the driver's counter steer, and as he narrowly avoided crashing into the other driver, she hit him perfectly off-center on the right third of his bumper. The other car had maneuvered to match Carsem and tried to stop her as she opened the throttle full bore into the bumper, continuing to accelerate as the car in front of her dipped and began to roll over, and over. She counted three complete flips before her attention returned to the final car falling behind her. It tried to match her pace but kept a safe distance.

The pursuing car followed her through Panama City. The day drew on through twilight and into the evening as she drove over the bridge, down to Yaviza, and through Darién National Park into the state of Colombia. She tried slipping off the highway onto the 82, winding through the mountains past the Cerro Tacarcuna ruins. Deep in the jungle, she caught his lights beaming down below on a switchback.

"*Soai.*"

She turned her lights back on and drove toward the wetlands of Bocas Del Atrato where she could get a ferry to Turbo. It was a race of attrition. Like the fox, she tried to stay ahead of the dogs enough to make them give up. With most of the crew dead or in intensive care, she assumed how it would end.

Carsem drove on across the raised bridges, reminding her of the deep south in the United States.

"Looks an awful lot like the Bible belt from up here," Carsem said, speeding a hundred feet above the flooded plain.

She flicked her eyes to the rearview mirror and saw, in the far distance, one other set of headlights. She was able to reserve a ferry to Turbo at the next exit. The sign read "*Corregimiento Bocas del Atrato.*"

Carsem drove up to the boarding area and was let on immediately. She knew this cruise at night wasn't going to be a safe Cajun Navy transfer, but even with the salacious glares from the crew, it was a better option than waiting around the swamp docks for daylight. The giant windlasses began to turn and haul up the incline. Carsem ran her hands over Sancho's back.

The windlasses groaned and stopped. The incline slowly let out. Carsem put on her jacket. She kept her eyes on the retreating drawbridge as she loosened the zipper covered vents of the left sleeve. She checked her side pocket for the knuckleduster as she stepped out of the car. She tossed a protein bar on the backseat floorboards and left the passenger door slightly open. Carsem stood casually behind a ship's rib on the other side, with the hull at her back. She could hear the hotrod whine ridiculously as it pulled into the maw of the ferry. Its rally lights flooded the otherwise sparse compartment with light.

The lascivious crew had other things to do topside. Two doors opened on the coupe, and three men emerged. Two walked like pit fighting dogs on leashes held by the third, just waiting for their cue. The boss was whistling. The echo turned up the volume for Carsem, and she smiled.

"*Estás sonriendo ahora perra, solo espera...*" the boss said.

[You're smiling now bitch, just wait...]

The Oldsmobile acted like a bulwark as they approached. The men had to come around the ends of the car one at a time instead of side-by-side. The boss took the far side, around the front of the car. He was half-way across when the stooges cleared the rear bumper. Carsem stepped out along the side.

"*¿Qué? ¿Lo que vas a hacer?*" the frontman said as someone used to abuses of power.

[What? What you gonna do?]

"Che," Carsem said.

[This.]

Her left palm flipped and her arm shot out, sliding the twelve-gauge down her sleeve. The report was deafening as a flash-bang grenade in the ship's hull. The first man's left leg disappeared into the bilge. The boss was drawing for a shot but couldn't reach over the roof. He blasted the windows out toward her in a hail of needling gunfire. The ricochets whizzed chaotically. Carsem felt something pull her across the deck toward the car like a string. She saw blood spray from the amputee's chin.

The second stooge opened fire wildly with the needle gun as Carsem's double-ought buckshot shredded his T-shirt. A third round flipped his cap back and twisted his friend's arm. Carsem threw herself back against the bulkhead, sheltered by the rib while she sought out the other man. He was writhing on the ground in a smear of blood. Sancho was locked on his crotch, having crushed the man's right wrist. He was failing at holding his right hand against his neck, which bubbled through his fingers. The raggedy heeler mutt looked at Carsem for approval.

"Good dog," she said.

She knelt beside him. She snapped her fingers and waved her hand. Sancho released his grip and backed up. The man's anguished face turned to her and blossomed wide-eyed in fear. Carsem slipped the metal shank over her fingers like she was showing off a silk stocking.

∼

The *drogas'* tiny car whizzed to life. Carsem drove it into position directly behind the 442. The music feed was playing oldies at a volume she could hear. Johnny Cash's voice wavered, through "God's Gonna Cut You Down."

Carsem looked over at her passengers. Blood loss made them immobile, and they were falling fast into the abyss, but she saw their eyes. They knew what was happening.

"*Destinado a suceder*," she said as she stepped out.

[It was meant to be.]

She put the car in neutral, stepped out, and closed the door. She walked to the tethered handheld control module and pushed the big green button. She lowered the incline until it was flat with the deck, then stepped into the Oldsmobile. Whatever had been damaged was back in place as the simulated 442 roared in the hold. She put the muscle car in reverse and slowly crept back to the sound of crunching hempglass. The light coupe rolled slowly across the deck until the back wheels found the edge of the incline. The headlights came on as the dying man in the passenger seat struggled with the controls.

A little more throttle and the lights drifted across the fantail, then stern of the ship. Carsem pulled the car forward, closed the incline, and waited in the driver's seat cradling her shotgun.

The crew slid down the ladders as the ship prepared to make port. It wasn't their first time leaving the gangs to their own work below decks on the crossing. They looked part crestfallen, part horrified as they surveyed the hold. It wasn't at the blood on the deck, or the drag marks, but when they saw Carsem sitting behind the wheel of the 442. They clotted up at the end of the ladder, unsure of what to do next. The deckhands' leader arrived and ordered the men about as if nothing was amiss. One deckhand started spraying with a hose.

As the incline descended to the dock, the chief nodded and casually raised two fingers to his brow in salute as Carsem backed out onto the loading zone. Only then did he reach for the comms handset and ring the bridge.

Carsem looked at the dog, now sitting in the passenger seat. "We need a pit stop, and I think we just got noticed, Sancho."

CHAPTER 9

Birth of a Nation

1015 22 JUN 2075

"They're backing out of the deal?" Keiko asked.

The Forum was a hall whose walls could expand to allow nearly five-thousand people to attend government functions. In its reduced state it housed the fifteen senators and the Triumvirate alone. The massive, telescoping venue was shaped in undulating waves of shimmering metal plates. When stretched out, it looked like the segments of a lobster tail. The plates were louvered to adjust airflow and natural light through the structure. Collapsed, there was a hall big enough for two basketball courts, with a separated office hall facing the Security Forces building across a courtyard. A retractable wall was left open between the two. The Triumvirate left it retracted so any citizen could observe their leaders directly—and to remind them they served at the request of the people. It was in this working space the Triumvirate conducted its official business. Here they could communicate with the offices of Giresun's government from across the island and under the waters off their coast as easily as if they were in the physical wing next door.

"Looks that way," said Chris. "The insurgency thing?"

"The insurgents are a smokescreen. Fake news," Columbia said.

"It's *bullsoai*," Keiko agreed. "They left that behind in the last century. With the power grab after the North destabilized the drug trade, the de Silvas united all those little Guevara wannabes and *caudillos* as muscle."

"What they're doing now looks a lot like insurgency," Columbia said. She leaned back in her chair to watch her fellow leaders. While the Triumvirate's workspaces formed a triangle at the center of the room, Columbia's desk sat on a slightly elevated dais between Chris and Keiko.

"That kid? He's banking on the name his granddaddy made. Hasn't done anything himself, just wants to get into the scene now that the GA has done the work," Keiko said.

"I caught some of his feed. Some populist stuff mixed with a whole lot of gaslighting about the usual Bolivarian rhetoric couched in pre-Columbian conjecture," Chris said.

"Right. Punk kid making a play now that Dad's out of the way. Who's controlling the strings?" Columbia asked.

"Not sure, except these two are never too far away." Keiko flicked a media feed's still onto the holo from her wrist screen. Elana Chávez and Samuel Brönner stood behind Armand de Silva at a podium in Lima.

"She's a professor of history, archeology, and anthropology at Cusco. He's been muscle for a long time for de Silva. Worked for Dad, dirty as hell," Keiko continued.

"Why was he in Lima?" Columbia asked.

"He's been using the cartel to provide humanitarian aid to the villages around GA, but now he's upscaling to the inner barrios of cities like Lima and Rio," Keiko said.

"Prime territories under their control, right?" Columbia asked.

"We've used their networks there for training missions—sex, drugs, you name it," Keiko said.

"Looks like he's trying to do some good? Did he turn?" Chris said. Her voice rose slightly out of control for a split-second. She recovered with just a hint of self-conscious blush.

"Any decrease in trade?" Columbia asked.

"No. In fact, they may be coordinating the uptick in murder for hire, but we're not sure yet," Keiko said.

"Let's keep on this. Keep the bots on a random search pattern. I don't want them to know we're looking for them," Columbia said quietly to Keiko.

Keiko tapped out the directive to the Security Forces. Chris went back to working at her desk. She sipped at a glass of water and avoided eye contact. The Forum's large hall appearance and in-the-round seating had the reverse effect of the old audience chambers. Rather than making the supplicants feel small, the effect was reversed for the Triumvirate's three Consuls. The empty seats bared down on them, a constant reminder of their role and duty to the sixty-thousand people of the island—they were accountable. Never mind transparency laws permeating the entire culture of Giresun. Fully assimilated after a couple generations, it rarely intruded into people's lives anymore. The psychology of the empty audience watching them was far more acute.

CARTAGENA, COLUMBIA PRESIDENTIAL PALACE

1724 22 JUN 2075

The President's cabinet had carved out spots around, but not *in* the office. Ignacio Guzman took over an entire Chesterfield sofa, while aides came and went through the ornate French doors with papers for President Calderone to sign or updates for his review. The executive branch was buzzing, while the vice president relaxed like a bear in a beehive.

"The entire western states seem unable to function now, *presidente*," an aide said.

"This is really getting out of hand. These marches… what do they want us to do?"

"The same thing they always want, these Bolivarian types," Ignacio Guzman said. "A North American lifestyle at a South American price."

"This little punk," President Caldarone said.

"Son of an established drug lord," Ignacio said.

"*The* drug lord," Hubert said. "His grandpa saw to that."

"Yes," Ignacio measured his words.

"The bastard is kicking us when we're down. This disease—goddamn jungle!" Hubert yelled.

He threw an ashtray at the wall. The crystal shattered like ice glittering across the parquet floor. It barely left a scratch on the centuries-hardened wall of the presidential villa. Colombia had built a few things to last despite itself. The room's fine furnishings were evidence to it. Unlike most, these were relics from the Belle Époque, not replicas. Despite the ornate gilt and filigree, the pieces were solid and expertly crafted. A substantial setting despite its Baroque aesthetic. They had survived the tumultuous history following their manufacture nearly two hundred years ago. The furniture would likely outlive them all.

"Still no idea," Ignacio said.

"Anything, anything at all we can pin to him, or the cartel?"

"Nothing," Ignacio said. "It's all aid work. He's made himself unassailable through the media. Everyone loves this kid—a prince, looking to undo the wrongs of his forebears. We can't create anything, either. He's built a pyramid of glass around him, all transparency—"

"You remember the time we went to Manaus to see *La Gioconda* for the bicentennial?" Hubert said. "The one about the jilted lover—"

"The girl Gioconda, who loves her mama so much that when her friend saves the mother, she steps away from her suitor, Enzo, as payback to her friend, only to be pursued by the villain Barnaba instead... so she kills herself," Ignacio said.

He stared off through the tall windows overlooking Cartagena.

"I want to be Enzo but it's like it's all destined to end up like Barnaba," Hubert said.

Ignacio held his tongue as he watched the president from the overstuffed leather sofa.

CARACAS, VENEZUELA

The motorcade arrived in the next barrio slum of Caracas, in the foothills around the city center.

"What's this one called again?" Armand asked.

"Juan XXIII," Brönner said. "Buildings so stacked against each other, one good earthquake and it'll fill in the valley below with a landslide."

"Is it here too?" Armand asked, trying to straighten himself up in the car's seat.

"Starting to. Ten percent dead in the *barrio* next door," Brönner said. He pulled up a PAPR mask and donned double gloves, while Armand slipped on a more refined filter mask. "Everything is set. You good? It could get a little... rough."

"Nice," Armand said through his amplified vents. "You've got your dose? Just in case?"

Brönner stuck his gloved hands in a bin of fine powder. It left no visible trace but caught the light like dust in a sunbeam.

"Of course. This close to death?" Brönner said. "In my pocket. You?"

Armand held up an ornate over-sized ring. "Old school. Family heirloom."

"Poisoner's ring," Brönner said as he raised an eyebrow.

The truck stopped. The doors opened from the outside as security, outfitted with masks and gloves, waited outside.

"*Buenos dias, mi familia. Encantanto de conocerlo,*" Armand announced through PA speakers hidden outside of the vehicle.

His words were met with cheers. Armand reached past the security team to shake or touch hands with as many outstretched ones as he could find. A hysterical mother managed to lift, nearly throw, her baby over the fence of men.

"*¡Señor!*" she screamed.

Armand caught the baby and cradled it gently in his arms. The child was obviously infected. As if to declare it so, the baby vomited on Armand's shirt like a possessed thing. Armand slipped his finger across a hidden chamber in his ring. He took the occasion in stride, and while wiping the baby down first, he soothed it with his hands, letting the child suck on a finger before handing it back to the mother. "*¡Gracias!*" the woman said, over, and over.

Armand pulled her across the picket line to find her husband holding the other arm.

"See to it that they are given food, water, all of it. Don't let them leave," Armand instructed an aide.

The aide nodded and led the little family toward the vans and tables further down the column. Armand returned his outward attention to the crowd.

Brönner split his attention from Armand to watching the baby and its family.

Armand finally made it to the dais set up off the back of a cargo carrier. As he mounted the ladder, Brönner touched his hand and twitched his head toward the family. Armand nodded.

"Hello, hello, hi everybody!" Armand said through the speakers, standing above the crowd. He mugged for the cameras now transmitting his face to the feeds of countless millions across the world. "Did you all get something to eat, to drink? I hope so. If not, please see my friends here, they'll help you out. That's what we're doing here. Everyone else seems to have forgotten about us, the ones who organized for this promise of unification. But now—it's looking a lot like the old world, isn't it?"

The crowd answered with a roar.

"They're doing a lot about this mysterious thing, huh? 'It came from the jungle...' Like it's some wild thing to haunt us in the night. I don't see the bourgeois people downtown dying in the streets though, no?"

A woman screamed. Several lights panned to find her—the mother and husband were holding up their baby to the light. A production assistant approached Armand from the nearest wing of the stage. Armand waived, and Brönner guided the family toward the ladder.

"What's the matter, *señora*?" Armand asked.

"My baby—she is so good, look! You touch her, now she's good! She's dying, now she's better!" Her uncontrolled joy crackled across the *barrio's* air.

"I'm sure it wasn't me," Armand said. "I'm glad she's doing better. She looks happy."

The woman was unable to talk through her tears. The assistant returned to usher them off stage. At the end of the street, Armand saw the flashing lights of a cordon of police arrive.

"Now, kind folks, it looks like our friends have arrived to have a say too. Please, don't judge them too harshly, but just do as they say. Hopefully not too many of us will get hurt, eh?" Armand raised his hands and waited as a platoon of police in riot gear threaded their way through the crowd. As they passed, the villagers raised their hands to follow suit with Armand.

The officer in charge stepped up on stage and was followed by four other officers. Armand slowly lowered himself to his knees.

"Armand de Silva," the officer in charge began. He was surprised to find his voice amplified across the barrio, and the world. "You are under arrest by order of the Gran American cabinet and Presidente Caldarone."

The ephemeral mic went silent.

The crowd put down their hands and turned them upon the cordon of police running from their command post to the dais. Gas canisters erupted from the police vehicles as batons flagellated from behind plexiglass shields. Water cannons blasted a clear path for the police gauntlet to return with their captive. Protesters were swept into the gutters. The police's crowd control turned into melee combat.

Wearing his PAPR mask and gloves, Samuel Brönner kicked his open bucket high into the air toward the rioting crowd and away from the police cordon. White powder streamed from it in a cloud over the masses, like chalk dust bombs in *Carnivale*. Police teams were loading what people they could from around Armand into cattle trucks.

Brönner saw the family with the baby pressed into a trailer and smiled. Seconds later the crowd exploded as the police opened fire.

Brönner launched a flare over their heads. What vehicles could move did, though a few including the tractor-trailer Armand had stood on minutes ago were left behind, overrun by the crowd. News crews stood above their heads and broadcast the riot to the world.

AMAZONAS, BRAZIL, PRIVATE PRISON

0855 27 JUN 2075

The cell was separate from the others. The mint green paint was peeling in chips from the concrete bricks and the steel bars around Armand. The heat outside made the walls cry tears of condensation, slowly dripping over the chipped masonry as he sat alone. He had been there for three days. A sink and a tin cup kept his thirst at bay, but so far there was no food. Armand knew just because he couldn't see them, someone was watching.

He hummed along to *Des Colores* sporadically. There were only so many ways to amuse yourself in isolation. Despite the open room, he occasionally flashed back to the confines of his disaster coffin under the rubble of the de Silva villa. He practiced slowing his heart rate and breathing just like Samuel showed him after the first panic attack.

The rise and fall of the sun and moon outside the high-set, barred windows of the jail cell convinced him that time still passed. Rather than pace his cage like a circus tiger for those who stood watching, Armand desperately fought to control his actions beyond breathing, like Brönner had shown him.

"Dim your eyes," Samuel had said. "Focus on clearing your mind of all the noise. Slowly bring your thoughts to the movement of your chest, quiet the impulse to breathe until you can hear your heart instead of feeling it.

"That's it. Now, focus on the heart, feel its beating. Picture it in your mind and, slowly, slow it down, until you can hear the space between beats. Keep practicing this until you can count slowly between breaths and heartbeats. Master your body, and you will master your power. With power and self-knowledge comes purpose, Prince."

Armand could almost see Brönner sitting next to him on the floor.

～

"It's zero-nine hundred," the guard said. "De Silva's doing push-ups and leg-tucks against the bars. Does he have a watch we don't know about?"

"Creepy. He's got this whole routine down, like a *po-gai* monk," said his partner.

El Comandante crashed through the door. "Changes?"

The two guards in the surveillance station snapped to out of their seats.

"Nothing sir, he's going through his routine. Right on time," the first guard said.

The commander grunted in response, peering closely at the monitor's displays. Everything and every angle were watched through minuscule cameras dotting the isolation room. The official stance was it gave the prisoners their safety without compromising the reinforcement of isolation. In reality, it was just another endemic injustice in an already cruel system.

"Orders, sir?" the second guard asked.

"The government is sending a cadre. Make sure they have access to whatever they need," the commander said. "They will be here tomorrow."

"Yessir!" the guards saluted.

The commander slammed his palms on the computer desk, staring at the display. He stood up, straightened his tunic, and walked out the doorway without another word.

～

Armand could hear the footsteps outside the window as the party arrived. He did not move. The door was unlocked, and a guard held it open while another guard was the first other person into the room in four days. Four men in dark suits followed the guard while his mate closed the door behind them.

"Armand de Silva," one of the suits announced.

Armand did not respond.

"That is you, isn't it? I'd hate to think we had the wrong person in here all this time."

The third man held a covered tray. Armand could smell the food from across his cage.

"It was. You can call me Pachutec," he said. "I have had an awakening by the spirits of my ancestors."

"That's cute. Sure , Pachutec. Whatever you say," the man in the suit said. "You can call me Sancho. I have some questions for you... Pachutec. If you answer them well, I also have some delicious food here. I understand the accommodations aren't quite what you're used to?"

Pachutec was betrayed by his stomach. It growled louder than their conversation.

"Very well," Sancho said. "What are you doing in Colombia? We know of your travels throughout the rest of Gran America. Not buying the philanthropy angle."

"Too bad, because that part is real," Pachutec said. "The people bought into the lies for the thousandth time. They immortalize Bolivar and imagine a heaven on Earth, but no one delivers more than promises. I've got plenty of money and resources. Is it so bad to feed the hungry and cure the sick?"

"For the son of a drug lord? Yeah, not buying it. Your dad was an evil prick. You have given with one hand and taken away with the other. Nothing more than a street kid's shell game," Sancho said.

"True, my father did a lot of things to unify his empire. Now I can do something with it," Pachutec said.

"Which brings us to the point. What is it you're after?" Sancho asked.

"I want to give the people what they want."

"Not much happening from here," Sancho said. He flicked the chipped iron bars.

"But it continues out there. That's what I want," Pachutec said.

"Power does not abide sharing"

"I've got my own power, more than I could care about. Tell Calderone I don't care about sharing his power or have any care about his government. He can keep it."

"What about your followers?"

"What followers? I just give out food and aid. Are you seriously telling me that the unified government of South America is threatened by a fed populace who are getting vaccinated? If that's true, you've got bigger problems than me."

"Enjoy your food," Sancho said.

The third man set the tray into the pass gate between the bars. The guard on the inside rapt the door. It opened to let the official party leave. Pachutec waited until they were gone and opened his tray. He smiled, unfolded the napkin, and slowly ate for the cameras.

∿

"Uploading," Brönner said. The bugs the cleaners had planted transmitted the video feed from the prison to his mobile van. The national news was covering the fallout from Juan XXIII as riots had rocked across Gran America and President Calderone had desperately tried to reign in his earlier authorization of deadly force. Hundreds had died in the wake of violence after Armand's arrest by police.

"If you thought that the death of that little girl and her family in prison made the world take notice..." Manuel stopped talking and looked at Brönner. "When do we go get him?"

"Patience. All those pretty people are going to do what they always do. Interfere in a weak government. They'll ask us to take him back."

CHAPTER 10

The Woodshed

1033 30 JUN 2075

The barber took the towel off of Pachutec's face.

"All done, *Señor Pachutec*," the barber said. He laid the towel over the shoulder of his red polo shirt.

"Thanks, Raphael," Pachutec said.

The old man rinsed off his things in the cell's sink. The guards watched to make sure everything made it back safely into his bag.

"He's the only one who gets it right," Pachutec said, admiring his cut and shave with his hand. "Well, gents, it's been a month. I'm all cleaned up and fed. Either it's the stockade or a press conference, but looks like we're ready to go outside, no?"

The suit by the door knocked, and a guard opened the cell from the outside. The barber went out first, followed by the guards who bookended Pachutec into the streaming sunlight. The smell of fresh-cut grass wafted by as he exited the concrete paddock. The suit followed the entourage across the neatly trimmed lawns toward the backside of a raised stage. Pachutec could see the cameras and the aerial antennae from their vans over the stage.

"Up you go," the suit said as the guards fell back. He ushered Pachutec onto the steps.

Before his shoulders cleared the stage, the audience erupted in cheers. Car horns blared behind them. Pachutec waved to the people while ensuring he didn't break the fourth wall by looking directly at the cameras. "I'm here for the people, not the publicity," was the message.

"Ladies and gentlemen of the press," a secretary announced from the podium, "President Calderone."

The leader of Gran America appeared before the cameras on stage. The crowd failed to react.

"*Buenos dias*, people of Gran America, South America, Central America, and the world. I stand before you today, a humbled man. As leaders, we listen to counsel and form our opinions based on the best information we have available to us. In this case, many mistakes were made. I listened to the wrong people and bad information.

"Over the last several weeks we have tried to make up for these shortcomings and repair our trust. Many investigations are ongoing still. Justice will win out. And to that end, I do not wish to dwell on fault but on what we can do better going forward. It is with a contrite heart that I bring forth *Señor* Armand de Silva now, whose efforts to ease the pain and suffering of our most vulnerable were seen as a wolf in sheep's clothing. May I present our friend—" The crowd did not allow the president to finish his remarks. The president eventually acknowledged he was beaten and motioned for Pachutec to take the podium with him.

President Calderone paused for the cameras with an arm around Armand. They raised their opposite arms together. Calderone waved with an open hand. Pachutec held his fist aloft.

Pachutec moved toward the microphone. "*Me genie me llaman Pachutec—*"

[My people, they call me Pachutec—]

Was all he could blurt across the airwaves before the mic was cut. Security officers were pushed back as tough-looking men in red polo shirts and khaki pants stormed from the side of the platform, encircling Pachutec. The prison's security guards were overwhelmed and helpless to stop them on live broadcast around the world. Samuel Brönner directed his organized mob to bring Pachutec down and to their awaiting motorcade. President Calderone watched in disbelief, surrounded by his own double cordon of secret service and police, helpless to intervene. It was like fighting the tide as it washed his control out to sea.

Guns were drawn but no resistance was given by the red shirts. In the face of the world, Calderone knew he had suddenly lost his victory to the jaws of defeat. His handlers and the police forcefully ushered him into the awaiting motorcade. In seconds the line of presidential vehicles were pushing through throngs of people beating impotently against the outside.

"What the *po-gai* just happened?" President Calderone asked.

He sat in the back of the limousine while aides typed on their screens to both assess and control the damage done.

"Do you want to continue to elevate Gran America, or is this the inflection point where you go full Chavez?" Ignacio Guzman said.

"*Po-gai*," Calderone said.

"You already took care of that," Ignacio said.

"Instant reactions are cratering, GA and abroad," an aide said, wearing an eyeglass interface with her screen. "We need to turn this around right now."

"What would you have me do?" the president said.

"Fall on your sword. Resign. Preserve the State. Do what none of your predecessors in kind could pull off. What made Washington so great? He moved on. He let the republic stand on its own. It's not an election, but at the expense of your legacy, Gran America may survive," Ignacio said.

"I'm not sure that's going to be enough. The whole country is ready to make this kid king," the aid said.

"*Po-gai soai!*" Calderone screamed.

Everyone else in the vehicle tried to disappear.

❀

"Thanks for picking me up," Pachutec said jokingly. He gently walked through the crowd as Elana pushed him along, flanked by their own security. Pachutec followed Elana into the armored behemoth after one final wave to his people.

The motorcade of armored trucks sped along the brick-red dirt roads away from the prison complex and reporters. The thick quartz windows were beaded with condensation. The armor plating snapped brush and cracked tree limbs through the jungle road. The combat-tuned suspension could not overcome the ruts in the dirt. The occasional deep gouge jostled the passengers against their restraints. In a moment, the jungle swallowed the evidence of the compound and political drama into its green maw.

Pachutec bounced against his seat, startled by four loud pops as they bounced off the roof.

"Aerial drones. You're okay?" Elana said. "Our analysts say that the Air Force is up to something. Now that we're out of the cameras' eyes, we're just taking a look around above the canopy." After a long pause she added, "Pachutec, huh?"

He smiled. "Who better to lead the new Incan empire?"

"You know you misspelled it," she said.

"I wanted similar, not same. Making our own way, honoring the past, right?" Pachutec said.

"Smart guy," Elana said.

"Speaking of which, how's it playing in the streets?" Pachutec said.

"You're practically a saint. The people expected the food and supplies to stop, like a Bread and Circuses rap. Their bellies are full, and they're open to suggestion."

"Then let's give them something to do."

~

After several kilometers, a de Silva airfield appeared before them, carved out of the jungle. A Sikorsky S-70 helicopter was sitting on the tarmac with the pre-flight warm up complete. Its rotors began to spin as the entourage left their vehicles. Brönner coordinated the personnel as some walked quickly to the helicopter and others rearranged themselves in the motorcade.

"What's that?" Pachutec said.

"I hear it too," Elana said.

Three Super Tucano attack planes buzzed overhead, banking sharply as the motorcade was spotted. It would take a minute for them to turn around, even with the propeller engines.

"Air Force. Time to go," Brönner said over the roaring helicopter. The incoming aircrafts' noise was louder than the Sikorsky as they banked back toward the airfield. Dust plumes pocked the dirt runway as the fixed-wing fighters strafed their guns at the entourage.

"What are you doing?" Pachutec yelled over the noise as Brönner took him by the upper arm and forced him into a dead run. They zig-zagged away from the main body of guards and aides. A couple of guards stood to return fire, then crumpled to the ground under the aerial assault.

In the time their lives bought, multiple aerial drones launched from the other vehicles to form up with the scouts. As Brönner, Elana, and the remaining half-dozen aides strapped into the large helicopter bay, Pachutec watched the drones attempt to crash into the oncoming attack planes. The Super Tucanos dodged the incoming drones, barely. With their low speed but superior lift, the pilots pinwheeled like acrobats above the airfield. It kept them busy and took their eyes off of the S-70. Pachutec watched over the shoulder of an aide who sat between him and the helicopter's thin fuselage. The acrobatics eventually led the planes to wildly throw fire toward the rising helicopter.

Once airborne, the cabin was rocked as countermeasures dropped off. The aide was streaming the incident live onto the net, further shifting the balance of power in favor of the people's newest champion. In a straightaway, the old fighter planes easily outpaced the tech. The combat drones, with their artificial intelligence and quick reaction time, were deadly in a dogfight even in small numbers like this. It was a battle of attrition. One Tucano crashed into the airfield as it collided with three drones. Forced into a stalemate, low on fuel, the Tucanos retreated.

The helicopter crew, aided by controlled aerial drone counter-measures, were victorious. The cabin joined in a triumphant yell as the Air Force disengaged from pursuit. Brown hills and arid plains stretched out under the low-flying S-70. The landscape was dotted by collections of green, like the dense forest hiding the airfield and the outskirts of the prison. Brönner keyed his mic.

"The villa, please," he said.

Crossing the border into Peru would take them out of Calderone's official range while he tried to convince the senate to authorize force across state lines. Thanks to the de Silva information campaign, he now had plenty of bigger fires to put out.

With the immediate danger past, and despite the deafening engine noise inside the poshly appointed cabin, Pachutec fell soundly asleep.

GIRESUN ISLAND

0201 01 JUL 2075
René walked home from the party. Things had gone off without a hic-cup, at least not one the hostess or guests had noticed. Everything was coming up roses. The night was cool compared to the day. The island was under a near-constant breeze from across the ocean because of the crescent-shaped mountains behind the city. The stars filled the sky above. Thanks to the meticulous urban planners, the geometry of lights in Giresun was angled to provide pedestrian illumination while preserving the night sky. She held her heels in her left hand, keeping an eye out for anything she didn't want to step in. Otherwise, René was lost in thought.

She didn't notice the errant footfalls. By the time her skin was prickling up, it was too late. Something solid clipped her hard over the back of her ear. On the way down and out, she caught the mottled gray jumpsuits of the Security Forces.

The nauseating whiff of smelling salts assaulted her. She couldn't see, but René felt an eye mask or blindfold around her face. She vomited a few times and felt it land in her lap and run down her chin. Apparently, she was secured to a chair of some kind. René felt the heat of lamps on her. They did nothing but exaggerate her nausea.

"Coming to," said a husky female voice.

"...you dumbasses..." René said groggily.

"Hmm?" said the husky one.

"...lights and a blindfold?" René said.

"Oh," the husky voice said. Suddenly someone punched her squarely in the side of her face. Her cheek and jaw went into convulsions for an agonizing minute.

"In case the blindfold slips. Let's get to the point," the husky woman said.

"Whatever you say. S and M party? Need catering?" René said.

A closed fist slammed into her forehead like a hammer. The back of René's head bounced off a wall at her back. She knew she was in a seated position, facing the right way up. There was a wall behind her and at least two people in the room—why else would she have announced her "coming to"? They were apparently professional, so they wouldn't use comms for this with the emissions surveillance on the island. René couldn't smell anything but her own vomit, and her ears were ringing from the hits she kept taking.

"Who do you work for?" Husky asked.

"Self-employed," René said. She choked down more bile.

This time someone ripped her sleeve off. A rubber hose slapped across her arm like a chain whip. René knew it wouldn't leave much of a mark, but the pain was searing.

"Before that," Husky asked.

"I was homeless," René said. "Lived in a car."

"Who hired you to interfere with the First Consul in Cartagena? We know Samuel Brönner has been in contact with you. We know the deal."

René added "government or Security Forces" to the list. Through the haze of her likely concussion, she recalled the glimpse of uniforms on her way down to the pavement.

"Dumb luck," René said. "Wrong number, wasn't interested. Typical macho cis, can't take no for an answer."

"C'mon. Be honest," said a new voice. It was carefully measured and cultivated. René's blood ran cold.

"Looks like I'm trying to get in the way?" René said.

"Stay out of it, slitch," Husky said.

René felt a rag loaded with something like varnish press over her mouth and nose. She reflexively tried to twist out of it and hit her head on the wall again before slipping away into a gray then black nothing.

∽

Abby was on her screen talking with Sim(on). She cradled René's head in her lap in the middle of a cobblestone street. René startled and vomited at the same time. She tried to look around but couldn't quite get her bearings.

"Easy, you," Abby said. Tears fell from her face onto René's as Abby smoothed her friend's hair. "Medics are on the way." Abby let out a throaty growl. "I don't give a *po-gai*, SIM! Get it done!" Abby screamed and hung up.

René heard the ambulance before slipping out of consciousness again.

CHAPTER 11

Rest and Recovery

0931 01 JUL 2075

"Not to sound ungrateful, but why didn't they just kill me?" René asked.

Diffuse backlighting provided illumination and the color of the recovery room. As routines changed, or additional services were needed, the color responded to cue in passing staff. René sat in a polymorphic hospital bed. Programmable hydraulic lifters mapped her body under a gel membrane. The system matched every contour and recalibrated with the movement of her muscles to hold her in a pressure-free posture no matter the angle. The blue blob felt alive under her until her senses accommodated the mattress. Then it seemed to disappear under her.

With a word, a sign, or the selection on a menu, the bed turned her, cooled or warmed as needed, and measured her vital signs through contact with her body. The rest of the room was as anthropomorphic. The typical medical equipment and bins had disappeared, replaced by integrated sensors and predictive routines based on the patient and what the provider needed. Abby and Sim(on) rose from a bench attached to the nearest wall. The upholstery deflated and folded back into the paneling.

"It would've caused more of a stir. Assault does still happen on the island, but murder is a big deal," Sim(on) said. "Plus it sends more of a message than a dead body."

René closed off her reaction, remembering what the second voice said.

"Look what you've done, clod," Abby said. She came to René's side like a mother.

"I'm okay," René said.

"Let me," Abby said. The worry on her face was more disconcerting than the disjointed feeling from René's concussion. Abby repositioned her sheets, there for the patient's feel and modesty more than anything else.

"Doc said you're going to be fine, that nothing was permanently damaged. They need to deal with some bruising and swelling in your brain. They've got it under control with their—" Abby cut off Sim(on) with a withering look. "Sorry," he said, returning to his screen.

"Can I get you anything?" Abby asked.

"I'm fine, sweetie," René said.

"The last time you called me that was when you'd done the open heat for the Security Forces obstacle course and fell off the poles into that nest of nettles," Abby said.

"Punctured a lung and a couple arteries," René said.

"I still don't know what possessed you to do it," Abby said.

"Trying something different," René said. Her gaze shifted to some faraway place.

"You've got that here. Stick to the parties," Abby said, holding her hand from the chair beside her bed.

"Okay, you ready to get out of here?" Dr. Way asked.

"Are you sure it's okay?" Abby said.

"It's been three days. Everything wrong has been corrected. The nanomachines have been passed. You're good to go when you're ready.

We have outpatient counseling and groups if you find you'd like to use them," Dr. Way said.

"I'm okay," René said to Abby. "Sure, doctor. I appreciate it."

The doctor tapped a few times on her screen and brought it to René for her thumbprint. "Okay, there you go. When you're ready, you're discharged. Just give a call if you need to set up a vid conf or an in-person? Nice to meet you all." With a curt nod, she was back out the door and on to her next patient.

"You're good?" Abby said.

"Yep, need to get back to the apartment," René said.

"I've requested extra security," Sim(on) said. He moved to the bedside to help lift her out.

René leaned into a huddle with Abby and Sim(on).

"Security Forces were there," René said. "Asked me about a guy—bad dude who I didn't shake before getting here."

"*Soai*," Abby said.

"I'm on it," Sim(on) said. He expanded his screen and flicked his fingers in whorls and snaps too fast for René to follow.

The threesome walked downstairs to an awaiting cab.

"Spill it," Abby said. The apartment was clear of surveillance according to Sim(on). If they could fool him, they deserved to listen, according to Abby. Everyone agreed the dog would have said something.

"Somebody or some bodies wearing SF jumpsuits hit me with a sap walking home from an event. Caught a glimpse as I went down, but I couldn't make out more. They got the drop on me. Some woman with a husky voice and strong arms worked me over a little, quizzing me about Columbia and this asshat Samuel Brönner," René said. "Was in a small space, nondescript as far as I could make out. I was vomiting everywhere, blindfolded, tied to a chair."

"Jesus," Abby said.

"No, they were both chicks," René said, then chuffed. She cradled her ribs and head. "Anyhow, the other was polished. A 'didn't-get-dirty' corporate type."

"You managed all this instead of losing your *soai*?" Abby asked incredulously. She got up and made a cold compress in the kitchen. "I'm all about the details. Ask my contracts," René said.

"Sure," Abby said.

"Someone big is mad," Sim(on) said. "But not at you."

"Who's hungry?" Abby asked. She placed the cold, wet rag on René's forehead.

René and Sim(on) raised their hands and laughed. While Abby busied herself in the kitchen, they huddled over his screen's display. Sim(on) shuttled his fingers across the rolling stream of information about events and Giresun news.

"I'm not seeing anything on the feed—like it didn't happen. They had to have been offline," Sim(on) said.

"You can do that?" René said.

"Sure, it just sucks. Really have to work at it, but yeah. You can make chloroform with bleach and isopropyl alcohol—sounds like what they did before dumping you on the street. No electronics, even neuro disruptors—they give off EM that can be picked up by our internal surveillance. Old school interrogation instead of computer-assisted in a neutral buoyancy tank... they knew what would show up. Even the time frame, just long enough to get the job done and quickly erased before anomalies started getting noticed. I bet they even spoofed the contact tracer—like, left their screens at home or something. You're right. Somehow it's tied in with SF." Sim(on) shot a look at Abby.

Abby walked over with a pile of "kitchen sink" sandwiches. "If you don't like 'em, it's your fault. I just grabbed what was available and slapped it between some bread."

"I'm sure they're better than the hospital," René said.

"You didn't eat anything in the hospital," Sim(on) said.

"Exactly," René said.

"Okay," Sim(on) said after taking a bite. "I'll call off the SF downstairs."

"No, keep them," René said.

Abby furrowed her eyes at René.

"Don't want to tip our hand," René said. "What, you guys don't read? It's like the main part of every mystery, crime drama, or spy thriller. Let the bad guy slip up in front of you, instead of sitting for days in a stakeout."

Abby retrieved the empty plate and went to make more sandwiches. She opened a bag of chips and poured them into a bowl. René sniffed at the aroma. When Abby returned, René scooped half of the bowl onto her plate.

Sim(on) stirred in his armchair across the coffee table. "I'm going to go check something. But I can't do it from here. Gotta get to work. Call me if you need me? Thanks for the sandwiches," he said to Abby as he grabbed another to go.

"You bet," Abby said, keeping her watch over René.

$\sim$

As Sim(on) got off the elevator, he passed two SF guards in the lobby.

"Have a good day. Looks like another winner," the automated door said.

As he waited for the cab to arrive, Sim(on) looked up from his screen before quickly dropping his gaze. He turned around, pretending to be on a call, and focused his camera feed on the reflection in the door. Sim(on) streamed it straight to the holo in René's apartment.

Nancy and N'gono stepped out of the transport van further down the curbside as Sim(on) back walked his way into the cab butt first. The gull-wing door of the cab closed just shy of his toes as Sim(on) cut his feed and set it on loop to the apartment so he could keep an eye on things. Looking at the mirror's reflection, he saw Nancy and N'gono in their gray jumpsuits taking the measure of the wide receiving area in front of the high-rise doors. They were milling about the tall Ti, gardenia, plumeria, and hyacinth planters and talking among themselves.

"Probably nothing..." he muttered as if trying to convince himself.

TRIUMVIRATE PENTHOUSE

1702 01 JUL 2075

"...so, what you're telling me is she's not a plant," Chris van Buren said. She sat on the rooftop terrace overlooking the island's downtown. She found the spot across the next hillock where René's apartment sat. The sides of her mouth curled up in an unfriendly way. The privacy screens surrounding the edges of the garden terrace were technically legal. They were incidentally made of metal that scrambled electrical emissions like a Faraday cage, but copper was a stylistic choice to complement the sunrise and set, she'd said. The hanging planters had earned the Consular residence's garden the nickname "Babylon" for its views and reputation as a secluded retreat for the Triumvirate.

"Ma'am, she doesn't have a record prior to arriving in Boston. She's a Kurd, like from there. Just a refugee," N'gono said.

"Wrong place, wrong time I guess," the Consul said. "The fly in the ointment."

"She's holed up in that apartment. We could—"

"No," the Consul broke in. "Nothing happens... for now. Keep watch—against these criminals roaming the streets—make sure you're seen that way."

"Yes ma'am," N'gono said.

"Was there something else?" the Consul asked.

"These other two—Abby Katz and Sim-on James. They're... not with the program," N'gono said.

"And?" the Consul said.

"Wrong place, wrong time?"

"If it needs to be. We're not trying to undo things, N'gono. Show our hand too early, and you'll bring the whole thing down," the

Consul said. "Now, you better keep a low profile. No more harassing Abby Katz."

N'gono departed, her boots clicking across the iridescent blue-tiled floor to the private elevator.

"Line secure," a computer-generated woman's voice said as Consul van Buren mashed four fingerprints onto her screen.

"So good to see you again *Señor* Guzman," Chris said.

"Likewise, *Señora* van Buren," Ignacio said.

"According to the latest news, it looks like things are going well," Chris said.

"For some. Not so much for others," Ignacio said. He had a thin cruel smile. It mirrored her own.

"Anything I can do here to help?" Chris asked.

"*Nada*, it's all coming together. Even they don't suspect."

"Good. You know how to reach me if that changes, but otherwise, we'll talk again as agreed?"

" Until then, *mariposa*," Ignacio said before disconnecting.

Chris let out a disgusted sigh after the screen went blank and she could stop pretending. With a little luck, the boys would wipe themselves out to the point she could finish the job herself. Consul van Buren poured herself a glass of white wine, adding a splash of seltzer and a few dashes of orange flower syrup. Then she retired to watch the sunset through the hanging gardens of Babylon.

CHAPTER 12

A Pattern of Shadows

GIRESUN ISLAND

1042 07 JUL 2075

The Capitol building was across a giant square from the Black Box. A strange, fractal pattern reflecting pool arched its way back and forth through the square. When viewed from above, it was breathtaking. Walking across the square required vigilance, with one wrong step ending in a watery disaster. The edges were a special material that absorbed the shock, so you wouldn't break a leg or gouge an eye out on the sharp-looking tendrils. The pool was an object lesson: every step the burgeoning nation took must be carefully examined, or disaster might strike.

Sim(on) walked gingerly across the pool-courtyard. The Capitol complex contained not only the Forum where the government conducted business, the Black Box, or the Triumvirate residence, but also the Archives, where records and libraries were kept on protected servers along with paper documents. The strangely angular postmodern gothic architecture certainly set it off from the Black Box and the combination of neo-federalist and biomechanics of the Forum.

The transparency laws guaranteed the right of every member of Giresun—someday citizens—to access the Archive's records at will. As part of the importance of accessibility, the work offices for each the Triumvirate's Consuls were adjacent to the central rotunda of the Archives. Littered with museum pieces and memorabilia, the Archives was literally the crown jewel of Giresun infrastructure.

A security scanner read Sim(on)'s retina while SF officers scanned the rest of his body and belongings.

"Have a nice day," he said. They nodded slightly in return.

Sim(on) walked down the central corridor and across the enormous rotunda to a bank of terminals in an adjacent space. There, he registered himself as an auditor and researcher and began pouring over transaction records and communications between Consuls and anyone, everywhere around the world. He watched as his personal research bots danced articles across the screen, making connections in a visual index like an old school threat assessment map. Sim(on)'s unconscious took over soon enough, as he lapsed into a memory.

"Eww! Why are you playing with him?" the girl yelled.

Simon pushed the ball back to the girl in the other square.

"Shut up, Aly. He's nice," Mel said. She bounced the ball back to Simon's square.

"But he's a boy... You know they're defective. Stupid mutants," Aly said.

She walked to the edge of the outlined space on the playground.

"He's not a mutant, Aly," Mel said. "You're not a mutant, right?" she whispered to Simon.

Simon shook his head no.

"He's got that mutant Y-comma zone. Teacher said so," Aly said.

"Yeah..." two of Aly's third-grade henchmen joined in.

"Can't be that bad if he can play nice," Mel retorted. She winked at Simon.

Aly and her droogs snatched up the ball in mid-bounce and ran across the playground to the field. Mel clenched her fists, started to give chase, then noticed Simon stayed put.

"If you don't stand up to them, it won't get better," Mel said.

"Sure. Eventually they'll do something really bad, then I can stand beside them and laugh and point," Simon said.

"That's not very nice," she said.

"Maybe. But it's kinda funny," he said. They chuckled.

As a dream within a dream, he returned to a different scene than the one happening in real time. A nondescript academic center engulfed him. The multi-purpose nature of the room left little impression, from the tan walls and drop-tile ceiling to the industrially bland carpet. It would probably last as long as the concrete floor under it. Computer screens lit a line around the room, sitting on a continuous desk. Partitions defined test-takers' workspaces.

Sim(on) remembered a dozen more instances like the playground sexism as he sat down for his placement exam. Life was the greatest simulation of all, always on, running around the clock. Giresun was founded as a refuge for women and those who had the imagination for creating something better but without the resources to see it through. Eventually, males started showing up.

"Usually on purpose. Well, sort of," Sim(on) said to himself.

The matriarchy did not let on they ruled the island until the last moment. It was like a sudden reveal in the augmented reality novels Sim(on) loved playing in as a child. There, the figments of those AR stories played with him and took part in adventures when no one else wanted to.

Sim(on) had changed his name with Giresun tradition on his sixteenth birthday. Old enough to know what he felt like being called, he kept the phonetics of his given name but added a similar layer of detail to his own story. His mothers were proud of his sense of humor. Despite the challenges he faced as a young man in Giresun, he remained positive, hopeful. For someone who retreated into an alternate life in the virtual world, why wouldn't the "sim" always be "on?"

The screen blinked. He felt sweat pouring off his body under the air conditioning. Pure adrenalized fear. Sim(on) was as prepared as he could be. If he failed, he could take the test once more and then have to find a new career path. Sim(on) selected his answers thoughtfully, focused like a laser. He diligently applied every heuristic the reviews had given him and mentally indexed every type of code the test covered.

It was all there in his head. He just had to overcome the fear and answer the question as written, not what he thought came next.

He was in such a heightened state he lost track of anything else around him. The room could be on fire, and he wouldn't have noticed. Suddenly the computer shut down. Either he had answered so many wrong the adaptive programming kicked him out, or he answered enough right the test was content he knew his soai. *Either way, it would be over in a moment.*

The proctor tapped him on the shoulder. Sim(on) gathered his things and walked out following her. In the waiting room, there were refreshments—the water cooler had been the only thing offered on the way in. Now there were sandwiches, covered terrines, and plates of snacks next to a cooler of drinks. Sim(on) sat down primly until he started to shake. He had to weather the come down before anyone else arrived. It would just be too much to have everyone watch as he went to pieces. When the shaking stopped, he took a plate and filled it up. He ate, then got a drink. An hour later, other test takers started coming in from the test room.

"Hey," he said nonchalantly.

A head nod.

Time marched on.

Another group came in from the testing room.

"O'Leary," the proctor called.

"Mintz," she called.

The names went on, slowly at first. Other proctors started opening the door and calling names.

"Hi," Sim(on) said to one.

"Haliday," she said.

"Oh, excuse me," Sim(on) said.

Fifteen more names were called. Three other students remained in the waiting room. The terrines had gone cold. Most of the snacks were either gone or in shambles.

"James," the woman said.

Sim(on) gathered his things again, having found their way out of his bag and onto the seats next to him among the used plates and drinks. "Here! Coming," he said.

Sim(on) awoke with a snort. He snored so hard he'd woken himself up. After hours and hours of teasing apart information, Sim(on) sat back to look at the projection of his work. There had been ten other people in the bay when he arrived. He was alone and apparently in the dark, according to the sky visible through the postmodern gothic windows. The information was clean, with no evidence of wrongdoing, inappropriate collaborations, or connection to René. Something was nagging at him, an itch just out of reach.

He got up to use the restroom, and there, it came to him with a shock. He hurriedly washed his hands, so fast he was still refastening his pants when he hit the hallway.

"It's not the connections. It's what's *not* there!" he said to no one. He stopped by the kiosk outside of the Triumvirate offices. He put his name in line for an appointment with the Proconsul. If she was in on it, then they were all doomed anyway.

Sim(on) packed up his mess and downloaded his notes to a solid-state crystal he'd developed. The file names and data tags were all readily visible, but the internal information was obstructed through strange refraction within the crystalline matrix. A computer with a long number algorithm would readily reconstruct it. Unfortunately for everyone else, Sim(on) had not disseminated the algorithm. Technically, it was legal as a work in progress, part of his professional development as a data security specialist. He would be required to produce the decoded documents on request, but until then they were safe from anyone trying to surreptitiously eyeball his work.

The day was gone, and the night was getting on too. Sim(on) looked over at the Archive's paper vault but couldn't bring himself the strength to tackle the physical stacks today. They would have to wait until his next day off. A strange rock caught his eye as he passed by.

"Weird," he said. The oblong piece of crystal-laden igneous rock ontinued to float on its ornate Greek revival pedestal, regardless of his remark.

DE SILVA RETREAT, PERUVIAN ANDES

1610 16 JUL 2075

"I'm kind of impressed that Calderone sent the planes after us," Pachutec said. An aide carried his bags from the helicopter. They hadn't been unpacked since before the riot, but "better to have them at hand and not need them" was the mantra of every executive assistant. Pachutec threw open the doors to the mountain hacienda's main house before the servants could catch up. The Andes rose severely, majestically behind and across a narrow valley from the palatial grounds. This refuge had served as Armand's childhood home. Away from corrupting influences, his father had said, where Armand could focus on developing his mind.

"It's good to be home!" he shouted. "Should I have ridden a palanquin, Elana? I mean, that is the sort of thing Pachacuti did, right?"

"You know it is," said Elana. She squinted her eyes. "But maybe that's a little too on the nose?"

"Aw, you're no fun. What do you think, Brönner?

"I'm not going to carry you," Brönner said.

Pachutec laughed and put his arm around both of them. "C'mon guys, let's enjoy the moment. We're about to birth a revolution! Fernando! Hey Fernando, get some *chicha* poured for us? And some *mamacos*, the hot kind, if we've got 'em?" Pachutec called out.

He sat down on a large sunken sectional sofa and turned on a vid projection, scrolling through international news reports.

"We put out the word?" Pachutec asked.

He indulged in a glass of the corn beer and watched the effects of their work play out on the world stage.

"...outside of Cartagena," a female journalist with a Venezuelan accent reported. "We've been receiving reports all afternoon following the press conference at the Colombian prison where Armand de Silva, known as Pachutec, was held as a political prisoner for more than three weeks following the riots shown here." She flicked a recording from her screen into the transmission. "*Presidente* Calderone has had no further comment since the Colombian Air Force attempted to attack the convoy Pachutec was traveling in. The young man was able to escape from a nearby airfield and is believed to be sequestering himself in one of his family estates.

"The Gran American President is no doubt shaken by the apparent loss of control in rural areas throughout the states. The people there report waiting for Pachutec to rise as their new *caudillo* as the government is blamed for reneging on promises of water, food, shelter, and medical assistance throughout the region. Meanwhile, the son of the deceased de Silva cartel leader has spent many months providing exactly that, starting with outlying villages and working across the country to their largest cities."

"Go, go, go," Pachutec said. Brönner and Elana rose from the couch and conferred with the aides who were setting up teleconferencing gear linked to multiple transmission sites.

"They're ready," Brönner said as he ducked his head back into the room.

The camera lights were fully tuned. Their intensity blocked out everything beyond the stage. Pachutec cleared his throat and smoothed his hair behind his ears. Unlike *Señor* de Silva, he was tuned in to the hide-and-go-seek games of international hell raising. Using dispersed encrypted communications with clear radio signals, he appeared anywhere he wanted to be. His enemies could not pin down his physical location because the signals they used to track him were fabricated through a mixture of digital and ancient analog tech. They were throwing their million-dollar missiles after ghosts and reflections of Pachutec.

"My fellow citizens, your words have touched me. All I have endeavored to do is fulfill the promises you were given. My resources are great, but they are not infinite. If it is your will, I will happily continue to serve with the machinery of this deformed union as my ally. Foreign interests are hereby put on notice. We will freeze prices, so our people can have their eggs tomorrow at the same price they paid today, and freeze assets of foreign companies who've stolen the treasures out from under our former leaders' noses. We will be in touch for negotiating fair settlements in the days ahead. Have patience, and use this time to think not what we have done to your bottom line but what caused it to be necessary." Pachutec ended with the cameras panning to frame the explosion of two different repeater sites across the valley as missiles screamed overhead. The cameras panned back, and Pachutec punched his arms up in victory before the signal faded to white. The Yankees were displeased, no doubt.

"How'd that go?" Pachutec asked as he left the patio and descended to the fallout shelter under the hacienda.

"We won't have a moment's peace for a while," Elana said.

"No troop movements though," Brönner said.

"That would be too much. Plus, they're sluggish. They know where we are. I hope the house survives. I do like it here," Pachutec said. They descended to a similar series of rooms, deep below in a vault inside the Andean peak. The construction was concrete with wood accents, and the smell betrayed its recent cleaning. Pachutec clenched and unclenched his fists, avoiding further small talk.

"Are you going to be okay?" Elana said.

"What, down here? Yeah, sure mama. It's a lot bigger than my bed," Pachutec said. "Fernando? Another round, *por favor.*"

CHAPTER 13

Rolling Thunder

TURBO, COLOMBIA

1945 06 JUL 2073
Bullet-riddled cars were not uncommon in Turbo. For untold decades, it was a hub of illicit trade, either to get to Central America or into *el Caribe*. As the tides moved inland from the waterways and harbor, the houses grew legs, then interconnected walkways developed into plazas. The once gridded neighborhoods of Turbo had borrowed a page from Venice, with canals supplementing streets and a *Carnivale* to rival its Italian cousin. Modern materials tried to emulate the gothic and renaissance aesthetic but fell short. Beyond the less ornate architecture, the key difference was its inclusion of land-based shipping. Turbo was a hybrid port with ships and cargo carriers of all types pushing goods across the border. Like the original Venice, Turbo was a consortium of shipping magnates. While the fat-cats had extravagant meals at renowned institutions further inland, their dock workers needed quick, easy to eat meals around the clock. Carsem pulled up to a local bakery drive-through.

"I'll take ten empanadas, whatever you've got, five papusas, and two large teas. *Gracias*," she said.

Carsem tossed a beef empanada to Sancho.

"Eat up. It's going to be a long drive," she said as the nav directed her to the 90 North.

For seven exhausting hours, Carsem drove as much through the windshield as she did the rearview. Nothing happened, and it set her even more on edge. She sped on across the jungle.

~

"Cartagena. This is as far as I can get today. Keep an eye out, okay? Hey, we'll stay somewhere nice, yeah? Less likely to mess with us in a public place."

Casa San Agustín was the longest-running luxury hotel in Cartagena. Near the University, it was the Colombian version of the old Waldorf in 1900s New York City. It served as a residence, luxury hotel, and rendezvous point for the wealthy and well-heeled. Carsem chose it both for the protection public space might give her, and because Sancho could walk in with her rather than being smuggled in a bag.

Carsem and Sancho walked up from the parking garage to where the main lobby stood. Photos of the hacienda-style architecture of the original hotel lined the walls of the hallway toward the lobby. The staff left out a dog bowl of water next to a dispenser of biscuits. Sancho nudged his lead toward the treats and sat.

"Oh, so soon? Eh, whatever, mutt," Carsem said. She dropped a couple biscuits down for Sancho as she took in the lobby. Women in tailored business attire littered the space, some lounging on furniture artfully scattered around the lobby. A few were obviously security, judging by their wide-legged stances and hands clasped in front.

"Must be a convention," Carsem said.

Sancho lapped at the water bowl. A woman in a chartreuse pencil skirt suit walked over. From the watchful gaze of several others, Carsem could tell the lady was a big deal.

"Can I pet your dog?" the lady asked.

"Of course. Sancho'd love that," Carsem displayed on her screen.

Sancho didn't mind, except to take a quick glance at Carsem and then the stranger.

"He knows who's boss, eh?" the lady said through her own device.

The other woman was able to relax with Sancho, and Carsem saw the stress leave her body for a moment. After longer than a casual passerby would have stopped, and certainly before Sancho was done, the lady dusted the dog hair off her hands. Standing back up, she offered a hand to Carsem.

"My name is Columbia."

"Carsem." She shook the other woman's hand. "I think you've got a new friend, eh Sancho? Sounds like you're in the right place."

"Funny. Nice to meet you both. Bet you couldn't tell, but I love dogs. If I see one, I've just got to see about saying hello. I appreciate your indulgence. It's my first time to Cartagena. Sancho's made sure I got off on the right foot." Columbia said.

"Me too," Carsem said.

"Business?" Columbia asked.

"No, just passing through," Carsem said. Something had changed in the air. Carsem felt it and tightened up Sancho's leash.

"Trouble?" Columbia asked.

A blast rocked the building. Debris rained down in the lobby, and outside chunks of concrete fell. The guards were on Columbia before anyone saw she was holding a dog. The leash pulled Carsem toward the lobby doors. Vehicles pulled up to the building as the entire lobby seemed to form a cordon around the better-dressed women.

Carsem desperately focused on keeping up with the pull of Sancho's leash. The smell of dust, smoke, and acrid chemicals assaulted Carsem's nose. She coughed as her body reacted to the confusion in a mixture of a soldier's instincts and crippling dread. She drifted in and out of disoriented shock, always fighting through tunnel vision to keep up with the leash.

"Get down! Get down!" a grizzled woman with short hair and dark skin shouted above the din. She began to fire over their heads in the direction of the hallway Carsem had just walked through. Carsem saw another woman shoot toward the valet and concierge desk as men in paramilitary uniforms returned fire. For a moment Ani and Anan appeared in the battle, and Carsem almost lost her grip. She blinked rapidly, shook her head, and they were gone. The scrum holding her dog moved toward the front doors, pulling her along with them. Every guard's weapon was drawn in overlapping fields of fire as they drug on toward the waiting vehicles.

One guard moved to open the double French doors and was blown back into the lobby in a volley of splintered doors and broken glass. The explosion reset Carsem's focus. Her mind raced behind her eyes. This fight definitely wasn't for her, and so far these women were willing to take her with them. Besides, Sancho was still in the other woman's arms. Carsem didn't have much of a choice.

Three squads of men closed in on the entryway, forward, left, and right. The women warriors were firing full auto but barely making a sound. Their pistols seemed to have no recoil or need for magazine changes. Sancho began to bark. Carsem's focus was knocked away from the battle in the street to meet the gaze of the dog. One of the guard women held a large jagged spike of wood and stalked Columbia from behind. She moved to drive the shiv under Columbia's ribcage from the right. It would pierce her kidney, liver, and puncture a lung with one strike. Carsem had learned the same stab from a Mossad agent years ago, through a cross-training program for the women Peshmerga.

"No!" Carsem screamed. On pure instinct, Carsem stepped between the attacker and Columbia. She captured the knife-hand under her left arm and held it as hard as she could against her body. With her left leg, Carsem wrapped around the attacker's right leg from the outside, creating a pivot point between the other woman's legs. Carsem threw her body weight forward and felt the captured knee crack next to hers.

The would-be assassin was no fool. As she went down, she grabbed Carsem by the right lapel and drug her to the sidewalk. Carsem continued to pin the attacker's arm through the roll. She lost her balance, and the other woman abandoned her makeshift weapon. The assassin switched hands, holding Carsem down with the freed right hand as a long knife suddenly appeared in her left. She drew down a slash toward Carsem's face. Carsem stared her opponent in the eyes as the blow fell. Someone fired in the maelstrom, just as Carsem was about to be cut down. The knife fell to clatter onto the pavement instead. The body's deadweight fell to the side as Carsem realized she herself wasn't dead. Other women laid on the ground, bloodied messes from the gunfight. Carsem couldn't turn her eyes from the one who half-pinned her to the concrete.

Calloused hands were picking her up then, carrying her in a daze to a large black transport of some kind. Women in form-fitted black body armor were pulling others from the battle zone. Some were helped to their feet while others were carried out of sight like heavy sacks. After a moment, Carsem's mind caught up with her body. Something was licking her fingers.

"Sancho!" she yelled. Tears fell unbidden from her eyes. She looked up, and Columbia sat with a medic applying a bandage to her shoulder. One already sat over the left side of her head. "What the *po-gai* was that!"

"I'm so sorry, Carsem," Columbia yelled.

The guards and medics just piled people into the vehicles and tore off to the private terminal of the airport.

Under the cool air of the wide-open space, Carsem sat on the tarmac with Sancho's head in her lap. She was occupied with sorting out what had just happened. Medics checked her bandages and draped an impossibly thin blanket over her shoulders. She pulled it tight around both of them.

"Carsem?" Columbia said loudly. Aides and medics tried to keep up in her wake. Security guards were circling, keeping watch with their eyes and screens, scanning the dark beyond the airstrip.

Carsem nodded with her fist.

"Do you sign?" Columbia gestured with her index fingers in a circle toward her body.

"A little." Carsem flicked her thumb up like a reverse snap.

Columbia sat down an arm's length away from Carsem. Sancho lifted his head, groaned, and laid back down. She was welcome to stay.

"Someone tried to kill me?" Columbia signed.

"No *soai*," Carsem yelled.

"With a knife," Columbia signed.

"Yes," Carsem signed. "That too."

"You stopped them," Columbia signed.

"Maybe," Carsem signed.

"You did. I owe you. Come with us?" Columbia signed.

"You had my dog. Where?" Carsem said.

"A new life, away from all of this," Columbia signed.

"As a pet? No—" Carsem signed.

"As a whole new person, in my country," Columbia said loudly. "Or wherever else you'd rather go. Just come see what we have to offer first? There's a lot of possibility for a person like you there."

"Nothing left for me back here," Carsem signed. "Still, I'm going to need to think about it."

"Let's get you fixed up at least. When you're recovered, and when you're ready, you tell me. No hard feelings either way. Deal?" Columbia asked.

Carsem nodded her head.

GIRESUN ISLAND

1812 23 JUL 2075

N'gono sat on the bench by the red kelp vendor facing the water. The deceptive smell of bacon wafted from their air fryers. The boardwalk was doing good business. Kids played in the sand and surf as she watched the sunset. The sun and shadows started to play in contrast across the shopfronts, sand, and skin.

"I know there's a whole continent just over there," N'gono said.

Chris van Buren sat across from her, facing the boardwalk watching her screen's scrolling feed.

"Just like I know that's not bacon," N'gono said. "But I can eat it."

"Just bide your time. Everything is in place," Chris said.

"Like last time?" N'gono asked peevishly.

"No. This time we're handling it, not those *vaqueros* riding in like—" Chris was cut off.

"It has to be a complete victory," N'gono said.

"It will be. All of the pieces are lining up and won't be detected until it's raining down around their heads," Chris said.

"I've done my part. I have your three-hundred," N'gono said. "These like-minded patriots will follow me, even against their sisters."

"Hopefully the eighty won't notice what's happened until the other twenty percent have made it to the end," Chris said. She continued to scan her screen's feed. "Regime change in GA..."

"There will be hell to pay," N'gono said.

Further down by the florist, Nancy crumpled a red kelp wrapper and tossed it into the nearby trashcan. N'gono got up, smiling ear to ear, and walked over to Nancy. They laughed loudly. A Security Forces patrol walked by, nodding to Consul van Buren. She smiled and nodded back before shutting off her screen and walking over to the kelp vendor.

GIRESUN ISLAND, TRIUMVIRATE PENTHOUSE

1922 30 JUL 2073

Keiko stared at a holo projection of line charts. She flitted one on top of another in contrasting colors, then rapidly switched back and forth between reports, attaching some as data points and others as connections between the charts. From up here, shadows stretched across the tiny city through the windows of the penthouse. Night was falling. In the purple and orange of twilight details were replaced by shifting projections like clouds taking shape. The Triumvirate continued their day's work after dinner while scattered around the penthouse's vast common room. Columbia washed dishes in the kitchen while

Keiko sat on a sectional couch. Chris sat at a concealed secretary's desk against a wall.

"You look like an insane conductor, Keiko," Chris said. She walked across the room. "Feeling okay?"

"Just trying to make some pieces fit. That deal could've really worked for us, you know?" Keiko said.

"Yeah, sounds like they're having troubles beyond our interest in helping," Chris said.

"We really stepped in it, yeah?" Keiko collapsed her files and put them away.

"Just glad you weren't hurt," Chris said.

"You too. Weird about Columbia," Keiko quietly said to Chris.

"Any idea what went down? I mean, about the Security Force woman who tried to kill her?" Chris said.

"Pretty basic. Our would-be assassin owed a lot of money to some of the seedier citizens. You know those soldiers, hookers, and blow," Keiko said. "Anyhow, it made her easy to manipulate. Fold in some extortion, blackmail, they made her desperate enough to do anything to get out from under their thumb."

"Yeah, sure, whatever," Chris said. "Drink?"

"Already got one," Keiko rattled an old fashioned glass with a large ice cube in it. "Thanks anyway."

"Just refilled," Columbia said. She sat down on the sectional, out of Keiko's flailing arms' reach.

"You keeping in touch with any of those chumps from the mainland?" Chris asked.

"You know me, always keeping an open channel," Keiko said. She sipped her drink and went back to scrolling through her screen on a wide setting.

"I'll leave you to it then," Chris said. She noticed several messages tagged from outside Giresun by the relay servers as she got up to pour her own glass. Her eyes dilated and her hands started to shake slightly as she walked back to the bar.

"Keiko, little too convenient? Even if she was desperate enough to try to kill me for it, there was a lot of money in that show. Keep digging, but be quiet," Columbia said in a whisper from her side of the couch.

"Agreed. Too organized for a rogue SF to have arranged. Not everyone was happy about that last vote," Keiko said.

"The statehood measure? Why would we give up independence to a nation that still epitomizes so much of why the Founders left the rest of the world?" Columbia said.

"You're preaching to the choir, boss. I'm just saying, free trade, travel… it'd make a lot of people rich overnight," Keiko said.

Columbia stood up and refilled her drink. "And end up beholden to a bunch of men as second-class citizens? Or worse, again?"

"Greed is a powerful addiction, boss," Keiko said.

"One we haven't got a cure for yet, either," Columbia said. She squeezed Keiko's shoulder and left the room for her suite.

CHAPTER 14

Checkmate

1832 20 JUL 2075

"How did this happen?" President Calderone asked.

Morning streamed in beams through the high windows of the government palace. A night's worth of work and worry littered the president's office. Instead of giving visitors an exalted vision of the president, the vaulted ceilings and arches simply made Hubert Calderone feel small. An aide came through the giant wooden door, took the contents of the out basket and quickly left, averting his eyes and trying desperately not to be seen.

"I can't escape the feeling we've been played," Ignacio Guzman said once the door closed.

On the wall screen, a segmented display of news agency coverage from around the world about Gran America scrolled through footage of peaceful protests and violent retaliation from law enforcement and military agencies throughout the confederation. Calderone watched from his ornate carved desk, drinking from a cut crystal glass. An unstopped decanter of cognac sat to the side of his view.

"It's like they just cherry-pick the shots to play, over and over and over..." Calderone said. "I just spent all bloody night trying to get the legislature caught up and to make sense of all this. Rampant disease, unrest, and here I am trying to get the medical centers to see people for free..."

"Here's what the citizens are producing," Ignacio said helpfully. Guzman flicked the local and national video feeds to the center of the wall screen from his hand. Local reporters were interviewing citizens on the street and, on some segments, turning to academic-looking political analysts for commentary.

"It's the best thing Chavez ever did, publicizing the news," Calderone said.

A local woman's framed face was enlarged on the wall. Interviewing the crowd, they talked about their gratitude for the free medical care and food in these troubled times.

"And we can point to it in the future, having restored it without the state censors," Ignacio said.

"All the good we did, summed up in this." Calderone swept his arms wide toward the wall screen. "*Ay*, and there's that *bastardo pachuco*!"

The woman began to elaborate the relief efforts were at the hand of Pachutec, the surviving son of de Silva cartel's boss. She explained while the government's response to caring for the citizens had not been matched by their ferocity against their comrades, the young man had continued his work to turn the family fortune into relief work across Gran America.

"Pachutec, Hubert," Ignacio said.

"He's a punk, and I don't care. He's taken it. Hasn't done anything he hasn't admitted to. It's all so useless," Calderone said. He took a long drink from his glass and moved to refill it. "What? What now?"

Ignacio increased the volume on the international news section of the wall screen. "The Union of Nation's Parliament has voted to sanction Gran America for its abuses. In London's White Hall, the international governing body has declared the economic blockade will only be lifted with the peaceful abdication of power by the current executive branch of the GA," the British reporter said.

"The UN has now officially joined with the northerners. They're calling for us to step down," Ignacio said.

The early morning light's beams turned to the glaring bright sun of Cartagena's full daytime.

"*Bullsoai*," Hubert said. He shakily filled his glass to the top.

LIMA, PERU

1840 20 JUL 2075

Pachutec wore one of his more beat-up couture linen suits on the ride to the Legislative Palace in Lima. As the official party, Brönner and Elana emerged from the back of the black truck first. A cordon of red-shirted security agents was waiting, holding back the crowd. As Pachutec reached the doorframe of the vehicle, he held onto the top of the door to stand up and wave to the crowd.

Enthusiastic cheers drowned out any other sound from the city around them. The columns of the palace thundered with their echo, while the people were a sea of red and khaki spilling over and across the Plaza Bolívar.

Brönner and Elana raised their hands to Pachutec to remind him to come down.

"This is incredible!" Pachutec shouted.

"Stay focused," Brönner said. He scanned the crowd and security for threats, like a barely tamed circus tiger walking among the crowd.

A raised dais was arranged on the few steps leading up to the palace. The governor and his aides stood as Pachutec and his entourage approached. When Pachutec's party had arrived at their seats, everyone attempted to sit down at the same time, though the effect was rippled by many of the chairs being too tight for the large old men to fit in.

The state's governor rose and walked to the podium.

"People of Peru," the governor announced over the crowd. He had to repeat himself to bring down the din. "Your voices have been heard. Over the last several weeks, the government... *I* have failed you. The disease killed hundreds of thousands. The government's panic has killed thousands more. After careful deliberation, and the consideration of many hundreds of your thoughts, encouragements, and points of view, I have made my decision.

"You may not agree with me, with this decision, but I hope you will trust me, for this is what I think is best for us, the people of the state of Peru. Though the record shows I have voted against the president, I have no hesitation to stand down for my part in these tragedies. It is with great honor that I present the savior of our nation, and his home state of Peru, *Señor* Pachutec."

The throng's voices overwhelmed the speakers again as Pachutec took the stage.

"*Mis amigos*," he began. "We are a noble people, with a noble past. We have been downtrodden for so very, very long. It was always my intention to simply lift us up together. When disaster struck, we redoubled the efforts we already made to address poverty and illness in our communities. Because you recognize this, we are now not just the voice of Peru, but of all this country.

"To correct our mistakes and wipe the table clear of our miserable past, we must not just change but start anew. This is why with my ascension to the head office in this great nation, the leaders of Bolivia, Paraguay, and Uruguay have signed with us to make a new land, an Incan land, restoring the former empire of the four quarters, a New Incan Empire!"

The thundering crowd was almost too intense to bear. The noise was so loud, taking a breath was a stifling task. For everyone but Pachutec, it was a stage show to endure and perform for the cameras. The self-made emperor would have floated on the crowd's emotions, the resulting crescendo of the entire cartel's endeavor to win the hearts and minds of Gran America over. Now they were witnesses to the cartel's apotheosis.

"Work is underway. Your streets are clean and there is food to eat, and you no longer have to wait for some *caudillo to* open a factory for work. We are going to work together to make all of South America, and beyond, the gem that it truly is. When you have enough to eat and a clean place for your children to play, come to the abandoned cities of old, where we can bring our culture back to life without inter-ference from the North. Come to places like Vilcabamba, where we will build our new capital on the ruins of the old, where we can start afresh without the weight of capitalist thieves on our necks. Come! There is much to be done, together! Long live the New Incan Empire!"

After leaving the stage, Brönner handed a key card to the former governor's top aide. A decided wave of relief cascaded over the governor's body as he scanned the card through his screen's hardware. In the second following the governor's transaction, his security men looked for Brönner without success.

CHAPTER 15

Salvation

GIRESUN ISLAND

2130 06 JUL 2073

The flight from Cartagena to Giresun was brief and uneventful, if rushed. The interior of the *Remora*, previously as well appointed as a business office with its gro-printed wood paneling and subtle decorative carpet, was littered with medical supplies, wrappers, and bloodied bandages. Keiko rang Columbia's screen constantly following the firefight. In the air, Columbia finally answered it.

"*Po-gai*, you're okay!" Keiko was visibly panicked on the display.

"Yep, thanks to a fellow traveler," Columbia said. She glanced at Carsem and caught her eye.

"So, what happened?" Columbia said.

"An old paramilitary group is claiming responsibility, but the paper trail is too neat. These guys haven't been outside of some basic kidnapping and ransom stuff for decades, then all of the sudden they're international terrorists?" Keiko said.

"K, don't. I hate to say it, but you know what I'm saying?" Columbia said.

"Mm-hmm. Okay," Keiko hung up.

Columbia's attention turned inward. She was quiet the rest of the flight except to pet Sancho at random.

The landing was the smoothest Carsem had ever felt.

"Okay, ladies, ma'am, welcome back to the island. We're going to get everyone checked out after we deplane. There's a clinic in the hangar, and after triage, you may be referred to the hospital. Clear?" the lead medic announced in the cabin.

The door opened onto a runway surrounded by ocean. Suddenly the breeze blew in through the doorway. With it came the warmth of the beach and the smell of the sea over the mechanical noise of engines powering down. The heat of Cartagena was missing, replaced by a coolness perfumed with tropical spices and flowers. The aides around Columbia comfortably shuttled Carsem and her dog across the tarmac to the hangar.

"Any dizziness? Trouble breathing?" the nurse asked. She looked at her screen while checking Carsem's pulse.

Looking over the nurse's arm, Carsem saw all her vitals displayed on the woman's screen.

"You have some kind of touch," Carsem said. She nodded at the screen.

"Electrodes on my fingers," the nurse said. "Hearing loss—before the attack?"

Carsem nodded.

The nurse splayed her fingers across different points around Carsem's ear.

"Okay, you're good to go. If you have any changes for the worse, come to the hospital. Otherwise, go home and get some rest," the nurse said. "Next!"

A security guard in a jumpsuit waved Carsem over to where Columbia was standing by.

"Okay, thank you," Columbia said, signing off on a screen held by an aide. She knelt down to pet Sancho, then stood up and motioned to a waiting car. There was no driver inside, but the door opened like a wing as they approached. Once inside, the vehicle hissed into acceleration. It was just Carsem, Sancho, and Columbia as the vehicle sped off into a city Carsem had never heard of before.

Outside, the practicality of an airport transitioned to a small city, with the same types of shops and businesses Carsem had come to expect in her travels. She noticed the typical brands were missing, as well as an absence of trash. Green plants were everywhere, but manicured rather than the riotous jumble of South American jungle or the encroaching decay of North America. Technology was embedded all around her as they cruised through the streets, relatively seamless with the natural flow of green spaces, vertical farms, walkways, and open areas.

Carsem rolled down the window. The air was cooler than she expected. She could still smell the ocean, but the warmth of the beaches was replaced by the humidity of a tropical landscape. Everywhere she looked there was plenty and no sign of people in need.

"What do you want to do, Carsem? I mean, like lifestyle, work?" Columbia asked. With a quick flick of her fingers, the words materialized where Carsem was looking, like an overlay. She turned her head, and the words followed her gaze.

"I don't want to do anything I used to. I'm done with that. If the world lets me," Carsem said. "This place, it's called Giresun? Is that the city?"

"It's both the island and the city," Columbia said. "It was settled by people like you—they didn't fit in where they came from for one reason or another, or needed to find somewhere they could grow, have a second chance, or a rebirth."

"I thought all the islands were used up," Carsem said.

"They kind of made their own, you could say. Look at what the ancient Venetians did. They took a handful of scrawny spits of land and turned it into a world power in their day. The Founders just did it with a little more technological advantage," Columbia said.

"Surely not everyone's an engineer or soldier," Carsem said.

"Everyone does the best they can, and there's plenty to go around. We just focus on having enough, not having everything," Columbia said. "So again, if you had a choice to try different hats on, what would be the first?"

"My uncle said I have an eye for detail. I used to put the holidays together for the villages where I grew up. Who did what, you know? Food, that sort of thing," Carsem said. "It was fun. I didn't have to think beyond the event, you know? Just focus on making sure everyone was taken care of, having a good time."

"Want to try doing something like that here? It'd be a discrete way to see the lay of the land around you—you know, like recon," Columbia said.

"You were a soldier?" Carsem asked. "No wonder you're unfazed by all of this."

"A long time ago. Then the people needed a leader more than they needed a warrior. So, here I am, helping you through the same thing," Columbia said. "I try to be whatever the mission needs me to be. There's a certain freedom here you don't get elsewhere. Our laws require that all citizens have open access to everything, and the reverse is also true. Living without secrets actually allows people to live here without fear of each other for the most part. You can be who you want to be, love whom you choose, and there's no reprisal because, well, we're all in glass houses."

"Is English, Spanish, Portuguese, or French the official language here?" Carsem asked.

"It's English. The genitive case in any language was just too much for the Founders to support," Columbia said.

"I should brush up," Carsem signed, staring out the window, starting to withdraw.

"You can find anything you want to be involved in here; doesn't have to be your job for you to contribute. I know you're not interested in your old life, but Giresun rescues human traffic and archeological artifacts too. It'd be a natural fit with your skills and disposition. You don't have to stay, we can take you anywhere in the world you'd like to go and get you started there," Columbia said. "But I see so much potential in you, Carsem. We'd be lucky to have you here, as a valued member of our community. Am I putting too much on you? It's a lot of change, all at once. Sometimes I just get carried away."

She watched Carsem for a moment. Columbia rubbed Sancho's head until he laid down on the floorboards again. He slowly nudged his way to Carsem's feet. Columbia had seen enough people through recruitment and watched many of them decline the offer over the years. She knew Carsem had bought into Giresun, even if she didn't know it yet herself.

"We also export a lot of our technologies. It's actually why we met. I was there to work a trade deal with the Gran American council. We've been exporting infrastructure tech since the Founders. Something to think about later if you're interested in business, medicine, or international relations. Giresun's latest program provides fiber-optic electric therapy to drug addicts who want it. Among other sensory repairs, it can rewire the brains of addicts to a state before their drug use diverged their neuropathology. Optogenetics—a great alternative to psychosurgery," Columbia said. "We combine the hardware with psychotropics. Reprograms the original experience, and emotional connection reframes the whole thing. But still, it's nothing new."

"Then why isn't everyone doing it?" Carsem signed.

"Because the systems of the world want their people docile and afraid at the same time. They're not interested in curing the problem. It doesn't consolidate or strengthen their power," Columbia said.

"Power to the people," Carsem said. She stared up at a lavish high-rise apartment building.

"Right on," Columbia said. "Here we are."

"Your place?" Carsem signed.

"No, yours," Columbia signed back. "Question—forgive me if it is rude?"

"Okay, sure," Carsem signed.

"Would you like us to fix your hearing?" Columbia signed. "The optogenetics program can sort it in outpatient, according to the physical we gave you at the hangar."

Carsem just stood there, bewildered at the thought.

"Let me ring up the hospital. You know, Consular privilege," Columbia signed.

The clinic waiting room was unlike any doctor's office Carsem had been to before. It had the usual air of one, though the walls were decorated with local painter's works, occasional sculpture, and music softly playing over hidden speakers. A woman in scrubs opened the door to the rest of the clinic and stepped forward to where Carsem could see her.

"Carsem?" she signed.

Carsem stood up from the chair, smoothed her pants, and walked toward the open hallway.

"Hi, I'm Joan. I'm a tech here. We're going to test your hearing in the room two doors down on the left."

Carsem nodded.

When they entered the room, the nurse indicated for Carsem to have a seat on a hospital gurney. It resembled a lounge chair more than a bed. Joan picked up what looked like a scanning thermometer with a long point.

"I'm going to gently place this in your ear. I'll need you to hold steady for a moment. It is going to test the mechanics of your inner ear." The nurse's words hovered in the air between them like they had in Uncle Raz's office.

Carsem nodded again.

The device felt like a thermometer for all the world. Joan removed it, walked over to a screen, and angled it so Carsem could see.

"This shows us what is going on with the small structures of the ear," she said, pointing to a graph. "And here is the nerve, sending signals from there to your brain. Let's try the other side, okay?"

After repeating the process, Joan said, "...and with that, I'll let the doctor know we're ready for her."

Carsem felt out of place, still wearing the clothes she'd been through combat in. She realized how dirty she was, surrounded by the comfortable but hygienic medical bay. A light breeze blew through the room, out under the door. Suddenly, two quick knocks, and the door opened.

"Hi Carsem, I'm Liz Way. I'm going to be your doctor today if that's all right with you?"

"Hi, Doctor," Carsem said quietly.

Dr. Way was dressed in a pair of avocado green coveralls. A visor covered her eyes with a projected display like a screen. As she moved, Carsem saw the display was providing analysis to the doctor. Liz didn't miss a beat, keeping her banter rolling seamlessly as the information scrolled past her eyes.

"How did you like the test? Pretty easy?" Liz asked.

"So simple," Carsem said.

"Looks like the nerves are locked in the on position—they're firing sound impulses at your brain constantly. That's why you're always hearing that ringing, a form of tinnitus. The good news is that we have a treatment."

Joan came back into the room with a thin plastic box. She set it on the table and opened it to reveal a mouthguard.

"Mouthguard for my ears?" Carsem asked.

"Kind of," Joan said.

"With a push of the button here," Liz demonstrated, "an electrical signal is sent via bone conduction to reset the nerves. Sometimes one, but oftentimes a few treatments are needed to eliminate the ringing sound."

"That's it?" Carsem whispered.

"We're going to do a little fine-tuning. The device will be for maintenance, like a retainer or brace, until everything settles down. Joan here is going to get you all prepped, and when you're ready, I'll be back to take care of the procedure. Then, you'll be back on your way. It's really not a big deal." Dr. Way signed, "Don't freak out."

∿

Carsem had a hard time not freaking out. Her head was locked in a vise-like cage of stabilizers. Rods pressed against a network of plates, formed to her head. It was like being paralyzed, except she could still feel her muscles move. A neural block prevented her from feeling anything happening to her face. A pair of microsurgical tools were in her mouth while another set sat in her ear canal. A third pair made a small incision at the hairline behind her outer ear. The process was apparently as routine as teeth cleaning, and over in about as long.

"There, all done," Dr. Way said.

The doctor sat where she would be least visible to her patient and watched Carsem for a moment.

"When do I start to feel my face again?" Carsem said.

"About fifteen more minutes. I'm going to ask you to just sit here 'til then, and after we'll send you out on your way," Dr. Way said.

Then it donned on Carsem. A smile transformed her face from the bottom of her soul, while tears ran to drip off her chin in rivulets.

"I'll stay," Carsem said.

GIRESUN ISLAND, SAFE HOUSE APARTMENT

2103 08 JUL 2073

An SF legal officer and Columbia were projected into the living room of Carsem's apartment.

"Sorry for the holos," Columbia said. "We need to keep this under wraps until we find out what or who was behind the attack and what's actually happened."

"It's okay. Believe me, it's not the first time I've talked to ghosts," Carsem said.

"Carsem, Columbia has explained too, I'm sure, that Giresun is founded on transparency, so this secret meeting and what we're doing here... eventually it will come to light, and there will be consequences for keeping this private," the officer said.

"Yes, but I'm fine. Whatever I can do to help," Carsem said.

"We're doing it for many reasons," Columbia said. "We have to protect you, Carsem. We don't know who's involved, and they will no doubt try to keep it that way."

"It also sets a trap for those behind the plot. I get it," Carsem said. "I'm protected in some ways, but I'm also bait in others."

"You're going to be an anomaly. Eventually someone's going to see it and get curious," Columbia said.

"Besides the stone-age cloak and dagger bit, this paperwork guarantees a trail of evidence, accountability, and that will be necessary when we take out this existential threat we seem to be facing," the officer said.

"Down to brass tacks then," Carsem said.

"What will be your name here in Giresun?" the officer asked.

"I had a friend in New York when I was there for school. She was Algerian. We were both visiting students from poverty, anomalies. Her name was René," Carsem said.

"René it is then," the officer said. "Just René, or is there more?"

"Anderson," Carsem said. "René Anderson."

"Okay, René Anderson then," the officer said. "Now, there's just a little more to go. It's a surprisingly short form to commit potential treason, or at least a serious felony."

TRIUMVIRATE PENTHOUSE

2103 17 AUG 2073

René sat on the veranda overlooking the central settlement of the island. The ocean tossed around the shore below. She could see surfers riding the breaks off the reefs. Just some light stuff, around six feet probably. A storm looked to be gathering upwind.

"Might make it tonight," she whispered.

Columbia walked onto the suspended patio from the Triumvirate's penthouse complex.

"Ma'am," René said.

"How are you adjusting, René?" she asked.

"Well. It's an amazing place you have here," René said.

"We can speak freely here. Executive privilege."

"I need to do something. I actually miss driving around with my dog. I feel like I'm pretending to be someone I'm not. Don't get me wrong, it's everything I dreamt of…"

"—but now that you have it, you're not sure what to do with it?" Columbia Honalee put her hands on the guardrail a casual way off from René's.

René nodded.

"Event planning, right? What you wanted to do if you ever got settled? Things are steady here, and events are part of what happens when people are at ease. We can get you work. I'll introduce you—or have one of the aides do it if you feel like I'd be in the way?" Columbia turned and smiled at René. "The rest—it will come in time. You do not need to go back to anything, but the past has a way of calling to us. Many who come here have a need to change their identities to sever ties with what brought them here. You have the freedom to choose what parts to keep," Columbia said. "It will take time. Thanks to you, I have a little more, and I'm happy to share."

René stared off at the growing illumination from the city below. Lights began to phosphoresce under the water in clusters out to sea.

"I like the new shoes," Columbia said.

"Thanks. There's so much to choose from," René said. "I need to start doing something other than shopping, going to the beach, and working out."

"Let's get you hooked up with some work, then," Columbia said. "Nothing too crazy. There are some parties coming up. Want to start with one of those?"

René continued to keep her eyes locked on the panorama below. Her hyper-alert senses began to shake her body with anticipation of a threat. Sometimes the apprehension alone was enough to set her off. Memories demanded her attention over reality in an instant. She was thrown violently into a lucid dream.

Carsem heard the plank steps to the flat roof creak. The family set up their sleeping quarters around the top of the squat, jigsawed building to escape the trapped heat within. Everyone was asleep or near to it, except Carsem. Rumi's death still kept her up at night. His loss was a personal pit of despair. It stayed with her constantly. It likely wouldn't let her sleep until just before dawn.

The cool air had just started to dissipate the residual warmth from the concrete blocks around her. The canvas partitions for her spot on the second roof steppe lightly rippled in the desert breeze, full of the scent of sage. She was downwind from something sour, more so than everyone else under the water rationing. A shade drifted across the canvas, hunched low. It tried not to be seen, but Carsem knew. Like the blunt-nosed vipers she'd watched as a girl, she made ready. Her hand slid Rumi's kindjal from its scabbard while she coiled her legs and hips. The man quietly lifted her makeshift door and reached for the blanket. In the dim starlight, Carsem recognized her second uncle Kazem. No one liked him. Sick of the water rationing, he'd taken a bath in the cistern weeks ago. Now, they all joked, everything tasted like his dirty laundry.

He reached for her. She threw her heels with all her speed and strength into his solar plexus. With the momentum, she rolled backward into a crouch, the twelve-inch dagger flashing in the night. Her savage eyes turned quizzical as Kazem staggered bodily, collapsing the awning around him and falling silently off the edge of the roof, wrapped up like the garbage he was. Carsem peeped over the edge. The lump of the canvas wasn't moving. She crawled toward her disheveled bedroll. The kids stirred. She watched and waited, but they stayed asleep. Carsem lay with the unsheathed kindjal in her hand staring at the stars for the rest of the night. She would deal with the consequences in the morning.

"I'm not looking to be paid back, René. You saved my life. I can afford to give you a new one without any strings attached."

René did her best to calm her subconscious down.

"How's that guy from the cartel business, the one who called you after we got back? Still bugging you?" Columbia asked.

"Sometimes. It's weird. He went from baiting me to phishing," René said.

"Power play—some of the intel says they may've been behind the night we met," Columbia said. "Even if they weren't, they probably wanted a piece of it and are looking at you for a way in. Typical espionage BS."

"I… I haven't said anything, or replied to anything," René said.

"Don't worry about it. We're good," Columbia said. She slugged the last of her drink. "Ready for dinner?"

"Starved," René said, slightly shaking.

OUTSIDE OF SAO PAULO, BRAZIL

2200 07 JUL 2073

"...and we're in," Nancy said.

"Remember, just a training raid. Get the target out, neutralize the local *soais*, cover our tracks, and cancel secondary effects," N'gono said. "Nancy, you're just to observe and make sure these kids get back. I will be watching."

The rest of the team's blacked-out screens buzzed. They were piggybacked onto the local network, monitoring traffic while blended into the signal like background noise.

N'gono stalked through the remaining jungle until she saw the thugs playing cards by an open door. Inside, a sweaty, mustachioed man was holding a broken broom handle over a teenage girl. The other men ignored her pleas and turned up the radio. Their heads swiveled as three women in scant nightclub dresses bobbed and weaved their way along the road. Like a pack of dogs, the men excused themselves from the card game and circled the women.

"Hey *chica*, nice ass!" one called.

When he was ignored, another man called out, "Hey! He was just talking to you."

"*Perra!*" the third shouted.

The women dropped to a crouch facing their targets. The trainees fired, and all three men dropped dead in the street. N'gono took notes on how well each of the trainees had performed, then popped the bone conduction microphone at her neck twice. The man at the table lolled his head back while his cards dropped to the ground. There was barely a report from the sniper trainee across the road. N'gono couldn't see the girl anymore, but the man inside kept breaking past the doorframe.

Nancy's microphone popped three times.

N'gono walked without a sound past the security fence while the women in dresses drug the bodies toward the patio.

N'gono swung around the door. The girl screamed over the radio. N'gono popped her microphone twice. As she walked the girl out of the house covered in an afghan, a truck advertising contract framing stopped in the alley. The team slid the panel door shut as the house and the bodies on the porch burst into flames.

The girl was in shock. Nancy tended to her wounds and gave her a vial of pills.

"*Toma estos. Todo lo que te dio se irá. ¿Entendido?*" Nancy said.

[Take these. Everything he gave you will go away. Understood?]

The three women pulled the gray security forces coveralls over their club wear.

"*Sí,*" she said. "*¿Esos hombres?*"

[Yes. Those men?]

"*Nada,*" Nancy said.

[Nothing.]

"*Mi Madre es...*" the girl said.

[My mother is...]

"*Nuestra próxima parada. Entonces, paz,*" Nancy said.

[She's our next stop. Be at peace.]

CHAPTER 16

An Inconvenient Truth

GIRESUN ISLAND

2157 31 JUL 2075
Giresun kept cleaning up space junk and debris for the majority of
the world and a hefty payday. The duties were part of the security
operations center, though the program was the responsibility of the
mining industry. A portion of Sim(on)'s display was from a low Earth
orbit satellite. Abby recognized the unit as a salvage net. What wasn't
in the contract specs was what happed to the material after their satellites sequestered it. An onboard power source smelted the material
and molded it into balls, covering it in heat shield material. A drop
rail inside of the spacecraft's antenna acted like a bowling alley ball
return, dropping a nine-kilogram solid metal sphere seven-hundred
kilometers within two meters of a target with the kinetic energy of
over two-hundred and fifty hand grenades.

"I've got eyes and ears on you. Go," Sim(on) said.

Two mic clicks popped.

"There are three groups of ten in those containers. Not a lot of
movement. Recommend medical. No evidence of hostiles inside.
Watch yourself." Sim(on) said.

A high-altitude drone transmitted live video in simulated daylight from its synthetic aperture RADAR, interpolated by Sim(on)'s computer program. Abby sat behind him in the ops room.

"Picture's clearer than ever, Simon," Abby whispered.

Sim(on) shook his right hand in a shaka for thanks. Technically, non-Security Forces people weren't supposed to be in the Black Box. Abby was quick to remind the guards the transparency laws meant she could observe.

"Overwatch, a little help?" N'gono said over the mic.

"Coming in," Sim(on) said.

Sim(on) noted through the aircraft hangar style Quonset hut it was movie night in the sex trafficker's depot. All of their captives were packed for delivery. He sent a line of four balls from end to end of the building. The drone footage showed the facility next to the shipping containers explode from the inside out, lifting the half-tube twenty feet into the air before crashing down on its frame again.

"Subtle," N'gono said.

"Sending in the cargo lifts now." Sim(on) remotely activated four construction lift drones to break from the holding pattern he'd flown them in. The security forces platoon breached the containers at the same time. Searching the prisoners revealed no further combatants, and the medical team attended to the drugged women, boys, and girls. The rest of the soldiers prepared the containers for aerial pickup and pulled security around the landing zone.

"This is going to make someone really pissed," Sim(on) said.

Sim(on) waited in the rotunda again for an appointment with the First Consul. He held the data on a chip, inside of an official courier case. The raid was more useful than just freeing the prisoners set to be sold for sex traffic and worse; it provided a treasure trove of information about the de Silva cartel. Sim(on) had spent the previous night correlating the de Silva organization's activities with the rise of Armand "Pachutec" de Silva. He was sure the triumvirate urgently needed to be aware, and some of the correlations suggested it needed to be brought in person at once.

Despite his excitement and impatience, the scene looked exactly like the last time he'd been here, the same sparse visits by ordinary people. With the transparency of Giresun's culture, no one seemed to care about the inner workings of government because everyone knew it existed and could be checked on. In the espionage novels he'd loved as a kid, Sim(on) learned hiding in plain sight is often the most effective concealment.

An hour went by. Then two. Refusing to give in to the bureaucratic pressure, Sim(on) checked in at the Black Box to let his supervisor know he was taking the day off after the mission.

"I heard it was a late night, but uneventful," his supervisor said.

"Yep, just need to calm down. You know how it is," Sim(on) said.

"I'm here if you need me," the supervisor said.

"Thanks. See you tomorrow," Sim(on) said.

Sim(on) walked over to the receptionist kiosk. His name was still on the waitlist, though it was highlighted to indicate his priority.

Something clicked inside his subconscious. He walked over to the paper records archive and checked his screen. It would announce if there was any change in his waitlist status. Assured he wouldn't lose his place in line for it, Sim(on) began to dig into the paper records about the Triumvirate themselves.

Three hours went by. Sim(on) was surrounded by sheaves of paper on the parquet floor of the archives. His skin became cold, clammy, and ashen as he spread out three files next to each other. His heart raced as he collated the information in his thoughts. Absent-mindedly, he wrote a short letter of introduction to the Triumvirate members, attached his analyses from the mission, and pressed send. He removed his name from the queue.

Sim(on)'s hands trembled as he scanned the paper documents into his screen. He deliberately put the documents away in the precise order he had found them and returned them to their magnetic codexes on the shelves of the hall. Sim(on) walked out of the Archives without a word and headed to the Admiral's Daughter. He sent the location to Abby without explanation.

PERU, AMAZON SIDE

2309 09 APR 2044
Young Sam Brönner squatted quietly in the large well of tree limbs. The night was in full bloom in the Amazon. The air, a blanket of inescapable heat, steamed around him. The canopy here let in enough light he could see. He silently watched a jaguar stalk its prey below. The bugs and other nighttime creatures were nearly as loud as the city streets of Cusco or Lima during the day. Sam liked the creatures of the jungle more. They were easy to understand and free of anything but their purpose. Fully immersed in the reverie of the night, Sam could smell the soldiers' bivouac upwind of his tree. Purportedly jungle experts, they stuck out to him like the pimples dotting his face—sore and embarrassing. With the jaguar passed, Samuel slowly moved down from his perch like a sloth. A memory broke into his concentration.

"Was siehst du, Samuel?" his father asked.

[What do you see, Samuel?]

"That animal," a five-year-old Samuel said.

"That is a sloth," his father replied.

The old fascist stalked across the copse of trees, quietly drawing his bolo machete. In one smooth stroke, the animal was cut down. Herr Brönner returned to his son, half-dragging the dead headless animal.

"Now it is dinner. Clean it and bring it inside to your mother," he said.

"Ja, papa," Samuel said. The emotion was vacant in his voice, but older Sam remembered as he silently stalked his way through the jungle underbrush. The strong take what they need from the weak. Strength is power. Mastery of self is strength.

The teenage boy saw two men and a woman in the camp. One was awake, but barely. Their fire was meant to be concealed, hidden in a covered earthen dugout. It would have worked, except it smelled different from the jungle. So did the people. The Shining Path had been warned about crossing into the Brönner hacienda before. Now they would find out why. Communista were not welcome.

Samuel circled the camp. He took some sticks and lashed a frame, then wove large leaves into the cords. A bent sapling acted as a spring to make the covered frame pop up suddenly when the cord was cut. Once the trigger thread was covered in honey, sausage grease, and cheese from his rations, Sam set two more traps in an arc around the sentry. He snuck back to the opposite side of the bivouac.

He did not have to wait long. Some opportunistic pests sprung the first trap. The sentry left his post to investigate. He was gone just long enough for Sam to slip in and jam a pick through the temple of the other sleeping man. The boy was efficient, leaving no trace of a disturbance in the moonlight. The second and third traps snapped to in quick succession as Sam returned to the opposite tree line, and the sentry had emerged. This time, the soldier broke out a flashlight. Sam's heart raced as the adrenaline from the first kill and the increased threat washed over him. When he went for the woman, she turned open-eyed to him with a pistol in her hand. Expecting an attack from one of her comrades, Sam gave her a start. Sam had no mercy.

Her pistol went off as Sam knocked it out of line with his head. Instinct took over, and soon she stopped moving. He left his ice pick where it was, forming a grisly shadow in the dancing flashlight's glare. Sam scrambled for the pistol, a beat-up Makarov nine-millimeter, and rolled into a prone shooting position. It put the fire pit between himself and the running man. Dirt kicked up around him from the soldier's shots. Sam took a second to aim and fired. The communista crumpled to the ground. A black stain spread across the left of his sternum. Sam stood over him and fired a second shot to ensure the job was done.

Sam checked their supplies, ate their food, and read their pamphlets to see what all the fuss was about. When he was fully ready, Sam walked toward home, melting into the night.

"Vater wird stolz sein," he said hopefully.

[Father will be proud.]

Brönner looked out across the valley at the stunning, severe landscape of the Andes before him and was pulled back from his memory by a door slamming shut. Surrounded by comfort and luxury, Samuel spent most of his time in the villa out on the veranda or walking the grounds, for his connection to the wilderness. The vitality of life on the margins sustained him. The fight between just enough to survive and death had been his home since he was little more than a boy on his father's *hacienda*. The day's news reminded him of how quickly they could all be reduced from this highborn life back to the natural order. It did not frighten him, merely interfered with his desire to be left alone.

"It's out. Everyone knows we're still in the business, the drugs, the sex, the hits. They're calling for my head, just like they did with Calderone," Pachutec said across the expansive outdoor entertaining area. "Except that was us too!"

"Let them clamor and bang their pots," Brönner said. He sipped a cup of coffee.

"What?" Pachutec came around to confront him.

"I said, let them rattle their sabers. The UN has nothing on us. Calderone was looking for a place among them. All we were after is here already. They are impotent," Brönner said. He drank deep of his coffee. His icy blue eyes cut Pachutec to the quick. The young man's composure and rage cracked as if he'd walked around a corner to suddenly face a wolf.

"I actually agree," Elana said. She walked up to the two men. "There's nothing they can do and not betray their own."

Brönner swallowed the last of his coffee and set the mug on the rail.

"I know where the leak came from. It is dealt with, along with anyone who knew about it outside of what I am telling you. An organization as big as this, there are eddies like in a stream. Sometimes they end up with extra toilet paper or chairs, sometimes it's a forgotten data backup," Brönner said.

"But the image—" Pachutec said.

"The image is fine—get out in front of it. Admit it, and everything else. The only power their words really have is that they expose something. If you expose it, you take their only power," Brönner said. "Someone hit the depot, but before they blew it to hell, they looked inside first. Like I said, sometimes secrets get out. But they only have as much power as you're willing to give them."

"We can announce legislative measures. Legalize it all, across the NIE," Elana said. "Spin it as forward-thinking, decriminalizing things that the *bourgeois* used to hold down the *proletariat*. The old saw that sex work is just work, that no one should tell you what you do with your body—drugs, sex, whatever. It's so outrageous they'll probably overlook the racketeering and all that. There it is, your first major act of legislation."

"Do it," Pachutec said. "The worst they can do is send another airstrike."

"That would go over even less well than this," Brönner said.

Elana left with a phone to her ear, organizing the draft of the legislation.

"Armand—" Brönner said.

Pachutec leered at him.

"Armand," Brönner said firmly. "We need to discuss the plan for Giresun. They're the ones who've done this. They've been harassing us for years. It wasn't clear until now, but Ignacio Guzman called me. We have much to discuss."

CHAPTER 17

The Price of Admission

DE SILVA RETREAT, PERUVIAN ANDES

2143 01 AUG 2075

"Can you please get these sycophants out of here? *Gracias*," Pachutec said. "*Soai*, I can't believe how hard it is just to get around now. Someone's always asking for this, for more of that, or just trying to get my atten—hello, what's your name?"

Elana pulled a young woman with two too many undone buttons out of the expansive conference room turned business office and out into the hallway.

Pachutec shrugged with his hands as she disappeared behind the ministerial aides as they ushered out the crowd of businessmen and lobbyists. Brönner squeezed through on the side of the door as it was shut.

"We need to control Giresun," Brönner said, ushering Pachutec out onto the veranda.

They stared at the Andean mountains across the valley. The echo of rocks falling pierced the silence at odd intervals. The air was thin and cold. Standing outside made the comforts of the indoors call to Pachutec like a siren.

"It's just a tiny island, bunch of women," Pachutec said.

"It's so much more than that," Brönner said. "They were in negotiations with Calderone's people and the delegates. They have technology that surpasses the others. Things beyond the farming, mining, and information support they offered. They're not interested in dealing with us."

"Why not? Money is money," Pachutec said.

"Not to them," Brönner said.

"What, some kind of zealots?" Pachutec said.

"I guess, maybe. Not religious," Brönner said. "They are an island of women, led by women. Arguably they've achieved more in fifty years than we have as a continent since the first man set foot on the ground here."

"Impossible," Pachutec scoffed. "I rule the entire Gran American confederation. In less than three years I went from the son of a drug lord to controlling most of a continent. Besides, don't we have a chief of staff for that sort of thing now? What does our State Department do anyway?"

"They won't sell or share, so we must take," Brönner said.

"How does that make us different from the imperialist Yankees?" Pachutec said, pouring a pisco sour. "No, we should try to win them over, or at least go through the proper channels like every other proper government in the world does. Get the Secretary of State in here, and let's get the diplomats working it."

"The Incas built their empire on coercion, but when necessary, they violently overthrew those who opposed them. This tiny island has dealt the first blow, drawn first blood. We must overwhelm them, but without destroying what they have in the process. We need to bring home their skills as the spoils," Brönner said.

"And turn into *conquistadors*, like Pizzaro?" Pachutec said, incredulous. "This is where we show the world that this new Incan empire is an improvement on the old models, like Gran America. The country is better off now, and the people are in control of their destiny because of me. We need to show the world that our way is better than the old habits, that we're something different."

"Do not turn your back on what brought you here. The lesson to display is to not forget where you come from. You want the people to take pride in their brave new world? Don't be ashamed of how you became their leader. No, turn the tables on the world stage. Do unto them what they've done to you. You want to be the new Incan Emperor? It's time for some display of strength."

"Very well. They're not our people," Pachutec said. "But they have no allies either. We can display our strength without causing a war. Just a bunch of women in need of a reminder of the natural order. Coordinate with O'Higgins. Have him begin preparations and gather the fleet as directed, but *en masse* as he sees fit before detouring to the island."

"As you say," Brönner replied.

OFF THE COAST OF ECUADOR

1037 04 AUG 2075

The ocean swells threw the flat-bottomed landing ship side-to-side and front-to-back with an irritating lack of habit. Elana had worn out three nausea bags when a seaman handed her a small plastic bucket.

Pachutec admired the absence of land, the bewildering tapestry of the open ocean. "It's so different from flying over it," he said.

"The ships with deeper keels are less… chaotic," Brönner said. Even he looked a little green.

"Here." The ship's medic opened a small packet of plastic sheeted aluminum foil. He peeled off tiny gossamer gel pads from the foil and motioned for access to their ears. Placing them on the skull behind their ears he said, "This will take a few minutes to take effect. But you should start feeling better soon."

A larger warship, having breached the horizon, was moving toward them now. As it drew near, it loomed over the tiny-by-comparison LST.

"Ah, I see what you mean about the ships," Pachutec said.

The bosun's mates passed lines across the gunwales of both ships, then created what looked like a makeshift crane and elevator between them. A whistle sounded.

"Lady, gentlemen, if you will pass this way. We are ready to transfer you to the *Cochrane* at your pleasure," the Chief Bosun said. A system of winches, pulleys, and sheets worked to transfer the container up, across, then down onto the deck of the frigate *Cochrane*.

Emerging from the elevator compartment, Pachutec was greeted with official fanfare on the *Cochrane* and cheers from both crews. He raised his arms in a V and shook as many hands as he could reach.

"He's loving this," Elana said.

"And they love him, for now," Brönner said.

"Go on, make nice," Pachutec said before joining the official escort at the end of the sailors' gauntlet.

"Your Excellency, I am Admiral O'Higgins. I command the GA fleet, and this is our flagship the *GAS Cochrane*. Welcome aboard," Admiral O'Higgins said. "This is my Executive Officer, Commander Cantos. He will escort you around the ship, your Excellency."

"Thank you, Admiral. I appreciate your making time for us to observe the fleet. I was reviewing the training schedule," Pachutec said. They walked through the pressure doors and into the officer's mess. Pachutec motioned for the Admiral to have a seat, taking his own.

"I saw the report from my aides. I understand that with the new additions to... the New Incan Empire, you would like to take a tour of the ports starting here on the Pacific, around the horn, then up the Atlantic coast?" the admiral said.

"Yes, I thought it would make for a good show of unity, of solidarity across the nation," Pachutec said.

"No doubt also a bit of admonishment for the hold-outs?" O'Higgins asked.

"A little bit, I'm sure," Pachutec said, smiling. "What do you know of this island?"

Elana passed a folder marked with the official seal and stamped "*Confidencial NOEXTRA.*"

The admiral opened the folder as an aide moved to help. The admiral waved him off with a slight gesture. "Giresun," the admiral said. "It's a man-made spit of land just off the coast of Guiana, about four hundred and fifty nautical miles, past Devil's Island."

"The people there?" Pachutec asked.

"Mostly women, from what I know. Industrial work, well paid," the admiral said. His face was set like a poker player, looking to bait the new commander-in-chief into showing his hand first.

"They were in negotiations with the previous government. I want to… encourage them to join us. Do you know the history of the Yankee fruiters and how Hawaii became part of the United States?" Pachutec asked.

"Of course, it happened in our own history as well. We just didn't get the same result."

"What do you say we see how the run goes, and maybe I'll ask for the fleet to put in at their port if negotiations stall?"

"Aye, sir."

The two sat for a moment, just eyeing the other and the documents laid out on the conference-turned-dining table.

"Well, unless you have anything else to discuss, Admiral, I'm famished. I'd love to see the rest of the ship and meet her crew before heading back to the land?" Pachutec said.

Elana and Brönner stood.

"Of course, sir," the admiral said as he looked at his executive officer, who stood by the door. "Cantos, if you'll lead the way?"

"Aye, sir." Commander Cantos stood and opened the door. A petty officer dogged it open and returned to parade rest next to it. "If you will all follow me, please. Watch your step and your head. The doors on ships can be tricky to navigate," Cantos said.

Admiral O'Higgins remained standing at the table while the rest of the ship's officers trailed Pachutec's party. He looked at the provided intelligence photos, maps, and documents while trying to sort out a plan of how to avoid creating another banana republic.

VILCABAMBA, PERU

1038 05 AUG 2075

Elana Chavez stood on the platform raised at the new national capital in Vilcabamba. Cranes were pulled out of the screenshot, and while the edifice was complete, nothing stood behind the great gold-plated doors in back of Elana's podium. Delegates from all the nations of the New Incan Empire were seated behind her. In the front row were the heads of the combined air force and armies of the empire—Admiral O'Higgins would join them virtually from the *Cochrane* as it rounded the horn of South America. The landscape just out of the construction zone obscured by the state-approved camera angles was still a riotous jungle. Some thousand citizens crowded up in front of the cameras. A cordon of red-shirted people stood at their backs and maintained the focus toward the steps of the new capital.

"*Buenas tardes, señoras y señores del Nuevo Imperio Incan. Jefes de Estado, nuestros ilustres comandantes militares, bienvenidos.*

[Good afternoon, ladies and gentlemen of the New Incan Empire. Heads of State, our illustrious military commanders, welcome.]

"For hundreds of years, discriminatory policies have provided an international means to keep the countries of South America in thrall. The progress of history slowly wends its way toward justice and equality for the common man. The legislation we announce today will begin to right those wrongs, to free us from the boot of the Yankee and European usurpers alike. We are those most harmed by their history of explicit and implicit colonialism, and we will restore justice to our people! Systemic racism has devastated the economies of our many nations in the past. As a unified South America emerges as the New Incan Empire, we will repair the damage from this historic, systemic racism. May I introduce our Emperor Pachutec!" Elana drew out the last like a *fútbol* or *lucha libre* announcer. It was the first time the formal title was used by the government. It went off like a rocket.

The cheers from the crowd so close by were deafening. Pachutec rose from the back of the dais, appearing to arrive out of nowhere, stealing the idea from his ancestors' love of forced perspective tricks. He threw his arms up in his customary, exuberant V. The English vents of his jacket flared only so slightly as their well-tailored gussets maintained the thin silhouette of his torso. Every detail was scripted, down to the physics of his trouser fabric. The young ruler was to be someone feared while also desired, unifying and charismatic. Elana was given carte blanche in achieving her goals.

The crowd eventually died down as Pachutec motioned for quiet, gently pushing down with his palms toward the podium.

"In a moment, we will hear from our Admiral O'Higgins on the flagship *Cochrane* as he circumnavigates the continent, establishing the sort of unity I see today among our Navy. But with the ability to use force there must also be as strong a sense of justice. That leads me to our first legislation, which I will sign into law here before you all, as a testament to my dedication to the people of our great nation.

"I am proud to say that our delegates have passed one of the most daring criminal justice reforms of any nation on the planet. This monolithic step will bring real change to our communities. In one swipe of my pen, we can begin to heal the injustices of the criminalization of certain personal freedoms. Freedoms decried as immoral, like our predecessors, guided best as they could by false myths and superstition, sought to dictate individual rights as morality. An overwhelming cry by the people of our empire resulted in our reexamining of the criminal codes, as we unify one law for the entire land. We hope that eventually our southern neighbors, Argentina and Chile, will see these efforts and finally concede to join us. If it harms no one, it is not a crime. And so, I formally announce that the criminalization of substances is at an end. Those imprisoned or taxed for the non-violent use, distribution, or growing of these crops will be released. Reparations for seized assets will be made."

The crowd exploded in shouts of support.

"Please, please, my countrymen. There is more good news. Please, use your devices to register at this location, so you may receive your benefits. The local police offices will not be handling these issues. You may, however, register online, and you will be connected with your benefits through the system. If you do not have access yourself, there will be kiosks located in your town or village squares or internet cafes in the city. There you can also review the law in full, as well as comment on our work to unify the codes across the nation and identify those wrongs committed under the previous codes if you choose. There is something of an amnesty at work during the transition. But we will be watching. The era of graft and bribery is at an end. Those entrusted with keeping the peace must do so without sacrificing the peace of the people in the process. What I witnessed firsthand, standing with all of you in Cartagena, must never again pass for justice.

"Recreational and medicinal use of substances is not the only decriminalization in this bill. Too long, because of the engineered social stigma of our forebearers and their contrived morality, we have punished those who for lack of other prospects use their bodies to pay for their family's needs or sustain themselves. The World Bank states that more than seventy-two percent of the people of the world, seven billion, struggle to find a way to afford two meals a day. They take jobs in dangerous places, working in conditions hazardous to their health, until they get sick and can no longer help with anything or anyone. And our predecessors punished them more for it.

"I declare an end to all of that. If you harm someone intentionally, then the law will come down on you in full force. If you do not harm someone else, then it is not a crime. Disruption of the peace is now the rule of law. Be at peace, and you will be left to thrive. We will help rather than punish you. Thank you for your continued support, *mis amigos. Buenos noches.*"

A cordon of security streamed in from the side of the dais and formed a gauntlet for Pachutec to exit through.

Elana took the stage, still clapping along with the crowd.

Brönner met him on his way past the capital façade.

"Tell the regional bosses that they can each take turns raking in profits for their sectors—we're a united country now. I just cornered the world's market on sex and drugs for them," Pachutec said.

As he left for the motorcade, Pachutec smiled as he heard the crowd spontaneously sing *Des Colores.*

CHAPTER 18

Threat of Violence

1024 01 AUG 2075

The Admiral's Daughter was as empty as the Archives had been. Sim(on) sat in the same booth he, Abby, and René usually took. The music from the virtual jukebox echoed over the empty dance space and cloistered booths. The place smelled clean, thanks to the circulating cleaning robots, though an undertone of the ancient dive lingered below. A large neon sign, a mermaid looking out to sea, hung on the wall behind the zinc bar.

"Here you go, hun," the manager said.

She acted as a waitress and bartender while the numbers were low. She went back to paperwork on a screen at the rail.

The door opened, casting a portal of sunlight into the dim bar. Abby emerged from it and made a bee line for their booth.

"What's up? I thought last night went well?"

"It did," Sim(on) said. He quickly took a bite of nachos and washed them down with the contents of his mug. He signaled for another from the bar.

The manager reached over and expertly poured another pint from the tap behind her back.

She dropped it off, exchanging mugs without a word.

"Slow down," Abby said to Sim(on).

"I found something out I… I don't know what to do with," Sim(on) said.

"What?" Abby said.

Sim(on) ate a few condiment laden chips. He reached for his beer. Abby put her hand over the top of the mug.

"Is it about the de Silvas?" she asked.

"No. Yes, and no," Sim(on) said. "Pachutec is dirty. Never changed. We can prove it now, but that's not it," Sim(on) said.

"We should go public," Abby said.

"I did, took it to the Triumvirate myself. That's when I found this," Sim(on) said. He started his screen, flicked the document scans to Abby, then shut his screen off without a second glance.

"So that was your work? Man, the world is flip-flopping between Calderone and de Silva. Now no one knows who to back. The US is talking about intervention, of course—" Abby said. "What is this…?"

She looked over the documents.

Sim(on) tried to eat another chip, but it hung in mid-air until the weight of the nachos reached the breaking point and fell back to the plate.

"Abby… René… I found out why she was abducted. She's been working with de Silva. His man Brönner has been in contact with her since she came to the island. She's a traitor, Abby. She's betrayed *us*," Sim(on) began.

"—oh *soai*," Abby whispered.

"What do we do?" Sim(on) asked.

Tears welled up in his eyes and ran down his face. Abby looked at him, and she could not keep herself together. She scooted across the abused vinyl seat. As she pulled him in, her own tears broke.

CABO BRANCO COAST, BRAZIL

0839 08 AUG 2075

The NIE Navy regrouped with the Brazilian ships. Rather than steaming along with the coast gathering the rest of the fleet, they were met by the remnants at Cabo Branco.

"*Excellente,*" Admiral O'Higgins said as he stared through his binoculars to inspect the remaining ships. "Dispatch a *communique* to the fleet. Change course for Devil's Island. Let's run simulation *Camarón* and see if we can avoid colliding with each other. East Coast versus West Coast, target locks only."

"Aye, admiral," the conn crew answered.

"Commander Cantos," O'Higgins said.

"Sir," Cantos replied.

"Semaphore relay across the fleet. Captains, open orders at ENDEX," O'Higgins said.

"Aye, sir," Cantos said. He departed for the main deck.

VILCABAMBA, PERU

2214 11 AUG 2075

"I want—I need to be there when it happens," Pachutec said.

Brönner stood close by the sound stage set. He watched as crew members shuffled about behind the cameras moving lights and scenery.

Pachutec sat behind a field desk in a campaign tent surrounded by symbolic artifacts and potted jungle plants. "These propaganda spots for the vid feeds... everyone wants them, though it's weird, no one pays attention to the message so much as seeing who's in it. Apparently, words are meaningless here," Pachutec said.

The camera director gave him a thumbs-up. Pachutec took off the cravat and Ecuadorian straw hat, tossing them onto the desk, where they rolled off onto the fake earthen floor. He walked out of the tent with Brönner. The film crew packed up the set as the director gave the go-ahead. He walked toward the mixing booth.

"Good shoot, your Excellency. We should be rolling out the new spots by tonight!" the director said.

"Something real, more than this. That's what I need," Pachutec said. "How else are they going to take me seriously?"

He wiped base makeup off his face with a handkerchief while stage crews dismantled the scene in the sound stage.

"I'll get Elana to clear the schedule and coordinate with O'Higgins," Brönner said.

GIRESUN ISLAND, FORUM

1610 13 AUG 2075
Columbia stood at the podium while flanked by Keiko and Chris on the sides of the dais. The Forum walls had expanded, drawing the senators' rows out toward the cavernous back end of the stadium. The official seats of government were arranged like a lotus flower, with the Triumvirate as the central bud. The enormous tracked wheels of the clam-shelled enclosure ground to a halt as the retractable walls rose. Ports in the floor made a "whoosh" sound as air handlers pushed air through small subterranean vents, cooling the space with geothermal updrafts. The temperature within the Forum was significantly cooler than the midday heat of the tropics. Thousands of women, children, and men milled about and into the Forum, most taking snacks and drinks from the purveyors beyond into the enormous hall. Projections of the dais and senators blinked on around the expanse so everyone could see both in-person and better-focused versions of what was happening. The master-at-arms blew an anachronistic conch shell horn, amplified a hundredfold to bring the session to order.

"Good afternoon, citizens of Giresun," Columbia began. "Thank you for gathering here today. We are moving ever closer to the world recognizing our sovereignty as our own country, free from the interference many of us have endured around the planet. We strive to make the world a better place. A world that has oftentimes ignored, berated, and abused us.

"We face an existential threat today. I make no false claims about it. There are more than a few world powers who would see us in chains, brought back into their fold, returned to their patriarchy. I will not stand idly by and relinquish the great strides my sisters and brothers have made for all of the worlds. Our long fight against tyranny and the oppression of women, children, and the poor have put a target on us.

"Today I've learned that the New Incan Empire, the result of conflux of a criminal organization and failed statecraft, has mobilized their fleet against us. The declared purpose is a tour of their country, but make no mistake. They are gathering their forces into a wave aimed at the takeover of our island home.

"As a result of the hard work and valiant efforts of our Security Forces, we have exposed the corruption, villainy, and human rights abuses of the de Silva cartel. We have also made the connections and evidence public to the rest of the world, linking the de Silva cartel to the current government of South America—with the notable exceptions of Chile and Argentina.

"You have all no doubt seen this Pachutec caricature announcing bold new moves in the criminal code there, posing them as decriminalization of victimless crime. You know where Giresun has always stood on the use of substances and sex-as-work. Let me assure you that their proposals are not the same as ours.

"Pachutec has never denounced his family business, has never divested himself from it. In fact, he uses his father's palaces as *de facto* seats of government and the cartel's network to both incite violence and deliver relief to those affected. He has played the world, and now he's coming for us. We must all do our part. There will be an invasion. These ships will make port. But rest assured—they will not take us down. Like one of our championship fighters in the arena, we will beat them before a blow is landed and deliver a crushing defeat before they realize what has happened. All that will be left is their resignation."

The audience stood still for a moment, dumbfounded. A few children, no idea what to make of the adults' disbelief, began to cry halfheartedly.

CHAPTER 19

Confrontation

CABO BRANCO COAST, BRAZIL

1235 14 AUG 2075

"Sir, all ships have reported in at ENDEX," the radioman announced on the bridge of the *Cochrane*.

"Very well. Change course. We are heading to North five degrees, fourteen minutes, thirty seconds, West forty-four degrees, thirty-three minutes, seventeen seconds. Helm, plot a course," Admiral O'Higgins said.

"Plot laid in, sir," the helm responded.

"Full steam ahead," O'Higgins said.

"Full ahead aye, heading two-six-nine degrees thirty-seven minutes zero, aye," the bridge crew responded.

O'Higgins stepped out onto the catwalk. The water splashing onto the deck below with the smell of the open sea centered him. He was an ocean predator in the service of the people, whatever their names were this time around. His expression remained grim, and his burden was evident in the slow movements he took around the railing. He watched through his glasses as the *Cochrane* came about and counted off the other ships in view doing the same. In minutes the combined fleet of the NIE was steaming for a small island with no appreciable allies.

"God forgive us," O'Higgins said to himself.

GIRESUN ISLAND, FORUM

1300 14 AUG 2075

"Put your backs into it! We've got six more blocks of this to set up, and those mainland bastards are almost here," Master Sergeant Sarah Kelly shouted. The arena where she would conduct counter-offensive operations was nearly complete, and not a moment too soon. The security forces workers assembled sheets of wire mesh and fabric into hollow walls like a professional pit crew. Squads of carryall drones lifted and transported the walls into rows. First along the street, with regularly spaced intervals between sections, then a second and third row behind them into the adjoining streets.

Sarah walked up and down Main Street, inspecting the fortifications. Retaining walls were going up as barricades—rock walls made steady by wire mesh lined with kinetic energy-absorbing fabric. Swarms of carryall drones flew in wave after wave over the hollow walls. The VR-controlled drones swooped in to drop large stones into the shafts. A squad of SF construction specialists directed their movements through headsets and controls worn over their hands and forearms.

In front of the barricades, human crews used exoskeletons and six-legged automatons to stack hedgerows of dried acacia. The sight of their seven-centimeter thorns made her scars itch.

"We'll see how these *putas* can handle a little pain," an officer said as Sarah passed for the fourth time.

"They wanna take us, they're gonna beat us!" one of her soldiers yelled. Her augmented fists clanged together like a boxer's gloves before climbing into the ring.

"It's like the Promotion Challenge came early!" Sarah said. She let out a war-cry with all her might. It echoed around the heart of downtown. "Everything is coming into position," she reported back to headquarters. The AI had already displayed readiness and completion estimates for everyone to see, civilians and government, around the island's network. Sterile data was always paired with human, qualitative analysis. Over-reliance on one or the other always left gaps to be exploited by an enemy or fate.

"I know it's just a prediction, but we'll be ready if they come. If not, we'll have a Promotion Challenge like none other and room for a parade to boot!" Sarah said.

"Something tells me we'll have a lot of new recruits applying to the Security Forces after this, either way," Columbia said from HQ.

"Everybody's going to want some payback if these terrorists come for us," Sarah replied.

GIRESUN ISLAND COAST

1111 15 AUG 2075

Twenty-two hours later, the NIE fleet was within sight of Giresun Island. The water was steady without a cloud in the sky. The sun baked the decks of the ships while the sailors tried to keep to the shadows as much as possible as they waited in the calm.

"Sir, the island is now asking for you by name," the communications officer said.

"Has the blockade closed around the island?" the admiral said.

"Yes sir, the *Valdez* has just closed ranks with the *Santa Ana*. We control the sea," Commander Cantos said from the plotting table.

"Firing solutions are programmed into the computers for all batteries and missile tubes. Surface defenses stand ready," fire control reported.

"Damage control teams are prepped and standing by across the fleet," another voice said.

The tension in the conn was palpable, pervading everything like the smell of the ship itself. Admiral O'Higgins did his best to keep everyone ready without pushing them over the edge into panic or sniping at each other.

"If you would patch me through to their leader, Columbia Honalee," Admiral O'Higgins said.

"Aye, sir," the communications officer replied.

"Ms. Honalee on the line for you, sir," the lieutenant said. While sweat dripped from his body like he'd gone swimming, he managed to hold the handset steady, reaching it out to the admiral in his chair.

"Ms. Honalee, this is Admiral O'Higgins of the New Incan Empire," he said. "We have been conducting exercises in the coastal area between you and the mainland. I would like to ask to put ashore with a contingent of the winners of our simulations if you wouldn't mind sharing your hospitality?"

"Good morning, Admiral. We were friends to your predecessors, and while we are a small island, we would be happy to welcome a small contingent of your sailors. Will there be a diplomatic envoy as well? We would like to resume our negotiations with the NIE that we started with the government of Gran America, if possible," Columbia replied.

"I believe that can be arranged, ma'am. Will your docks have room for three ships?" O'Higgins said.

"That can be arranged," Columbia said.

"Excellent. We will await the envoy's arrival. Will you send the pilot now, or do you prefer to wait until the parties have arrived?"

"We can send the pilot boat ahead to guide you in and ensure the envoys are not kept waiting," Columbia said.

"We await at your service, ma'am." Admiral O'Higgins held out the handset to the comms officer.

The admiral sat in the command chair, deep in thought.

"Radio the mainland. We are cleared for them to join us," O'Higgins said.

"Aye, sir," the comms officer said.

1115 15 AUG 2075

"You see that? Folding in the face of overwhelming force. They have no choice," Pachutec yelled at the giant display.

The majority of the wall in Calderone's old palace office was a plot of the fleet around Giresun Island, with in-sets of real-time images of the fleet, of traffic patterns around the island, and dossiers of key players on both sides. Elana pulled the file for Chris van Buren onto her own screen, then sat down and began typing.

Brönner stood in the corner, watching a video of Giresun Security Forces training.

"Is that what's happening?" Brönner said. He checked his pistol, then took a weathered large bore magnerifle from a gun case next to Pachutec's desk. He checked the rifle and slammed the ferrous block home for emphasis.

"Pachutec, it is time to go," Elana said. She helped Pachutec with his jacket, then straightened his suit.

"This is the day that will set the New Incan Empire on its path to greatness, as much as a revolution, but with the power to sustain that change into a dynasty," Pachutec said.

"A momentous day. A day of destiny," Elana said.

"Guzman and the others are on the chopper," Brönner said.

Pachutec looked in a full-length mirror on the wood-paneled wall across from the desk. Elana and Brönner flanked his reflection looking back at him. An esteemed professor on one arm and the embodiment of deadly force on the other with him, Emperor, in the middle. Pachutec earmarked this picture for the official portrait folio.

"Stay here and keep the machine of our empire running?" Pachutec said to Elana.

She nodded meekly.

"To the isle of women, then," Pachutec said.

"This is old," Keiko said. "Old-ass tech. Smells weird. What'dya do, dig it out of an Archives display? It's gotta be... *soai*, was this Jane's? Like, *the Founder* Jane's?"

"It will keep you safe from small arms fire," Columbia said.

"You *did*!" Keiko said in awe. "The docents are gonna be pissed!"

"They can't be pissed if we stop an invasion," Columbia said. "And if we don't, you and I probably won't have to worry about some fussy old broads lambasting us in the public square."

They stood in a private room. An empty box sat on an end table while Keiko slipped into the thin mesh. Columbia turned on the control box, and indicator lights traced Keiko's body like map contours. They shut off in unison, except for the status light at the wrist controls shining green.

"Diamond batteries are still at full strength. Tell me again," Columbia said.

"I squeeze and hold the green light, close my eyes, and roll into a ball. When there's a break in the gunfire, I get up and maneuver. Don't do anything stupid," Keiko recited.

"Mean it?" Columbia asked, adjusting the fit of the front seam.

"Yeah, boss," Keiko said.

"Be safe. They're serious," Columbia said.

"I didn't get my scars yesterday. You know I've got this, Columbia. Speaking of no scars, Chris is in the bull pen out there," Keiko said.

"I know. She's digging her own grave," Columbia said.

"If we pull this off," Keiko said.

"If we don't, we'll be dead and won't have to care about it anymore," Columbia said.

"Truth," Keiko said.

"Still, get her traitors quietly isolated from the others as much as you can. Remember, for the most part they're doing the right thing in their own minds. They're still our citizens at some level. Let Sarah know?" Columbia said.

"Can do," Keiko said.

Keiko put her clothes back on, and they walked into the makeshift headquarters sprawled across the Triumvirate penthouse.

A woman bumped into Columbia. "Excuse me, ma'am. I'm so sorry," the woman said. She wore a SF jumpsuit, hair in a buzzcut. She meekly avoided eye contact with the Proconsul.

"No trouble, soldier. Be careful. Everyone's on edge," Columbia said kindly. Columbia noticed a bag of thin fire extinguishers at the woman's feet. As the soldier slung it over her shoulder, Columbia tried to repair her morale.

"Good idea, making sure we're prepared," Columbia said. "Keep up the good work."

"Yes, ma'am," the woman saluted. She went back to placing fire extinguishers across the room.

Chris escorted the woman out of the Penthouse. From her body language she was venting her own nervousness. Columbia couldn't stop her eyes from rolling before turning to the latest analysis report. She looked up, caught Keiko's eyes, and nodded.

GIRESUN ISLAND, TRIUMVIRATE PENTHOUSE

1200 15 AUG 2075

"They're coming," Columbia announced to the penthouse.

Security Force personnel moved quickly, hooking up equipment and testing connections here with others erecting barricades below. Acacia branches with their seven-centimeter hardened thorns were layered meters deep around the barricades. The first scars SF members took were from mock battles, drills, and competitions climbing through their nail-like spikes. A frontal attack with personnel would take a lot of effort or pain, as the branches absorbed the slashes of machetes and entangled people like concertina wire.

Chris van Buren was busy directing the set up of her station when she came striding over to Columbia. "We're almost set. Gunnery emplacements are camouflaged, civilians are sequestered with enough provisions to last several weeks, aid and fallback stations are almost complete. Drone air support will launch once the ships are docked, or if any get trigger happy. Any of these *po-gais* fire as much as a needler, and we'll sink the lot of them. I need to go check the redundancies in our comms gear."

Keiko was watching the two of them while trying to go unnoticed.

"Fine, good, go," Columbia blurted, trying to avoid Keiko's eyes.

A calculated number of moments later, Keiko was nowhere to be seen.

"*Soai*," Columbia said.

∿

On the way down in the elevator, Chris checked her screen. She had already turned it to Private mode. The projection along her skin glowed faintly in a polarized pattern. It only allowed her to see the display straight-on.

The message "Set 300 , MagPi" glowed on her smooth palms.

GIRESUN ISLAND COAST

1300 15 AUG 2075

As the security team shuffled Mez Calla, Samuel Brönner, Ignacio Guzman, Maxim Torres, and Pachutec from the *Sea King* helicopter onto the aft deck of the *Cochrane,* Admiral O'Higgins and Commander Cantos greeted the envoys. A pair of security officers carried a heavy cargo box between them.

"The official vehicle is in the bay of the *Sanchez,* the LST you rode on before," Admiral O'Higgins said to Brönner. "If you'd like, we can stow that on the deck 'til we transfer, or have it loaded into the Emperor's vehicle."

"I will go with it to the *Sanchez*, Admiral. Better to keep out of the pomp, hmm?" Brönner said.

"Spoken like a soldier who's been in too many parades," O'Higgins said. He waved Commander Cantos over. "Have Mr. Brönner, their belongings, and anyone else who wishes to be, transferred to the *Sanchez*. Our commander and staff will disembark from the flagship and meet their convoy on the docks."

"Aye, sir," Cantos said. He signaled to the deck chief, and men began preparations for transfer at sea while the *Cochrane* and its tenders broke the line toward Giresun.

The rest of the envoy were milling about, looking at things they had no connection to, pretending to be interested. Most were on their screens. A woman and a couple of men were typing furiously on projected keypads. Only one seemed to have any military bearing, an old-weathered man dressed like a *caballero*. Admiral O'Higgins noted while the ranger had passed his pistol to the master-at-arms on landing, he kept a knife sheathed in the small of his back.

"Politicians," O'Higgins mumbled before returning to the official party.

RENE'S APARTMENT

1404 15 AUG 2075

"We're just going to talk," Sim(on) said.

Abby cracked the knuckles of her hands in the elevator.

"Abby. We're giving her the chance to come clean. We're here to help her," Sim(on) said.

"*Po-gai*, yeah, I'm gonna give her a whole lot of help," Abby said. "She's been flipped! You want to coddle that? She's a collaborator! Everything we work for—the drugs, the hits for hire, the sex slaves— you said it yourself, Simon, she's been feeding them intel since she got here! She's betrayed you. Me. The whole damned island! This *soai* with the invasion, it's her fault. She's orchestrated it or gave them the inside track, the whole bombing thing in Cartagena was probably a cover for her to get placed next to the Triumvirate—"

"You're taking a lot of different pieces out of context and making your own narrative. You know that? You used to be good at this, remember?"

"Yeah, then I was betrayed. How's it feel, Simon?"

The elevator doors opened to René's floor.

"Hey René, it's us. We need to talk," Sim(on) said.

"The invasion's almost here," Abby said, red-faced. "What?" she mouthed at Sim(on) and shrugged.

The door opened. René stood aside to let them in. Her smile fell into confusion as Sim(on) walked through, followed by Abby who conspicuously avoided eye contact with her. René could see the redness in Abby's face spreading from a blush to a burn.

Sim(on) took a seat on the large couch, dragging Abby down to it by her belt.

Bewildered, René sat in an adjacent loveseat. "What's up?" she said.

"René, I was trying to find out who abducted you. I found something that led me to a whole line of stuff... I don't know," Sim(on) began.

"How long have you been working for de Silva?" Abby asked. Her tone was ice cold behind her body of simmering rage.

"What?" René was aghast. "That's not me! I can explain—"

"You're a lying sack of *soai!*" Abby screamed. She flipped the coffee table, and the cups on top, across the room.

"Abby!" Sim(on) yelled at her.

René sat on the chesterfield loveseat, stock still with her hands on her lap like she was being chewed out by the principal at school. Sancho leaped to his feet from the relaxed position he'd had. Ears up and alert, he growled at Abby.

"What? She's lied to us since we've met! She'd be lying to us still, except we found out. And we're right! There's no denying it," Abby persisted.

"There are good reasons! She was told to, she was reinventing herself, that's what this place is for other people—a chance to change and rebuild, to escape the past—"

"But she didn't tell us!"

"That's what that means!" Sim(on) yelled back.

"The dog! I bet the dog knew," Abby yelled. "Probably would've lied too, just threading us along."

"No," René said.

"What?" Abby yelled back.

"No, Sancho never lied. I have always been the same with him. Words don't matter to him. Actions do. He was with me before and through all of this. You're lucky he loves you—like I love you both—or he'd have ripped out your *po-gai* throat just like he did on our way here," René said quietly.

"Wait, what?" Sim(on) said.

"My name was Carsem. I was on the run, kind of, from some gangbangers. I didn't think much of it. I was a woman alone on the road, and a Kurd. That's just a way of life. You already know the pieces. Let me put them in the right order," René said.

Sim(on) lightly held Abby in her seat. He nodded toward René while his eyes bulged in contact with Abby's ferocious gaze.

"You found that I changed my name, where I was from, who buried my past," René said. "What you didn't find out was what happened before, why Columbia did it."

"We did! You were at the assassination attempt—" Abby said.

"No," René said. "I was there, yes. I got caught up in it. But what you didn't know was that it was a feint. What I know now is that Security Forces, or some of them, were trying to kill Columbia."

"A coup?" Sim(on) said.

"When their plan failed twice, we were almost to the extraction point. One of them tried to kill her with an improvised weapon, a broken piece of wood, right—" René leaped from her seat, dove around Abby, held her over the shoulder from behind, and knife-hand punched her upward between the third and fourth ribs, driving her to her knees. Abby sent furniture flying in a desperate effort to fight off René's attack. It was no use. René had her dead to rights. Sancho stood on the loveseat, teeth bared. Sim(on) froze. René released Abby, who twisted away into a crouch in case there was more coming. Abby stayed completely still as Sancho stared her down.

"It was my saving her that meant no one could know where I came from, who I was," Carsem said.

"But we have comms—you and the head of de Silva's security, Samuel Brönner, he's been your handler this whole—" Abby said.

"No, that's Columbia," René said.

"Wait, what? Now the Proconsul is betraying us?" Abby said, throwing up her hands.

"No, she's my handler," René let the words hang in the air. "I'm not even directly involved. SF's been using my likeness to feed information and gather intel from de Silva's organization through Brönner."

"So, what was the beatdown?" Sim(on) said.

"The mission's still going. I don't know. It wasn't the de Silvas, probably their people here," René said.

"Right. They have people here on the island," Abby said.

"Not exactly, okay," René said.

"There are people who don't like what's going on—trade, travel, joining the UN," Sim(on) said. "Would they be willing to risk a coup? They have to see that they'd have a counter insurgency on their hands... it'd never work."

"People do things that don't make sense, Simon," Abby said.

"All the time," René said. She shot an imploring look to Abby. "Especially when they're listening to the wrong people. The other consul, not Tanagawa, the other one—" She suddenly winced in pain, unable to concentrate for a moment.

"—van Buren," Abby said. Her emotions played across her face. She went to the kitchen and brought back a cool washcloth.

"Her. She, N'gono, Nancy, they're all working at betraying us to the GA, NIE, whatever." René sat back and held the cloth over her forehead and temple. "Tons of other SF are in with them too. Going to undercut us all and hand it over to this Pachutec *po-gai* on a platter."

"Not from the look of it outside," Sim(on) said. He looked up from his screen. "Sorry, I spent the last—hours? Days? —thinking you were an *agent provocateur*. It's going to take my brain a bit to stop fact checking you."

"That's why I was so easy to goad. I wanted to tell you. It hurt that I couldn't. I had to hide in plain sight. I couldn't say anything about my past, couldn't let you in—you don't know how hard it's been. You can't," René said. "You don't know about my dead family, the war, what it took to get here... at first I wanted to cut it all away. Never let it back into my life, leave it in my nightmares. Time goes by, and we are the sum of all our parts, right?" René blew her nose in a cloth handkerchief from her back pocket. "It's why I never asked about either of yours. I want to know, desperately. I want to share that secret with you, both of you, pain and all."

Rene blew her nose again and composed herself in the chair. She leaned forward and cleared her throat.

"The thing in Cartagena was a fluke. Complete accident. Wrong place at the right time. I thought they were there for me, but the bombs and an assault squad... that's too much for some pissed-off street dealers or mules. These guys didn't even care or know I was there," René said.

"Or that you are Peshmerga," Sim(on) said.

"What gave it away?" René asked.

"Nothing. You were flawless," Sim(on) said. "Just analysis."

"Well, you're right," René said.

René ran her hand over Sancho's head and muzzle. She turned a chair upright, sat down, and he reassumed his former lazy loll. The floor was covered with the ruins of René's living room.

"I am René Anderson," she said. "The person I was is left behind, along with her dead children and fallen husband. I have two members of a loving family that I would die to protect, a new home though still nationless. From the looks of things outside, I may not have any of that for long. But I love you, even if you can't love me anymore."

"We need to get to Columbia," Sim(on) said.

"What now?" Abby said.

"This isn't an invasion," Sim(on) said. "It's their endgame."

"Right," Abby said. "And..."

"And, it's going to happen inside, not outside," Sim(on) said. "The cabal is small, the actors, they have support across the island, but the ones actually doing stuff, that's a very small number. Like, five or six small. N'gono and Nancy..."

"Obviously," Abby said, suddenly turning the couch back over and sitting down. She felt dizzy with the change.

"At least one of the consuls, probably a commander in SF," Sim(on) said.

"But we don't know," Abby said.

"Right, and anyone below them might be acting out of orders rather than as a part of it—abused power," René said.

"That could be a lot of bodies," Abby said.

"Train hard, die hard," René said.

She reached out a hand without looking at Abby. For a second it hung in the air alone. Abby tenderly reached out and squeezed.

"We've got to get to the Forum, overturn this apple cart," Abby said.

"First, we have to get out of here. You know van Buren's people will be watching for us, probably in the lobby even," René said.

"Then we go out the window," Abby said.

"Too high from here. There's a common room a couple floors above the garden. We could jump," René said.

"Or rappel. Doesn't have to be fancy, but a broken leg would end this," Sim(on) said.

"We need to find something to climb down on then," René said.

"Then we get up behind Main. That's where everyone's going to be focused," Abby said. "I know someone who can get us through to the Penthouse—that's where the command center will be."

"That's where we could also meet the most resistance," Sim(on) said.

"Then we need to arm up, best we can," René said.

"Get what we can here, then gear up along the way if we can," Abby said.

"Ready to go *po-gai* up some holier-than-thou Security Force types?" René said.

"You know it," Abby said.

She drew René in and held her tight. Sim(on) wrapped his long thin arms around them both. Sancho whined at their feet 'til they broke up and petted him all at once.

René surveyed her demolished living room.

"*Po-gai soai.* You *are* going to clean this up," René said.

Sim(on) took an aerosol bathroom air freshener can out of the closet along with a shower foam spray can. Abby took a hammer from the toolbox on the floor.

"You wait here," René said to Sancho as she bent down to his level on the floor. "We'll be back. Ready?" she asked.

Sim(on) tested a lighter from his pocket, extinguished the flame, and nodded.

"We'll have to get around security, and that means dropping out of the second floor. I know where there's a balcony," René said as she opened the door.

"Go," Abby said.

Nancy stood leaning against the opposite wall and was armed with a duck-billed sawed-off magnerifle. She raised it to waist level and walked toward them.

"Back inside," Nancy said.

Sancho shot out like a bolt, crossing between their legs and flying up Nancy's chest under her guard. René, Sim(on), and Abby dropped to the ground as the shotgun blew a hole in the tin-plate ceiling. Sancho was locked onto Nancy's throat like a vise. Dark crimson poured out around his bared teeth as she gasped for breath through a crushed larynx and drowned in her own blood. She struggled to hit the dog, but panicked. Her eyes stared at the doorjamb as her strength faded fast. As soon as Nancy's struggle ended, Sancho let go and limped back to René.

"Good boy," René said. "Go sit." She pointed toward the love-seat. Sancho limped across the broken room and curled up on the leather couch.

René stepped over Nancy's body to scout the hallway.

"Clear," she said quietly. Abby grabbed Nancy by the hair and dragged her body into the apartment. Sim(on) closed the door after.

GIRESUN ISLAND HARBOR

1410 15 AUG 2075

The *Cochrane* was the biggest ship in the harbor by far. The pilot boat guided the frigate to the deep end of the marina along with its escorts. The *Sanchez* disembarked first, lowering its foredeck as trucks and armored personnel carriers drove off the ramp. They formed a cordon as the official vehicles peeled off for the dock. Military trucks, upscaled for their venerated passengers, flew a red and tan block flag for the New Incan Empire's government. Samuel Brönner sat in the front passenger seat, wearing his Makarov in the open and the large-bore magnerifle across his lap pointed toward the open window.

Three companies of infantry disembarked from the other tender, mustering on the opposite deck. Platoons marched forward into the industrial loading zone further toward the capital, slowly forming their units. Unloaded from the *Cristobal*, six-hundred soldiers stood in formation waiting for their orders.

Chris van Buren stood to the side of the gangplank. N'gono stood by her side, awaiting the NIE emissaries. Chris's coiffed hair and pantsuit looked less than authoritative next to N'gono's stocky body, tight braids, and gray jumpsuit. The sea breeze pushed things in the harbor around at odd angles while the lapping waves knocked them together. Neither woman looked at ease with their situation.

Pachutec appeared at the break in the *Cochrane's* gunwales, and as he descended to the dock the rest followed.

"I think the jig is up," Pachutec said, offering his hand to Chris. "It is so nice to finally meet you in person."

"Your Highness," Chris van Buren greeted him.

"May I present Mez Calla, the representative from the state of Ecuador, Maxim Torres of Brazil, Pepe Hererra of Peru, and my viceroy Ignacio Guzman. I believe you two already are acquainted," Pachutec said.

"Let us finish it then," Chris said. She lifted her arm toward the cars and walked side by side with Ignacio and Pachutec while N'gono was forced to walk a step behind.

The convoy roared to life as the official party approached.

"This is a lot more than we agreed to, your Highness," Chris said. "It might undo things."

As they entered their vehicles, the turret gunners emerged. Weapons were engaged as the convoy peeled off down the main thoroughfare toward the Forum, followed by the rhythm of six-hundred boots marching in time.

"It's all for show, I'm sure, Ms. van Buren," Pachutec said. "We aren't here for a military conquest. It's in everyone's best interests, and a little window dressing just sells it. Don't you think, my dear?" Pachutec patted N'gono on the knee.

N'gono was as cold and composed as a solid onyx sculpture as she stared directly into Pachutec's eyes. He removed his hand.

CHAPTER 20

Stand Your Ground

GIRESUN ISLAND, RENE'S APARTMENT BUILDING

1355 15 AUG 2075

René sized up the electronic door lock. She scooted back away from the doorjamb a little more and kicked, putting all her weight into her hips. The door lock snapped and shattered the receptacle. The door swung violently inward.

She strode over to the row of glass French doors that opened up onto a double-wide balcony that ran the length of the room. The view below was of the downtown's lush tropical gardens. Sweeping water features, carved stone tōrō, and natural stone outcroppings peaked through the grasses, moss, and thickets of flowering trees.

Sim(on) and Abby rushed up to stand by her.

"There's a janitor's closet in the hallway. See if we have a rope or something," René said.

"Found this," Sim(on) said, returning with a twenty-foot extension cord.

"Everyone good with a little jump?" René said.

"It's that or hang here," Abby said.

René tied a bowline hitch around the base of the railing. Holding the fast end in her hand, she dropped the rest of the coil. Approaching boot steps echoed down the street. René lifted a leg over the railing, holding on to the cord. Wrapping her ankle around the end, she let herself down hand-over-hand to the bitter end. Then she let go and dropped the other ten feet to the ground. Abby followed next, rolling like a parachutist through the fall. Sim(on) landed gingerly on his feet, earning a look of surprise from Abby.

"C'mon," René said quietly.

The sound of marching was drowning under heavy engine noise now. They sprinted ahead on the next street over, dodging supply lines as they passed barricades.

"You! You're supposed to be indoors! Take shelter, we're being invaded, you slitches!" a female Security Forces Sergeant yelled and then turned her attention back to the battery and impending battle.

"Come on, almost there," Abby said as she ran.

Sim(on) was having a hard time keeping up, so René and Abby dropped back to take his arms and help him catch his breath.

"That's what you get living at a desk," Abby joked.

MAIN STREET

1400 15 AUG 2075

A series of passes by one bomber and a handful of NIE fighter aircraft drew shadows across Giresun's downtown toward the Forum. The fighters peeled off as they reached the shield wall, circling back over the farm and industrial sites before drawing together back across Main. The thrumming blades of modern rotary heloes, with their concealed turbines and diamond shapes, echoed against the highrises of the city. They maintained a watch over the side streets, neighborhoods, and parks, hovering like noisy balloon floats.

The rhythmic step of the marching soldiers crescendoed as the troops entered the city proper from the docks. The last on-lookers withdrew into the buildings, while some ran for cover behind the Security Forces' barricades. Marching uphill toward the seat of government, the NIE soldiers were sweating and trying to keep their breath calm. The mechanized armored vehicles groaned as the coastal flats quickly developed into steeper inclines.

As the NIE invasion crested the first rise, they found a young woman in an SF uniform. She wore a crown of acacia thorns that shone in the sun like a halo. She stood by with a staff, refusing to move until the enemy was yards away. As the front line drew up to twenty meters, they could see rivulets of blood dripping down from the six-centimeter thorns. Her eyes were blacked out, and she issued a chant that was too low for the soldiers to hear over the armor's engines. A single knife blade stood at the top of her pike.

"Put down your weapon. Prepare to be taken into custody," the first armored vehicle's sergeant announced over a loudspeaker.

The woman nodded and kneeled on one knee while driving the butt of her spear against the pavement. A concealed tube behind the shining blade launched an incandescent flare, shooting a thousand feet into the air before exploding in a shower of fiery phosphorescence. She ran toward the onslaught alone and was cut down by a thousand rounds of automatic magnerifle fire as she threw the spear toward the sergeant's tank.

The blade cut through the armor plating like butter before sinking to its cross guard at the start of the shaft. Like a magician's bending spoon, the metal bar drooped 'til the butt cap reached the ground. The end of the spear drove itself like a drill into the road. Despite the roaring engines of the war machine, it was disabled, locked, and immobilized in the middle of Main Street. Soldiers crowded to help free the vehicle, only to spin around at the sound of grinding metal, explosions, and flying debris as all of the aircraft suddenly crashed into the streets behind the Giresun barricades.

A stream of incendiary gel blocked retreat, forming a kill box at the end of Main. Incensed by the destruction of their air support and with nowhere to go, the NIE soldiers charged up the street.

"Take the wall!" a platoon commander yelled out. His troops were met with a spray adhesive that bound them together against the road, forming a secondary barrier before the acacia hedgerow.

Armored vehicles drove around the side of the sergeant's disabled assault craft and were able to stutter their way to overcome the adhesive. They began to drive into and fire upon the barricades.

"Holy *soai*! We must've hit a cache of that napalm! Roast you—" the lead vehicle commander was cut off from his perch on the turret as women spilled from the barricades like a wounded hornet's nest. A magnerifle blew his torso to the pavement.

Smoke and flame surrounded the six hundred soldiers. A clanging drumbeat deafened their ears as the Security Forces ran through the smoldering hedgerows to meet the invaders in melee combat. Their magnerifles and needle guns remained at their sides as they hacked and slashed at the soldiers.

The women's eyes were dilated, and foam flecked their lips as they savagely harassed the soldiers up the hill toward the Forum. Shock and the surprise of the native defenses wore off quickly as automatic weapons laid waste to the club and spear-wielding locals. The NIE soldiers took occasional casualties. The invaders repelled the defenders and resumed their roll toward the objective. The smoke rolled out further ahead than their pace could match and continued to billow up Main.

TRIUMVIRATE PENTHOUSE

1409 15 AUG 2075

"Flare!" a lookout yelled from the balcony.

"Fire!" the fire control officer bellowed.

From the sides of the buildings across the downtown, finely woven titanium nets were launched by rocket-assisted bombards. Like glimmering tablecloths, the shining sails drifted over the hovering aircraft below. The effect was as coordinated as a ballet—the drapes eliminated the lift created by the encased turbines. Without the upward push, the metal gunships plummeted twenty stories straight down.

Bomber and attack aircraft made an early return, preparing for a strafing run combined with a carpet bombing. In seconds they were incinerated as camouflaged anti-aircraft batteries concealed in the shield wall opened. Their flaming wreckage plunged into the waters beyond the harbor. The secondary detonations of their ordinance, intended for the civilians of the island, ensured that the debris was so scant and widely spread the underwater colonies wouldn't notice.

"Launch. Target the ships. I want them to know they're at our mercy. Do not fire unless they launch, shoot, or so much as throw a rock. Hold position beyond the docks," the Giresun air group commander said.

Swarms of aerial drones spread from the left and right horns of the bay. From a distance they looked like a cloud of starlings, shifting and undulating in mesmerizing shapes. Each tiny aircraft was loaded with a small charge the size of two twelve-gauge shotgun shells. *En masse*, they were an unstoppable bombardment on demand.

FORUM COMPLEX

1439 15 AUG 2075

"Abby, I got 'im. They're not going to let us in, and we left the extension cord at the apartment," René said. "We're not going to climb in during a firefight."

Abby sprinted ahead.

"Sarah Kelly," Abby blurted to the sentry behind sandbags, a composite barricade wall, and acacia thorn mesh. The sentry disappeared. René and Sim(on) caught up with Abby as the sentry reappeared with Sarah in tow.

"Hell of a time," Sarah said. "What?"

"The Triumvirate's in danger," Abby said.

Sarah stared at her as if deciding whether or not to shoot her.

"Let her in," Sarah said.

"Them too," Abby said.

"Whatever," Sarah said.

Abby drew out her stride to catch Sarah as she descended the ladder.

"What," Sarah said, more statement than a question.

"There is a cabal trying to overthrow the government..." Sim(on) said breathlessly.

"Tell me something I don't know," Sarah said. "Sergeant, get these idiots inside."

"From the inside. The invasion's a diversion," Sim(on) said.

He flicked the analysis to her from his screen.

"Now, that's useful. Give them a weapon," Sarah said.

"Just one?" the sergeant said.

"Can you all shoot?" Sarah asked.

René and Sim(on) nodded. Abby just stared, non-plussed.

"That would be a piece, then," Sarah said. "Go. Find Columbia, tell her and only her." Sarah ripped an armload of dismembered limbs from a meat printer's bin and shoved them into a nearby mortar pot. "Get those fabb'ed body parts printed and into the cannons! They don't have to look nice for *po-gai's* sake! We're trying to fake our deaths here!"

TRIUMVIRATE PENTHOUSE

1509 15 AUG 2075

The penthouse looked like the bullpen from an old movie. People were rushing around. Everyone seemed to be deep in animated conversation with someone on a screen or hologram. They fed new information into projected screens on the walls around the room. Trash collected on the floor between makeshift workstations. A fire extinguisher peeked out from a pile of papers knocked onto the floor. The bright red amid the black, gray, and white bustle caught Sim(on)'s eye. Columbia stood watching the data aggregate, written large on the same screen she watched movies on Friday nights with her fellow Consuls.

"I thought they were my closest allies... friends, even," Columbia said. "Chris van Buren, N'gono, and Nancy, I need a social net for all three. Anyone in it who isn't in this room is a suspect. Tag them as potential confederates, capture not kill."

Abby reached for René's hand to give it a squeeze.

"Ma'am," René began.

"Oh, hey," Columbia said. She nodded toward the screen before making a point of witnessing Abby and Sim(on) at René's side. "Big show hasn't started yet, but I guess the cat's out of the bag, eh?"

"Figured it out on their own," René said. "You can strike Nancy from the list. She's off the board."

"Things like that never last long here," Columbia said, and shrugged.

"What? Lies?" Abby said.

"Lies, secrets, omissions, privacy, whatever you call it," Columbia said. "Bigger fish to fry. Excuse me."

"Get down!" Sim(on) suddenly yelled, striking out for the red canister.

René wrestled Abby and Columbia to the ground as Sim(on) scrambled to his feet. The thin red cylinder hissed, spewing gas from its nozzle. With a free hand, Sim(on) drew the needling pistol Sarah gave him and, aiming past dumbstruck Security Forces, blew out the glass patio door. Sim(on) threw the small bottle like a quarterback, which ignited as it streaked across the patio reception area and detonated. The windows blew back as the flames ignited the thermobaric bomb's trail into the penthouse. Sim(on) rose, laughing hysterically from the flaming detritus of destroyed paperwork.

Keiko arrived with a contingent of Security Forces who knocked him back down. She held a compact automatic, a Giresun-made SF carbine. The added dimensions meant longer charges and faster cycling than the pistol version. The tactical team approached Columbia with Keiko in the lead. Abby and René held their weapons trained on them.

"Columbia, you okay?" Keiko shouted.

"Good!" Columbia yelled back over the noise.

Keiko dropped her stance and signaled orders to the team. "Get the rest of the fire extinguishers—throw them out over the patio! Boobytraps!" She pushed through Abby and René to give Columbia a hug.

"Looks like you and your friends were in the right place at the wrong time again—could be catching," Columbia said with an arm around Keiko. "Don't look too surprised. Sarah's an old friend. She sent me Simon's analysis—Hey! Get off him. He's fine! —anyway, we knew whoever was trying to throw this thing was making their big play, but not how."

Security Force members got off of Sim(on) and tried to help him to his feet. He fought them off and stood on his own.

"One down, and about six-hundred more to go," Keiko said.

"I guess it's all out in the open now, eh?" Columbia said to René. "With a little luck, we still might be able to survive."

TRIUMVIRATE PENTHOUSE

1537 15 AUG 2075

"Bait, that's what we're using Keiko for," Columbia said.

"I'll be standing next to her. I'll be the one who does whatever handshake business. That'll be the cue. Everyone is ready for it, but no one knows the whole plan except for Sarah, and now you three," Keiko said.

"What's our next contingency?" René said.

"You don't need to know, and hopefully it won't come to that," Columbia said.

"Just move down and out to the Archives. It's actually designed for a nuclear detonation—those Moorish arches are twelve feet thick and have a water matrix as a radiation shield. It's really the safest building in or on the whole island," Keiko said. "The support staff, the senators, their families are all in the catacombs down there."

"You've done enough, more than anyone expected of you all. We'll work out something afterward..." Columbia said before speeding off with Keiko to a sound booth.

"Okay. Did she stutter? Let's get down to the library, kids," Abby said.

"Didn't even get one of those pimento cheese sandwiches you're always talking about," Sim(on) said to René.

"Too bad. They're amazing," René joked. "I'll see what I can do when they have the kitchen back up and running."

"She did say support staff... maybe the cooks are already down there—" Sim(on) said.

"Shut up," Abby said.

MAIN STREET

1542 15 AUG 2075

The NIE soldiers continued to move as fast as possible up the hills of Main Street as they could among flames, smoke, and non-lethal deterrents. Every time the invasion slowed their assault to regroup, Security Forces would charge from behind their barricades, through the hedgerows, and goad them onward. The fog of war was thick. The emotional reaction to the SF's harassment was to chase and attack, drawing out the NIE lines and reducing their munitions. Grisly, printed human body parts were shot from Giresun cannons as NIE weapons impacted. They littered the skirmish lines like roadside trash. From the ground view, the NIE soldiers were winning the battle.

Behind the lines, aid was given to the women and men who survived their run through the gauntlet. Casualties were low—running and gunning in a relay disguised the actual numbers. The NIE soldiers were given no quarter to assess or reprieve to recuperate, drawing down their strength.

Cutting-edge aid was given to stabilize the SF wounded. For Giresun that could be borderline to reviving the dead. Those too injured to continue were hustled into the shelters below the buildings one block back from Main, while troops took water and reloaded.

"Good work, ladies! Those *po-gai* slitches are playing the hand we dealt 'em. Find your positions and catch your breath for their return trip," the sergeants called out to the Security Forces over their enemy's impotent gunfire.

THE FORUM, ATRIUM

Abby, Sim(on), and René took the elevator down to the Forum and walked through the statue-lined hall to the Archives. They casually held their magnerifles at the ready. There were only three SF sentries, backed by automated defenses powerful enough to repel a company of tanks.

"Okay, come on. Get your asses in. It's about to get heated," the sentry on point said.

Abby, Sim(on), and René walked through as layered doors of honeycomb armor retracted behind the decorative cast bronze façade.

THE FORUM, FRONT STEPS

Pachutec and his entourage stopped at the steps to the Forum, walking with Consul van Buren. N'Gono stood at the ready, stuck in the middle between the NIE soldiers and SF defenses. The square was surrounded by acacia thorn hedgerows. The wind flapped decorative flags and banners. Maxim Torres was trying to ignore his soaked shoes from falling into a fractal pond on the way across. Brönner stood beside the truck, shielded by the door with his rifle concealed behind it.

Smoke drifted across the square, rolling over the steps to lull at their feet and eddied along with the fractal water features of the square.

"Nice trick," Maxim said. His flamboyant suit of gold and thin red stripes flashed in the light.

Pepe Hererra cleared his throat.

Keiko emerged, wearing matte body armor plates and an ornate sword scabbard at her side. Columbia followed closely behind. They stood on the last few steps, maintaining a symbolic high ground.

"Where is Admiral O'Higgins?" Columbia asked.

Pachutec smiled.

"He is with the fleet, of course," Pachutec said.

"Oh, I thought his sailors were coming ashore to celebrate their victory, and you and I would get a chance to talk," Columbia said.

"Well, I did escort these fine Incan warriors ashore..." Pachutec said.

"It doesn't look like they're here to celebrate. Are you here to talk?" Columbia said.

"They will celebrate later, I'm sure. And yes, I'm here to talk. To inform you that your goals have been achieved. For decades, Giresun Island has angled for acceptance among the world powers. The world has not deigned to acknowledge you, they have not seen your wonders, your beauty. But I have. I see you. It is with great pride and joy that I'm here today to inform you that Giresun is now part of the New Incan Empire!"

A knife clattered to the ground past Pachutec's feet at the same time as a single gunshot report. Suddenly weapons were drawn and trained in all directions. Mez Calla lay dead, his straw Stetson rocked in the breeze on the square.

"I'm afraid I agree with your late friend there. We must decline. We would rather die than be subsumed by another country, especially one built on the exploitation and perversion of humanity that you represent, *señor*," Columbia said.

Keiko dropped to the steps; a series of interlocking scales covered her body. As if by magic, Keiko was covered in armadillo-like armor. Bullets from the invaders ricocheted off with sparks.

The remaining NIE armored personnel carriers managed to get off a short burst of their chain guns before going dead in a hail of orange sparks. The needle-thin rounds launched at near relativistic speed by electromagnetic cycling guns around the plaza punched through and spalled within the vehicles' armor plating like it was tissue paper.

The steps behind Columbia were chewed to rubble as her hologram, made opaque by the smoke usually used for computer-generated concerts, was turned off. The smoke cleared, and the flames abated. In their place stood row after row of Giresun warriors. This time their magnerifles were drawn and trained on the soldiers.

"It was all a feint?" Pachutec whispered.

"We've been at their mercy this entire time," Brönner replied.

With their armored support and vehicles destroyed, the infantry was left exposed, walled in on three sides in a box canyon of concrete and steel. A whooping war-cry began to drift from the barricades. Drums pounded, echoing back and forth across the street in a terrifying call-and-response cadence. The NIE soldiers were called back by long blasts from their sergeants' whistles, and with no clear objective, they effectively scattered. Random assaults on the barricades closest to their formation left men strung up on the thorns as women wearing metal armor taunted them from their parapets.

"Fire!" a NIE officer screamed. He drew a ceremonial saber and slashed through the air.

A squad of committed troops took defensive positions between two destroyed armored vehicles. They attempted to mount a defense, firing at SF troops as they dove over the acacia thorn hedges. Three troops emerged between the barrier and the hedgerow with a large ceramic cube.

"What the hell is that?" one of the soldiers yelled.

"Shoot it! Kill them!" the officer called back.

A deep thrumming sensation buzzed through the men, making their hair stand on end. A conch shell horn sounded.

"EMP!" the officer yelled as it donned on him.

"Sir! The weapons are still powered, but they won't fire!"

"It's a depolarizer, you idiots!" The SF troops taunted the soldiers from their barricade.

"Stand and fight, you cowards!" the officer screamed back, drawing an ancient revolver and firing at the device.

"Should've stayed in school, baby brain!" one of the SF troops yelled.

The soldiers drew field knives and started a run at the hedgerow led by the officer with his pistol and drawn sword.

"Overwatch twenty-three. I have six tangos and their fearless leader making a charge. How should I respond, over?" a SF sniper called over her comm link.

"Overwatch twenty-three, this is FSO alpha. Engage, minimal casualty, over," the fire support officer responded from the command center.

"Acknowledged. Engaging," the sniper replied. She fired seven rounds.

In the span of two seconds each man lost a foot or a hand, vaporized behind a shower of gravel and debris.

The officer turned to fire in the general direction of the incoming rounds before twisting in an opposite spin into a heap against the hedgerow.

"Six tangos are retreating toward harbor, over," the sniper said. "Acquiring next target."

Further down Main Street, the NIE forces deployed high-explosive rocket launchers to break holes in the SF defenses.

"¡Fuego!" the battery officer yelled.

A dozen rockets flew through the hedgerow, sending burning clumps of bush in every direction. The impact of the rockets on the barricade blew back against Main Street. NIE soldiers were knocked off their feet, and Security Force troops streamed out from behind the wall like water from a broken dam.

It was immediately apparent that in hand-to-hand combat the SF troops were also far superior to the men of the NIE. Broken bodies were thrown into the invaders' ranks.

One lucky soldier pinned a young SF woman in a combination leg and arm bar.

"Gotchu now, perro," he said through clenched teeth.

A nearby woman wrenched her opponent's arm out of its socket, then dragged him over to the fight.

She flicked a toe-kick into the would-be victor's exposed temple and crushed his eye socket. His grip slipped, and she returned to her own baggage.

"You good?" she said, staring down at the man holding his arm.

"Yes, thank you," he whimpered.

"Shut the *po-gai* up," she said. Another toe-kick landed square in his crotch, scooting him across the pavement. "I wasn't talking to you."

The other woman gave a thumb's up as her rival rolled onto the pavement from her choke hold. As she rose to her feet, they stood arm in arm to watch the invaders stampede for the docks. They let out a triumphant war cry together, raising their spare fists.

"That's right! Go back to your weak ass lives!" someone shouted nearby as she knocked a crawling soldier over.

"Somebody better have my Hashenswill ready! On ice!" another SF troop shouted, already heady with the rush of the fight.

"And some ice!" her comrade joined after.

Automated litters retrieved the wounded and the dead for transport to the docks.

Garbage, flaming papers, and boxes streamed down on the retreating forces as the citizens of Giresun joined in taunting their would-be subjugators.

Chris and N'gono raised their heads from the pavement. Dead bodies of the NIE delegation surrounded them. Maxim Torres's body was missing.

Brönner closed the eyes of Mez Calla before turning back to the Emperor. He sensed their movement, drew his aim, and fired straight through N'gono's forehead, over the Consul's back. Chris reeled from the shock as her fellow patriot's dead eyes stared up at her.

"N'gono wasn't attacking. It was just Calla," she whispered breathlessly. The weapons fire pocking the ground around her snapped Chris out of her daze. "I can get us to safety," she croaked, lifting her hands at the wrist.

"Now," Brönner said.

"The Archives..." Chris said. She pointed at the Gothic looking building next to the Forum.

"Get up," Brönner said to Pachutec. The young man was unresponsive, shaking on his haunches.

Brönner sprung to his feet, lifting Pachutec with him.

Chris stumbled up and forward trying desperately to match his speed. "There!" she said.

The automatic defenses trained on the three approaching people. Chris brought up her screen and typed in an access code. A large tile in the façade popped with the whooshing sound of equalized pressure.

"Inside, quick," she said.

She pulled the hidden door wide, then slammed it shut behind her. They passed through a narrow channel before Chris opened a second door into the interior of the building.

"This place is a fortress. They'll have put the government and their families in here," Chris said.

Brönner's face was an emotionless mask as he carried and half drug Pachutec's shell-shocked frame through the hidden passage. His eyes were filled with the fixed gaze of a predator. They emerged from behind a tapestry in the main hall. People were milling about. Some had laid claim to corners and niches. Others played games or read books. Occasionally, kids screamed by rapt in a game of tag and oblivious to the rest of the world. Coming from the battlefield of the other side, reality seemed to slip. The three of them walked along the edge of the rotunda, away from the edge of the tapestry. They continued past an apparently floating rock sitting above a pedestal. Brönner lowered Pachutec against the plinth of a nearby statue.

"What now?" Brönner asked.

"We take charge and negotiate," Chris said.

"Hostages," Brönner said.

"Coin of the realm," Chris said.

"I'm about out," Brönner said, putting his Makarov in its holster.

"Don't tell me you can't kill without one," Chris said.

"It doesn't inspire the same fear for our purpose," Brönner said.

"Then we'll improvise. You catch 'em, and I'll provide the drama," Chris said, nodding to the rock.

Brönner and Chris stepped over to the rock.

"Some kind of art?" Brönner asked, looking at it.

"It's something... kind of a neat rock, I guess? Some kind of relic from the Founders. I dunno, that pomp and circumstance stuff, waste of time," Chris said.

"Ready?" Brönner said.

"When you are," Chris said as she pulled down the rock. It was surprisingly light, almost buoyant.

As if on cue, Pachutec let loose a long-delayed scream from his horror on the steps of the Forum. It shook the room awake. He curled into the fetal position at the plinth and hid his face. Brönner snatched two kids running by and violently smashed their heads together. They screamed in torment as he held them. The little girl who'd been chased bit down with all her strength into his forearm. He hit her in the face with the back of the boy's head. Dazed, she spat wet, sticky bits from her mouth. Blood dripped from her lips as she vomited on his shoes.

The crowd moved forward to attack as a mob when Chris raised the rock over the children's heads.

Abby, Sim(on), and René stood up from their makeshift bivouac. A rations bar wrapper fell from the back of René's pant leg.

"What now?" René said.

"Probably some kid ran into a wall," Abby said.

"Is it them?" Sim(on) said. "Everything outside is blacked out. Technical difficulties, the system says."

René stood on tip-toe to try and see over the crowd. "I think we'd hear some more screams if it was," she said.

"That's Chris van Buren!" a woman shouted.

"The Consul?" a confused man said.

Abby grabbed René's arm at the name. With a look, the three of them worked their way through the thickening crowd.

"Why? What do you want!" the crowd began to shout.

Abby was the first to get into the front ranks. René stood behind her until she saw the scene. Abby tried to grab René before she slipped away.

"*Soai...* the kids..." Abby said flatly.

"You!" Chris shouted at René. "You did this! This is all *your* fault!"

Horror and pain swept over René's body and unconsciously propelled her beyond the front line. Once out in the open, she walked slowly toward the hostages. René smiled at the boy and girl, alternating with blank stares assessing Chris, Brönner, and the crumpled whimpering body on the floor that she assumed was their leader.

"Yes! Take me! Take me instead of the children. I'm worth more. Columbia will do anything to keep me safe. Just let me go in their place," René said. Tears poured down her face. She looked down at the children as blood began to drip from their noses. René kept shaking her head, trying to focus on the present and not drift into the past.

"Hold them, woman. If you move, I will shoot you and them," Brönner said.

René covered the injured boy and girl with her body and held them close under her.

Brönner's arm was bleeding steadily in rivulets from where the girl bit him. He wrapped it in a bandana from his back pocket.

"We could've had everything, a proper place in the world," Chris stood over René and the children with the rock. "All this *po-gai soai*, something to prove because we're women. Not everyone is an Amazon, and not everyone should try to be. So I never charged over a stack of thorns. I've got other skills, what makes for civilization. That's what I wanted. I wanted to bring us into the actual world, not some petulant 'she did it her way' *soai*. Now it's all *po-gai*'ed. I'm done trying to save you from yourselves."

"Your mate used a bioweapon on the people they said they were there to help! You helped create a plague that destroyed villages and killed millions!" Sim(on) shouted, pushing his way to the front of the mob. "Samuel Brönner!"

"What kind of a degenerate animal would choose that?" Abby shouted, joining Sim(on). "I'm talking to you, you dumb slitch!"

"It was grown and isolated in a lab, that's how we never saw signs of modification." Sim(on) spoke to the crowd. "If that's how they treat their own from the beginning, what chance do we have as a nation?

They will do what the unenlightened men have always done—squandered our wealth, our wisdom, and our love in exchange for power. What makes it worse is some of us agree to just let it happen!"

Brönner raised his Makarov even with Sim(on)'s chest and pulled the trigger. A sound like a child's electric toy car shrieked, along with the hollow click of the Makarov's hammer striking an empty chamber. Atomized red spray splattered across Brönner's face. He looked quizzically at his pistol, then turned as Chris van Buren crumpled to the ground over René. The rock fell to float across the floor like an air hockey puck. It stopped at Abby's feet.

Keiko stepped out from behind the tapestry to be passed by a squad of Security Force sentries.

"Did you think you were the only one who could hack your biomarker?" Keiko said as she unceremoniously rolled the other Consul's body off of René.

The rest of the Security Forces dropped Brönner to his knees on the ground. Brönner struggled, like a trapped animal. His eyes were wild, flashing with dilated pupils like the SF berserkers who'd harassed the NIE army with clubs and spears. Foam flecked his lips as he spat obscenities and roared against his acknowledged defeat.

The SF team's sergeant sprayed Brönner with a slimy, shimmering film. Hardening after seconds of contact, it formed a gel cocoon around his torso. He fought with his legs, twisting in a gyre to fell anyone he could reach. The corporal whipped around with a can of his own and secured Brönner's legs to the polished marble.

Keiko stepped up to him as he snapped his teeth at her, writhing like a snake staked to the floor. She stood over him, assessing and absorbing every detail of the tableau beneath her. Keiko drew the jian from her side. Its broad, flexible, double-edged blade sang in the air.

"Good! Do it! Kill me!" Brönner screamed defiantly.

With a dervish-like spin, her free leg lashed out to clip him across his jaw. The jian slid effortlessly across the tiles to fillet the gel from the ground. The impact of her kick sent his otherwise secured body rolling next to the cowering Emperor.

"Privates," Keiko said. "These kids need some medical attention. Sergeant, corporal, mind the prisoner."

Their parents were close behind as the sentries stood down.

"Oh my God, kids!" the man cried. He checked them over, competing with the corporal in assessing their injuries. Their mother simply slid in behind them both and cradled them in her lap against the stone's pedestal while others checked their wounds.

"Thank you," she mouthed to René, unable to find her voice and trembling behind a veil of tears. She reached for René's hand. René squeezed it tight, looking her in the eyes until she had to tear herself away.

"You okay?" Abby asked as Sim(on) put his arm around her protectively.

René nodded.

Abby passed her a handkerchief.

Blowing her nose, she cleared up her sobs.

"I... I want to tell you all of it," René said.

"When you're ready," Abby said.

"Guys... why is the rock pinging my screen?" Sim(on) showed them his screen. "Why is a rock asking for my network permissions?"

The gates at the far side of the Archives began to disengage their locks and retract. Sarah Kelly followed her troops in to provide whatever aid was needed, but she made a beeline for Abby, René, and Sim(on). She looked past them as the rock began to phosphoresce in pulsating patterns, like a cuttlefish above its pedestal.

"I need you three to come with me now," Sarah said. "Right now. Let's go."

Epilogue
What Lies Beneath

THE ARCHIVES, GIRESUN ISLAND

2000 15 AUG 2075

Sarah led René, Abby, and Sim(on) through the Forum and to an awaiting auto cab. The cab departed without a word between them. They each took corners of the seating. Sarah folded the middle row down into a table and turned her seat to face Sim(on) and Abby in the back row.

∼

Pachutec hadn't moved from the plinth he curled up next to since the citizens were cleared out. The original SF troops had drug Brönner with them, leaving a two-person detail behind to watch over the Emperor. The sentries charged with keeping him safe were visibly bored.

"I'd rather be stacking up acacia thorns," the man said.

"You *are* a thorn, Tom," the woman said.

"Bring the prisoner to the helipad," the radio squawked.

The sentries squatted down toward Pachutec, one by his head and the other across from the plinth, even with his shoulders. He tried to spin away, but the sentries easily blocked him in against the statue and lifted him bodily off the ground. Pachutec tried to fight them off.

"Stop that," the woman said. She jabbed a knife-hand punch in and up around the right side of his ribcage. Pachutec howled in pain. He offered no further resistance but became dead weight as the SF sentries lifted him off the ground and carried him to the Forum's elevators. An aircrew waited for them at the top of the lift. When it opened, Pachutec was crumpled in the corner like a kicked dog.

"Resistance?" the crew chief asked as the aircrew drug him the rest of the way to the transport.

"Nah, broken," the male sentry said.

The sentries walked back into the elevator without a second look at the fallen would-be-emperor. The aircrew threw Pachutec into a transparent box. The lid sealed and locked with a few commands on the chief's screen. Together they hoisted it to clang against Brönner's box already in the hold.

"Manifest complete," the crew chief announced. "Let's get the show on the road. I want to be back for the party, not the cleanup!"

TRIUMVIRATE PENTHOUSE

2013 15 AUG 2075

"So, we have an accord?" Columbia said. She stared across her desk at Elana Chavez's image as if she were staring down a tiger.

"Not that I have much of a choice, considering your absolute defeat of the Emperor, but yes. We have an accord. The NIE will continue as a matter of regional stabilization, but under my leadership. Maxim Torres, the delegate from Brazil will be my second. We have a non-aggression treaty with Giresun Island. We also agree to officially recognize you as a sovereign nation and forward you to the United Nations as a sponsor for membership. NIE will rescind the last several edicts, policies, and regulations pertaining to illicit trade and human trafficking as stated in your terms. And we formally request Giresun's help in dismantling the de Silva cartel in exchange for our assistance in a unified South American continental government."

"Madam, we have an accord. I look forward to working with your government in the future. We will be watching," Columbia said. She disconnected the transmission without further ceremony.

Columbia stood up and surveyed the men and women cleaning up the destruction. She walked across the isles of detritus onto the patio. The Proconsul surveyed the city below as similar crews cleared the streets and dismantled the fortifications.

"I'll be with you shortly. There's one more thing I have to take care of," Columbia said to her streets. She turned and left, walking to the private elevator in her office.

GIRESUN ISLAND, DOCKS

2023 15 AUG 2075

The vehicle drove itself down toward the bay, then changed direction for an outside edge of the cove. Sim(on) was the first to break.

"So... how much trouble are we in?" he asked.

"None. This is... an induction of sorts. Just be patient. You're not in trouble, and you're not going to be harmed, but it's best if... we just wait until we get there," Sarah said.

"Does it have anything to do with that?" René said, pointing at the horizon past the bay's pincer-like arms.

On the open seas, the entire NIE fleet was sinking rapidly, as if the ocean disappeared beneath them.

"Probably," Sarah said. "Yeah, that sounds about right."

"What in the hell?" Abby said, crawling across the table for a better view, using the back of René's chair to latch on to. "Are you seeing this?"

"Got it, drone feed," Sim(on) said staring intently at his screen. "Something big just happened to the water. They're too heavy somehow," he said in awe.

The car turned and pulled them out of sight of the harbor's cove.

"They're popping back up?" Sim(on) said in disbelief. "What the hell is this?" he said to Sarah.

"I'm not sure. Like I said, it's probably going to get answered here in a minute," Sarah said. "If I had to guess, I'd say either a giant fissure of gas, or a huge pocket of fresh water was released under the NIE fleet, then dissipated before killing them all. Like a giant swirly after getting your ass kicked on the playground."

The auto cab dove into a tunnel as it reached the shoreline. The road was pitch black, no lights. The automated car did not need them. Signs and automated gates were in place to warn curious citizens away, and anyone in the path of on-coming traffic wouldn't be for long. Suddenly, a blue light appeared ahead, growing into a tunnel, which turned into a tube under the ocean.

"The subs," Abby said.

Sarah nodded.

"The subs?" René said.

"You guys, the NIE fleet is limping along, like two-third under the waves," Sim(on) said.

"Told ya. You have no idea," Sarah said. "Underwater habitats, mining, and refining along geothermal vents. It's how we actually get the raw stuff for our factories up there. Very hush-hush."

The auto cab parked and opened its doors. A giant, double airlock sat across from the apparent loading dock as the wall of the platform.

"But you're about to find out," Sarah said.

Columbia was waiting on the other side of the second airlock. She gave each of them a muscular hug.

"I am so glad to see you all," Columbia said. "And it seems like this momentous day's not over yet..."

THE END

The adventure will return in *Bleeding Through*, Book Two in this continuing series.

Acknowledgements

I'd like acknowledge those who have given this book, and the stories within it, legs strong enough to move forward:

LTC Jennifer McKeel, Cameron and Kaitlyn McKeel, Norene Green, John G. McKeel, Debbie Norris and Jim Antholz, the Bentz family, Chris and Alessandra Kelley, the Hilleboe family, Erron Huey, Joy Rodriguez, Christian Deichert, Eric Koester, Mike Butler, Haley Newlin, Carol McKibben, and the whole team at both bSchool and New Degree Press.

I'd also like to gratefully acknowledge my family, friends, fellow soldiers, sailors, nurses, and supporters:

Anna Buitendorp, Marcus and Cheryl Tyler, Dana Rosenberg, Linda and Neil Williams, John and Heather Bollman, Krista Bullard, Mike Corum, Debbie Norris and Jim Antholz, Tam Mattox, Wayne Janoe, Mike Jones, Sarah Baylus, Mike Maloney, Richard Grigsbay II, Eleanor and Lilly Healy, Eugene Hunter Jr., Shawn and Gloria Killeen, Eric Koester, John and Veleda Simonson, Norene Green, Randy and Melissa Hilleboe, Kelly Williams and family, Joshua Lee Dilday, Christian, Kelly, and Carey Deichert, Brian, Julie and Halie Kelley, Adam and Brandy Lisser, Chris and Sara Smith, Kevin Tucker, Stephanie Hilleboe, the Rutledge family, Jan and John G. McKeel, Michelle and Paul Martin, Uriel Gerard, Jonathan Newey, Jacky Lee, Desiree Gonzales, Bailey and Angelia Brown, Charlotte Bentz, Roman Daszczyszak, Aaron Ross, Vicki and Mike Baylus, Tina Shawndell

Howard, Leiloni Stainsby, Heather Graham, Joshua Cordeiro, Shane Thideman, Jeff Beck, Lyle Williams, Grace Fecteau, Melissa Koenig, Joshua, Alice, and Owen Niekranz, Amie Smith, Tom and Lori Hilleboe, Karen Morris, Phil and Brandy Deppert, Edward "Massey" and Nicole Maschek, Stephen Hancock, Evan Heald, Tom Trinkle, Jeremy and Meloni Armstrong, Dustin and Michelle Bierlair, Kim Stavros, Todd Wilson, Molly Levine, Nichole Reid, Joy and Abe Rodriguez, Erin and Keith Verrier, Patrick Williams and family, Rowan Delaney Howard, Chantry Howard, April Seely, and Micah Beasley

Lastly, I'd like to acknowledge a few sources of inspiration:

Terry Moore, David Brin, Ernest Cline, Suzanne Collins, Mark Adams, Neil Gaiman, Dave Eggers, Tim Ferriss, Charles C. Mann, Jared Diamond, Steve Phillips, and Thaddeus Russel.

Appendix

CHAPTER 4

"De Colores." Pacific Historical Review. University of California Press 82, no. 4 (November 1, 2013). https://online.ucpress.edu/phr/article-abstract/82/4/646/80906/De-Colores?redirectedFrom=PDF.

Made in the USA
Las Vegas, NV
14 September 2021

30253545R00134